Forgotten Deeds

PARISI FAMILY BOOK 2

ANDREA HAGAN

Tradepaper ISBN: 978-0-9994116-9-8

For all the good girls who secretly like being called bad names.
This book is for you, you dirty little slut.

Before you begin reading…

If the dedication offended you, please turn back now. For a full content warning, go to andreahaganauthor.com. Click on FAQ.

CHAPTER
One

Darius

Shifting closer to the door, my left trainer is now stuck in God only knows what kind of bodily fluid. I yank my shoe free, positioning myself in the darkest corner of the alley.

The back door to Glitter strip club opens, and out struts a red-head with huge fake tits to match her collagen-filled lips. "Amethyst," I call, stepping out from the shadows.

She jumps like a scared cat, dramatically placing a hand over her heart. "Sorry, you got the wrong woman."

I'm on her in a flash, dragging her to the back of the alley with my gloved hand over her mouth. A shame, as I'm curious to know what those lips feel like. If I cut them off her face, would they ooze poison like a pufferfish? Shaking that thought away, I focus and say, "Mr. Parisi warned you to keep your mouth shut," I menace. "Now I hear you've been running your flap about his girl, Nicky Thomas."

She struggles against me, but freezes with fear when she

spots the calling card on my forearm. Ah, so my reputation as the Parisi family enforcer precedes me. How nice.

I inhale deeply, savoring the smell of this woman's abject terror. Fear really does have a smell—pheromones secreted to send out a non-verbal SOS—and for me, there's nothing sweeter. "This is your last chance," I warn. "Next time *Diávolos* comes calling, he'll make sure to collect. Keep your fucking mouth shut. Understood?"

Amethyst bobs her head, and while my fingers are itching to unsheathe my knife and find out about those lips, I reluctantly let her go. The woman sprints away from me; turns out she does have half a brain cell.

I start to walk away when I hear it—a tiny *whoosh* of air. Spinning around, I hustle to the end of the alley to find a petite woman with a halo of blonde hair crouched behind the dumpster.

Offering her my hand, she just looks at it. "Don't be afraid." Jesus, did I really just say that?

She hesitantly takes my hand, and it feels like she's scanning my soul for every bad deed I've ever committed. I hope she's got all day, because it's a long fucking list. Not that I would complain; it wouldn't be a hardship to look at this beautiful thing for hours on end. Likely in her early twenties, she's tiny compared to me—I'd guess five feet four inches—with long, light blonde hair curled into loose waves; pouty lips; and hauntingly pale blue eyes. I can't make out much about her figure with the baggy sweater and pants she's wearing, but that only piques my curiosity.

Her body trembles under my scrutiny as she stands, and suddenly, I don't like the smell of fear—at least not coming from this sweet little angel. She looks down at our hands still connected, her eyes traveling up my forearm, stopping at my tattoo. Dropping my hand like she's been burned, she takes off in a dead sprint.

I easily catch up to her, my arms banded around her petite

frame before she can make it out of the alley. "You going to keep your mouth shut about what you heard, *aggeloudhi mou*?" Leaning in, I inhale deeply—fear, mixed with lemons and something else I can't quite place. A clean smell; it's nice. She struggles against me, and my dick turns to stone. Interesting.

"I didn't hear anything," she whispers with a shaky voice.

"Good girl." I reluctantly release her from my arms, and she scurries to the door, punching in a code before disappearing inside the club.

Silly little angel, thinking she can run from the devil.

Lily

Entering the dressing room of the club, I try not to hyperventilate. I just came face-to-face with the devil. Hades, more accurately, since he was Greek.

I don't know what kind of shit Amethyst has gotten herself into, but now the bitch has dragged me into it—with a man who looks like a Greek god, and whose menacing voice sounds like the epitome of death and destruction.

Good girl. Replaying those two little words in his gravely tone has my pussy clenching.

Ugh, what is wrong with me? Pretty sure that man wouldn't give a second thought before snapping my neck like a twig. Besides, haven't I learned my lesson about bad boys? "Bad" is in the description for a reason.

I shake those thoughts from my head, changing into my stage clothes—what little they are. Slipping on the see-through fishnet dress over my bra and thong, I fasten my pleasers. Moving in front of the mirror, I touch up my makeup, adding one final coat of pink lipstick while marveling how my life has taken this turn. I never would have envisioned myself as an exotic dancer; I'm pretty reserved in real life. Then again, I never would have envisioned myself being threatened by the god of the underworld in the back alley of a strip club.

After some quick stretching, it's time to hit the floor. Giving myself a once-over in the mirror, I mentally slip on my dancer persona. *Bubbly. Flirty. Confident.* I repeat my mantra as I step into the hall, passing the club owner's office.

"Hey, beautiful," Leo calls, only because I'm sure he doesn't remember my stage name. I've only been dancing here for about a week. My old club—Joe's Cabaret—shut down out of the blue, leaving us dancers scrambling to find something else. A few of the girls came to this club with me— Amethyst included—but I don't know what happened to my friend Candy. Maybe she got out of the biz. Smart woman.

"Hey, Leo. I'm going to hit the floor," I tell him in a no-nonsense tone.

"Sure, sure. But know my door's always open if you ever have trouble covering your house fee. We could work something out," he tells me with a slimy smile.

"No thanks, I'm good," I say, walking briskly on. Oh, I know all about that open-door policy, being that I walked in on Amethyst blowing Leo my very first day at this club.

Stepping onto the floor with strobe lights flashing and music pumping, I try to get into the right headspace. The *hustler* headspace. I hate having to start from scratch at a new club—I've lost my regulars, and that's where a big chunk of my money came from.

I scan the crowd, making eye contact with a middle-aged man seated solo. Could be promising, and so I plaster on a fake smile as I shake my ass over to his table. "Hey, there. Having a good time?" I ask, giving my hip an exaggerated pop.

"Great time now that you're here," he says, looking me up and down with beady little eyes. "You're new. What's your name?"

"Pearl," I say with a practiced smile.

"Pretty name. You like pearls? How about a pearl necklace?" He snickers like he's done something big there. I really didn't think my stage name through, as I've received some variation of this dumb question every time I've stepped foot onto the floor.

"Sure, I like all kinds of jewelry, but diamonds are a girl's best friend," I say in my best "dumb blonde" impersonation, pretending to miss his sexual innuendo. "How about a lap dance?"

"Depends. You do extras?"

"Extras" code word for sex acts. "No," I say firmly.

"Then you're not going to last long at this club," he says dismissively, waving me away.

"Get the fuck out of here." A menacing voice sounds behind me.

I freeze. Why, for the love of God is the devil back?

"Who the fuck do you think—" The man stops mid-sentence when he gets a good look at Hades. Jumping out of his chair, he high tails it to another section of the club.

"Now that the asshole is out of the way, I'll take a lap dance," Hades says, taking a seat.

"Why?" Trying to nonchalantly scan the crowd for the bouncer in case I need help, I don't see him. Dammit.

He raises an eyebrow bisected by a small scar. "Isn't that what one does in a gentlemen's club?"

"Aren't you the same *gentlemen* who just threatened me?" I say, channeling bravado I didn't even know I possessed.

"One and the same," he says with a wink, making my stomach do a little flip-flop.

"A hundred bucks for one song," I challenge. My lap dance price just increased—call it hazard pay.

He pulls out a hundred dollar bill from his pocket and slaps it on the table.

Fuck, he called my bluff. I grab the cash and tuck it away in my g-string. A new song comes on, and that's my cue. I begin to sway my hips to the music as he watches with rapt attention. The man has me on edge, but I try to ignore my nerves and lean into my Pearl persona.

It's not working. Not with the way he's looking at me like I'm the sexiest thing he's ever seen. Which doesn't make sense, because there's plenty of sexy dancers at this club with bigger and better tits and ass than mine. Than Pearl's, I correct myself.

Ugh, I'm too much in my head. *Bubbly. Flirty. Confident. Dammit.*

I nervously step closer to him, dropping to the floor and spreading my knees as I grab onto his muscular thighs and bounce my ass, smiling up at him. To my complete mortification, my stomach growls loudly. Damn, I hope he didn't hear that over the music; I should have eaten something earlier.

He glances over my shoulder, someone snagging his attention; he must have noticed the bigger and better T and A. His eyes lock back with mine. "I want this moved to the VIP room."

"Sure," I say, dropping my hands from his thighs and standing to save a modicum of my pride. "Which dancer would you like so I can let her know?"

"You, of course," he says with an amused expression.

Flustered, I blurt out, "Ten thousand dollars for an hour in the VIP room with me. Still interested?" I usually charge a thousand dollars for an hour of my time, but I've tacked on an extra nine grand to ensure I'm *not* alone with this dangerous man.

He rises from his chair, and without a word, he turns on his heel and walks off.

CHAPTER

Two

Lily

Scanning the crowd for another customer, I try not to analyze why Hades blowing me off has left me feeling, I don't know. *Disappointed?* No, that would be insane, so it's got to be something else.

The hostess seats a man solo at another table, and she motions discretely for me to come over. Perfect. I make my way across the floor, but before I can do my introductory spiel, that menacing presence is back.

My body is on high alert as I slowly turn around to find the god of the underworld with receipt in hand. "Lead the way," he says with a naughty twinkle in his eyes.

I snatch the receipt and nearly faint when I spot the amount—he really paid ten thousand dollars. "I don't do extras," I warn him.

"Good girl," he leans in, whispering in my ear.

My skin prickles as I take a step back. "As long as that's clear, follow me," I say, leading us to the back. My flight or fight is telling me to run; the ten grand is telling me to keep going.

The ten grand wins.

We check in with the VIP hostess, who's all smiles until she spots my customer; now she looks like she might pass out. Same, girl. Same.

"I'll be receiving a delivery," he notifies the hostess, and she nods and smiles tightly before escorting us down the hall.

"You do drugs in here, you get kicked out," I warn him as we enter our private room. That was true at Joe's club, but I doubt Leo gives a fuck what goes on as long as he's making money. But I'm standing firm on this one regardless.

"Fair enough," he says, taking a seat on the faux-leather couch.

"Pearl, just a second," the hostess says, grabbing my arm and dragging me into the hallway. "Be careful with him," she warns.

"Who is he?"

"*Diávolos*. Crazy motherfucker. Hooked up with the mob. Word is he tortures poor souls for fun. Cuts out their organs and sells them on the black market, but he keeps the hearts and eats them." She pauses dramatically before whispering, "*Raw*."

I don't know if the hostess is trying to help me, or if she's trying to scare me off another dancer's turf. "Thanks, I'll be careful," I tell her with a nod.

Stepping back inside the VIP room, I close the door behind me, but linger close by—just in case I need to make a run for it.

"What's wrong? You look like you've seen a ghost," the man comments.

Not a ghost, but maybe something worse. "Do you torture people for fun?"

"For fun?" He considers my question. "No."

"Then for *work*?" I ask, my hands trembling as I bring them behind me—grasping the door handle.

"Love what you do, and you'll never work a day in your life," he tells me with a wink.

Before I can dart out of the room, he says, "I'm joking. Come sit with me." He pats the spot beside him.

I could run, but he'd be entitled to a refund—a ten grand refund—so I put one foot in front of the other, feeling like a lamb offering itself up to slaughter.

Taking a seat next to him, I dare to sneak peek. He's dangerously handsome, but that just could be because he's *dangerous*. Curly black hair cut short. Dark brown eyes. Prominent nose that looks like it's been broken a few times. Square chin covered in a short, well-manicured beard. Pretty olive skin. That scar cutting through his left eyebrow. He's dressed in jeans and trainers, with a simple black T-shirt hugging his muscular physique; not that his casual attire makes him any less formidable.

"What's your name?" The man takes his time admiring my scantily-clad body, and I try not to squirm.

"Pearl," I somehow manage.

"Real name, not stage name," he challenges, his dark eyes pinning me to the couch.

"Brooklyn." I give my practiced response.

His lips quirk. "Real name, not first fake 'real' name.'"

"Tiffany."

He chuckles. "Now you're not even trying."

"I'm not going to give you my real name." Tucking my knees to the side, I ask, "What's your name?" My eyes land on his right forearm—that scary as fuck devil tattoo with horns and a trident. I've always wondered how the devil co-opted Poseidon's trident, but I keep that musing to myself. The devil's mouth is open wide—devouring a man with ink-blood dripping gruesomely; below it, the word *Diávolos* is written in script.

"*Diávolos*," he says with humor in his voice as he flexes his muscular forearm; the action causes his devil tattoo to appear a bit too realistic.

Having been caught staring at his ink, I snap my eyes back up to his. "Real name, not nickname." Pursing my lips, I try to go for nonchalant—like me spending time in the VIP room with a man who refers to himself as the devil is an everyday occurrence.

"It's not a nickname, *aggeloudhi mou*," he corrects me.

"What kind of name is it, then?" I ask, instinctively scooting an inch or so away from him.

He doesn't answer my question; instead, he says, "My 'real' name is Darius Angelos."

"*Angelos*? A devil *and* an angel?" I raise an eyebrow.

"God has a sense of humor, no?" He flashes a grin, making the butterflies in my stomach take flight.

A knock sounds, and the VIP hostess enters carrying two large brown paper bags. "Here you are." She sits them down on the coffee table before practically sprinting out of the room.

Darius pulls out delicious-smelling takeout containers from the bags. "I hope you're in the mood for Italian," he tells me.

"You paid ten grand so we could eat?" My mouth falls open.

He lifts a shoulder lazily, fixing a plate and handing it to me, before busying himself with his own.

Waiting until he has his food, I take a bite of some kind of pasta and moan. "This is amazing."

"You have a man?" he asks, watching my mouth with interest.

The answer is on the tip of my tongue before I catch myself. "I'm not going to discuss my personal life."

He looks at me thoughtfully. "You're not a full-time dancer, but using this as a springboard for bigger and better things. Good for you."

Coughing, I nearly choke on my pasta. "What makes you say that?"

"Your speech and mannerisms give you away, *aggeloudhi mou.*"

"You've called me that a few times now. What does it mean?" I ask, deflecting.

Darius flashes a Cheshire cat smile. "Tell me your real name, and I'll tell you my nickname for you."

"I don't need a nickname, and this is a one-time thing, you and me," I warn him.

"Sure, *aggeloudhi mou.*" He playfully flicks my nose like I'm a naive child who's said something amusing.

Lily

A ringtone startles me, and it takes a moment to orient myself. I'm in the VIP room, my head on Darius' lap. He's on the phone, speaking quietly in another language—Italian, maybe?—while he runs his big hand through my hair.

Bolting upright, I check my bra and thong to make sure everything's in place. Nothing feels violated down there, but Christ, I cannot believe I fell asleep with a customer! So freaking dangerous.

He ends his call and looks at me with a wry smile. "My company's so stimulating I made you fall asleep?"

"No, it's just I never eat this late at the club. That, and I'm tired from—" I stop myself from revealing something personal. "I'm sorry."

"Don't apologize. I have to go. Until next time, *aggeloudhi mou.*" He stands, extending a hand for me.

Ignoring his gesture, I stand and beat him to the door, opening it. "No next time," I warn him.

He flashes an amused grin as he walks out. "Love offal, but liver is my favorite," he tells the hostess with a wink before sauntering away.

Darius

A bouncer tries to intercept me before I make it to the back—that is until he realizes who the fuck I am. He wisely steps aside and lets me through.

Leo's office is locked, but I know the little chicken-shit is in there. Kicking open his door, I flip on the light and stroll across the room to find him hunkered beneath his desk. "Well, well, well. Look who's hiding like a little bitch."

"Just trying to catch some Z's," he lies through his teeth, climbing into his chair. "About the money—"

"It's always about the money," I inform him, cracking my knuckles. Leo likes to play poker in one of the Parisi family's backrooms and has racked up quite the debt. Fine by me, as I haven't had the chance to fuck anyone up today, and I'm getting antsy.

"I'll have it by the end of the night when the girls turn in their house fees. I swear," he pleads.

I lean against his desk and say, "Here's the thing, Leo. *Diávolos* gives you extra time. Word gets out, and then everybody will want extra time. You see how that would be a problem for me, don't you?"

"I promise to keep my mouth shut," he says hopefully.

"Good idea." Moving lightning-fast, I jab him in the mouth.

Leo squeals as he covers his hand over his gushing bottom lip.

I make my way over to his filing cabinet, opening it and flipping through the files until I find what I'm looking for: Pearl's application and a copy of her driver's license. Committing to memory the information, I close the drawer and turn to Leo, who's holding a crimson-stained fast food napkin to his lip. "The new blonde dancer, Pearl, if anyone at the club gives her a hard time, I'll give *everyone* at the club a hard time. Starting with you." I give my knuckles another crack for emphasis.

"No one will give her a hard time," he's quick to promise.

My pager goes off, and I check the message. "It's turning out to be your lucky night after all, Leo. I'll be back later to collect—with an additional five percent annoyance fee tacked on for the trouble."

He nods, releasing a shaky breath. "Thank you."

"Better have the family's money in hand before you start thanking me," I warn him. "Oh, and this file cabinet stays locked from here on out," I order him as I head for the door. Never know; there could be all kinds of psychos out there.

CHAPTER
Three

Lily

"Oh my God, I can't believe you went to the VIP room with *Diávolos*!" Chrissy exclaims as we count our money at the end of the night. "He's one scary motherfucker."

"Don't be thinking you some hot shit, new girl," Star says from the doorway, giving me the evil eye as she flips her cigarette pack upside down and packs it with her other hand.

"Pearl is hot shit," Chrissy answers, and I'm silently willing her to shut up. "Who else has pulled in ten grand in an hour?"

All the girls in the dressing room gasp. Great.

"Bullshit." Star jeers.

"It's not, I saw the claim ticket with my own eyes," Chrissy goes on.

"Let's see it." Star walks over to where I'm sitting, snatching the ticket from my pile. Examining it, she grabs her lighter, flicking it as she lights the slip of paper on fire. My mouth hanging open, I watch ten thousand dollars go up in smoke. "No claim ticket, no payout." She smiles cruelly. "Welcome aboard, new girl."

"Star, that was a bitch move," Chrissy calls after her. All eyes are on me as I resume counting my money, willing myself not to cry. I do cry, then word gets back to the resident mean girl, Star, and she wins a second time.

Changing into my street clothes, I tip out everyone before walking to Leo's office. "Here you go," I say, handing him my house fee.

He takes the cash, jerking his hand away from me like I've bitten him. "Thanks."

"No problem," I say, wondering why he won't look at me. Debating if I should plead my case about the ten grand, I decide against it. Being new around here, I'm not sure what kind of "relationship" Star has with Leo. Plus, if word gets out I'm a snitch, my time here at this club becomes miserable, so I keep my mouth shut.

Stepping outside, I'm headed to my car, but stop short. On my windshield is a bouquet of pink lilies. Hands trembling, I grab the flowers, searching in vain for a card. I climb into my car, tossing the bouquet on the passenger seat. My stomach is in absolute knots wondering who's fucking with me about my identity. Unless it's just a coincidence? Or maybe those got placed on the wrong car. I'm sure that's it.

Driving home, I try to shake off the craziness of this night. Darius dropping ten grand so we could eat dinner together tops that crazy list, I think with a smile. But that smile is short-lived when I remember I'm not walking away with a penny of that money. I let the tears fall, allowing myself to ugly cry it all out before pulling into the driveway.

Quietly unlocking the front door, I step inside my house to find the babysitter asleep on the couch. "Hey," I whisper, nudging her.

"Oh, hey, Lily," she says, sitting up and rubbing her eyes. "Didn't mean to nod off." The babysitter thinks I work odd hours at a bar, which isn't an outright lie—there is a bar inside my club.

"No problem," I say, handing her cash for the evening. "How was Iris?"

"Good. She finished her movie, and then we read some books. She cried a little at bedtime, but she finally went to sleep."

Hearing my daughter struggled without me at bedtime is like a stab of guilt right to the heart. I hate leaving her on the nights I work, but Darius was right—dancing is just a spring-board to bigger and better things for me *and* my daughter. "Did Iris give you any trouble with the ear drops?"

"Nope. But I did have to bribe her with ice cream."

"That's fine. Thanks again, and I'll see you tomorrow night."

Locking up behind her, I tiptoe to Iris' room and quietly open the door. I walk over to her bed, adjusting the covers and moving a few wisps of light blonde hair out of my little girl's face. I don't want to kiss her with the grime of the club still on me, so I silently back out of her room and close the door.

Returning to the kitchen, I have every intention of tossing the flowers, but I can't bring myself to do it. Instead, I fill up a vase with water and arrange the beautiful lilies, sitting them down on the kitchen table.

A car alarm sounds in the distance, and I flip off the lights and hurry to the window. Newark has the dubious reputation of being the car theft capital of the world, and I'm praying mine didn't just add to the statistic. Peeking outside, I sigh in relief; my car is right where I left it.

Making my way to the bathroom, I let the shower heat up before stripping and climbing in. Giving myself a good scrub-bing, my mind goes back to the VIP room. God, I cannot believe I fell asleep with—as Chrissy called him—"that scary motherfucker." I was up the night before dealing with Iris' ear infection and trip to the emergency children's clinic, but men at the club don't want to know any of that. They just want the "fantasy woman" experience. Most men, anyway. I'm still trying to figure out what it is Darius wants.

Good girl. Those two little words sound in my mind.

"Well, stop it," I chastise myself.

Stepping out of the shower, I dry off before putting on a pair of panties and tank top. Giving my teeth a quick brush, I'm beyond exhausted as I climb into bed. Except I can't stop replaying the events of the evening. Tossing and turning, I eventually give up.

Marching to my closet, I grab the box on the highest shelf that houses my vibrator. I'm amped up from the club, and I need to unwind. It has nothing to do with Darius or his good girls, I lie to myself as I lay back down. Sliding my panties off, I turn on my toy and place it around my clit, using my free hand to lightly massage my breast through my shirt.

No, it has nothing at all to do with Darius and his big hand running through my hair. Or the gravely tone of his voice. Or the way he looked like he was going to devour me just like his devil tattoo, and maybe I wouldn't even have minded being eaten alive.

I imagine Darius spreading me out on the VIP room couch...

My fishnet dress is now bunched up around my waist, and he rips off my thong with his teeth.

He says something filthy-sounding in Italian—no, Greek—leaning his head down and swiping his tongue along my seam. I moan, holding onto his surprising soft curly black hair, and he growls against my clit. "Good girl."

Fuck, I'm wet. So damn wet. I turn the vibrator up to full speed.

His big hands spread my thighs open wider, flashing that naughty grin of his before he absolutely devours my pussy.

Gyrating my hips, I moan when I find the right spot; Darius' deep and dangerous voice the soundtrack to this little fantasy.

Darius

I have too many enemies to be caught with my pants around my ankles—that's the only reason I haven't pulled my dick out and jerked off to the hottest show in the world. Lily should really add curtains to her bedroom window, not that I'm complaining.

My face plastered to the window, I watch through a small opening in the askew blinds as she moves a pink wand around her pretty clit. I stifle a groan as her legs fall open— she must have found a spot she likes. Fuck, I wish I could hear her throaty little moans of pleasure.

Arching off the bed, Lily closes her eyes as she continues to run the vibrator over her clit. "Move it inside that sweet little pussy," I instruct her quietly, even though she can't hear me.

Her mouth falls open in a perfect O as she pushes the vibrator inside her.

"Good girl," I praise her.

Watching as her hot little body convulses, I turn around and walk off. It's that, or shoot a load in my pants.

Oh little angel, you're playing with fire tempting the devil.

CHAPTER
Four

Lily

"Mama!" The next morning, a little bundle of energy jumps onto my bed.

"Hey, sweetie," I say, kissing the top of my daughter's head and wrapping my arms around her. I desperately need about three more hours of sleep, but I'll take extra cuddles over sleep any day. "Did you have fun last night?"

"Yes! I had chocolate ice cream," she tells me excitedly.

"I heard all about it. How's your ear? Does it still hurt?"

"It's better."

"Good. Why don't you go potty?" I remind her.

"I already pottyed," she tells me.

"Such a big girl," I tell her proudly, smoothing her hair. "Then let's get ready—you're going to spend the day with your dad while I'm at class."

"Okay," she says, less than enthused.

"It's going to be so much fun!" I try to get her excited. Her dad's a shit co-parent, but he's the only father she's got, and so I try to encourage their relationship. It would help matters if he would pay some child support every now and then, and not miss so many visits because something from "work" came up.

"I guess," she says skeptically.

"Of course it will be! How about we go to the diner for pancakes first?"

That perks her up. "Yes! Pancakes!"

"Let's do it," I tell her.

We get ready, and after applying another round of Iris' ear drops, I give her two outfit options to choose from. I learned early on to choose my battles wisely, and battling over clothes with a precocious four-year old isn't one of them.

"This one," she says, choosing her polka dot dress and leggings.

I let Iris get dressed herself, and we walk to the door. "Mama, flowers!" she says excitedly, running over to the kitchen table and touching a petal.

"Lilies. Aren't they pretty?"

"I want flowers for my name!"

"Maybe next time." I smile at her.

We make the short drive to our favorite diner, and Iris eats her body weight in pancakes before we continue on to the park.

Iris runs to the playground, climbing the ladder to the slide. I wave at my independent girl, and she waves back with a giggle as she slides down like a little rocket.

Checking my phone, nine o'clock has come and gone, and no sign of her dad. My anger building, I give it a few more minutes before calling Harrison. It goes straight to voicemail.

Calling again, this time I leave a message. "This is Lily. Iris and I are at the park. You were supposed to meet us at nine. I'm going to wait ten more minutes; if I don't hear from you, we're leaving."

I hang up and stew for exactly ten more minutes, but no sign of Iris' dad.

"Be careful," I call to Iris, who's trying to climb up the big-kids rope tower. Losing interest when she doesn't make it very far, she hops down and returns to the slide.

Calling the babysitter, I say, "Hey, I know it's short notice and you weren't scheduled until this evening, but is there any way you could come in early? I have class at eleven, and Iris' dad was a no-show for visitation. I'll pay you double-time," I quickly add.

"Sweet! I have class, but I don't mind ditching."

"Are you sure?" I ask, feeling bad she's going to miss her college class so I can make mine.

"Yep. I can be there in about an hour."

"Perfect. We'll see you at the house."

Placing my phone in my purse, I panic when I don't see Iris. That is until I see Iris being pushed on the swing by *Darius*. Now it's time to fucking panic!

I run over to the swing set, grabbing the chains to slow it down. "Mama, I'm swinging!" Iris protests.

Pulling her into my arms, I glare at Darius. "What are you doing here?"

"About to go for a run," he says, glancing down to his long sleeve T-shirt that fits his muscles like a second skin, and running shorts. "But any time a polka dot princess needs assistance, I'm here to help."

Iris giggles.

"Thanks, but we don't need a knight in shining armor," I snipe. "Enjoy your run," I tell him, carrying Iris back to my car.

Hitting the unlock on my key fob, Darius is already there to open the back door for me. "Milady," he tells me with a dramatic bow.

Iris giggles again as she climbs into her car seat.

"Polka dot princess," Darius says with another bow.

Iris places her hand dramatically on her forehead. "I'm not really a princess! I'm Iris."

"Sweetie, we don't give our names to strangers," I remind her.

"But you know him, so he's not a stranger," she points out.

"Iris," he says her name reverently. "Not a princess, but a rainbow goddess! Does mama like Greek mythology?" Darius asks me, raising an eyebrow.

"None of your business," I say coolly.

"Mama, that's not nice," Iris tells me.

"Listen to the wise rainbow messenger," Darius tells me. "Iris, it was so nice to meet you."

I close the car door harder than necessary, and glare at him. "Stay away from me and Iris."

He leans in, whispering in my ear, "Why would I want to do that, *aggeloudhi mou*." His lips barely graze my ear, causing my nipples to pebble. He smells good; not cologne, but a manly smell mixed with something spicy.

Christ, who cares what he smells like? Fumbling behind me, I blindly reach for the handle, not wanting to turn my back to him.

"Smart woman," he comments as if he can read my mind. Opening the door, I stumble inside the car. "Be safe," Darius tells me as he closes my door.

Be safe? The only safe place for me is far, far away from that man.

"Mama, why are you breathing so hard?"

"Am I?" I say as I pull out of the parking lot.

Returning home, I turn on a cartoon for Iris so I can get ready for class. It's hot outside, and yet I choose a baggy sweater and loose pants. My Greek mythology professor's eyes linger just a bit longer than I'm comfortable. It's one thing to be leered at when I'm Pearl—that goes with the territory—but it's another when I'm wanting to be taken seriously as an academic; and hopefully one day, a professor.

The babysitter arrives, and I kiss my daughter goodbye and drive to class, replaying the park incident over and over. I also remind myself—over and over—*bad boy*!

Darius

Following Lily through campus, I don't know why she's wearing pants and a sweater, being it's nearly seventy-five degrees. But her hiding that tight little body does nothing to stop the college boys from taking a second look; and them taking a second look is doing *nothing* to stop the fury building inside me.

She steps inside the Humanities building, and I wait a few minutes before following. Just when I think I've lost her, I spot her blonde halo peeking out from a sea of students. She enters a classroom, and I take a seat on a bench at the end of the hall.

Pulling Lily's schedule from my back pocket, her only class today is a forty-five minute Greek mythology lecture. I kill time by fantasizing about *killing* all the fuckers who looked too long at Lily. With their dead eyes on us, I'd claim her as mine right there on the grass of the quad so everyone knows who she belongs to.

Fuck, where did that last thought come from? I don't know, but my dick's getting hard imagining it.

Lily

"Ms. Grant, just a moment." My professor stops me before I can make it to the exit.

"Yes, Professor Miller?" I ask warily.

"Walk with me to my office."

"What seems to be the issue?" The last thing I want is to be alone with this man if I can help it.

"I want to talk to you about grad school, but this discussion is better had in private," he says somberly.

"Sure," I say, my stomach in knots; I've yet to receive my acceptance letter.

We reach his office, and he unlocks the door. Following him past his T.A.'s empty desk, we reach his inner office. He gestures to a chair across from his desk, I have a seat as he closes the door. Those knots in my stomach have tied themselves into knots.

Taking a seat behind his desk, he says, "You missed my last lecture. Everything alright?"

"Oh, yes. Just dealing with a personal matter." The babysitter was unavailable, and of course, Harrison was too, but I never use my daughter as an excuse to garner sympathy.

He furrows his brow. "You feeling alright?"

"Yes. Why do you ask?"

"You've been wearing such heavy clothes lately, I didn't know if you were sick." He eyes my outfit.

"I never know with this building—one room's a sauna, the next an ice box," I say lightly.

"That's interesting," he comments, leaning forward. "You don't seem to have a problem showing a bit more skin at Glitter."

"Excuse me?" I say, nearly falling out of my chair.

"I've seen you dance a few times now," he tells me, and I

feel like I'm going to throw up. "You're quite the entertainer. I just hope it doesn't affect your academic future."

"What I do during my personal time is my business." I square my chin, but my heart feels like it's going to beat out of my chest.

He *tsks*. "A nice ideal, but we don't live in an ideal world."

"What are you saying?"

"As you know, I'm on the graduate admissions committee. This letter hasn't been sent out yet, but I'll let you in on a little secret—you've been accepted. But," he says, holding up my acceptance letter like he's dangling a carrot, "now that I have this new information about your 'extracurriculars,' I'm wondering if I should inform the committee?"

"Are you blackmailing me?" My mouth falls open.

His lips curl into a predatory smile. "You want me to keep your little secret, I'll need something in return."

"What?" I say in shock, refusing to believe this is happening.

"*Extras*. Isn't that what you girls call them?" His eyes travel to my tits, lingering there.

"I need to go," I whisper, swallowing down bile.

"Of course." He gives me a patronizing smile when his eyes meet mine. "Just let me know what you decide. Admission letters go out next week. Plus, your essay for my class is due soon, and of course finals are fast-approaching," he says, the threat lingering heavily in the air.

Nodding, I stand with shaky legs, somehow making it to the door.

"I wouldn't sit on my offer too long, *Pearl*," he calls after me as I dart out of his office.

CHAPTER
Five

Lily

Sprinting down the hall and out the building, I don't stop to catch my breath until I'm behind the wheel of my car. "Fuck!" I pull out of the garage, swiping angrily at the tears threatening to fall from my eyes. There was always a small chance a classmate would be at the club when I was dancing; but I fly under the radar at school, to where I thought no one would put two and two together. It *never* crossed my mind it would be a professor, and he'd use the information to blackmail me.

Driving aimlessly, I find myself in front of my favorite coffee shop, so I pull into the parking lot. Caffeine and sugar won't magically solve this problem, but it can't hurt.

Stepping inside, I place my order and snag a table in the back, mentally working through all the possible scenarios. It's too late in the semester to drop Professor Miller's class, so that's not even an option. I could report him, but it would be my word against a respected, senior professor.

I could go back to his office to "discuss" his offer, this time recording him on my phone; then I could file a complaint with proof he's a scumbag. Good plan, except that would only ensure my status as an exotic dancer comes to light. Sure it's not illegal, but Professor Miller was right about one thing —we don't live in an ideal world. I'd be judged, best-case scenario; worst-case scenario, I'd be passed over the graduate program because of my "extracurriculars."

Providing "extras" to his slimy ass isn't an option...but then what option does that leave me with?

Frustrated, I pull out my notebook and turn my attention to my essay. As Professor Miller so aptly pointed out, it's due soon. I'm focusing on Amekhania—the Greek Goddess of helplessness—with the overarching theme of oppression of women figures in Greek mythology. The irony isn't lost on me.

"Lily," a young barista appears, holding a plate with my amaretti cookies and espresso.

"Yes, thank you."

She sits the plate down, but doesn't leave. "Hi, I'm Valentina." She smiles brightly. "You come in here quite a bit; I thought I'd introduce myself."

"Hi, Valentina. It's nice to meet you," I tell her.

"You a college student?" she asks, eyeing my notebook.

"Yes. Undergrad. Hopefully a grad student next semester." Saying the last part has my stomach churning.

"Congrats. What major?"

"Classical studies with a minor in Greek mythology."

"Wow. Um, that sounds really boring. No offense," she quickly amends.

"None taken," I say with a little laugh. "How about you?"

"I'm about to graduate high school. But the exciting news is I'm starting my own event planning company! If you're even *thinking* of getting married, I'm your planner," she says excitedly. "Sorry, I can't help but work in a business pitch with everyone I meet now!"

"No chance of me getting married anytime soon," I warn her, "but good luck with your company."

"Thanks! Well, I better get back to work. Nice to meet you."

"Nice to meet you too," I call after her.

Spending a few hours working on my essay, I pack up my things and make the drive to Glitter.

I keep glancing nervously over my shoulder as I hurry to the club's back door, sighing a breath of relief when the devil doesn't appear. I've got enough shit to deal with without analyzing why I've masturbated to the thought of a man who might really be mobbed-up. Granted, most of the rumors about Darius sound like bullshit, but I'd be a fool to ignore the red flag of him dropping ten grand—*cash*—without so much as blinking an eye. Not to mention his "not a nick-name" nickname.

I try to sneak past Leo's office, but he spots me. "Pearl, just a sec."

Sticking my head in his door, I plaster on a smile. I swear to God, if another slimeball harasses me, I'm going to lose it. "What's up, Leo?"

"This is yours." He holds up an envelope, and I walk over and grab it. Peeking inside, I'm shocked to find stacks of hundred dollar bills. "From last night, minus the house cut," he explains.

"Thanks," I say, stunned.

He nods, indicating the conversation's over, and I keep walking.

"Heard a rumor about Pearl sucking Leo's dick," I overhear Amethyst lying as I step into the dressing room. "Maybe that's why he gave Star the boot. To keep his little BJ buddy happy."

"Amethyst, you are so full of shit," I say, and she spins around.

"Just what I heard," she says, examining her nails.

"I'd be careful, Amethyst. Pearl is *Diávolos'* girl," Chrissy warns.

Amethyst's eyes go wide, and I say, "That's right. Eat your *heart* out."

The girls gasp, whispering as I change into my stage clothes and stash my bag and envelope in my locker. I'm not *Diávolos'* girl, but I'm starting to see the upside of everyone at the club believing I am.

Hitting the main floor with a spring in my step, I approach the front door bouncer and say, "Hey, there's a man who's causing problems for me. If he tries to get into the club, could you turn him away? Name's Robert Miller. Early fifties. Around six feet tall. Lean build. Light brown hair graying around the ears. Fair skin. Green eyes. Preppy dress."

"I would do this why?" he asks in a bored tone.

Reaching in my g-string, I hand him a hundred dollar bill.

"Should've led with that," he tells me, stuffing the money in his pocket. "Robert Miller's a no-go."

If only handling Professor Miller were that easy in my other world.

Darius

Hearing every word the good professor said to Lily—I was standing right outside the fucker's office while he was threatening and sexually harassing her—I'm now outside his house. This neighborhood should really increase the HOA monthly fee, because the security around here's nonexistent.

I've already checked the exterior to make sure there are no cameras; good to go. I ring the doorbell, shifting my takeout bag.

Robert Miller opens the door. "Yes?"

"Dinner delivery."

"I'm sorry, you must have the wrong—"

I've already rushed inside the house with the door closed behind me before the professor can finish his sentence. Sitting the bag down on the entrance table next to a bicycle helmet, I sucker punch the man in the stomach.

He groans, falling to his knees.

My shoe connects with his face, and he tumbles over with a cry.

"Up," I say, dragging him to the kitchen.

"Help!" he screams, and I slap a piece of tape over his mouth before punching him in the kidneys.

Professor Miller's eyes snap shut in pain, and I drag the struggling man up the stairs, only to give him a good heave-ho back down. Hence the duct tape, because I knew he'd scream like a little bitch. He's still screaming like a little bitch, it's just coming out muffled as he bounces down the steps like a pinball.

Taking the steps two at a time, I join the good professor, who's taking a little cat nap at the landing of the stairs. Feeling his pulse—a shame; he's still alive—I drag him back up the stairs by his feet, making sure his skull connects with each and every step. I find the bedroom, dragging him inside and tossing him on the bed. Surveying the damage, I smile. Is he ever going to feel this when he wakes up from his concussion. The professor likely has a broken ankle based on the swelling, along with various abrasions and bruises all over his body; not to mention some nasty internal bruising, and a nice-sized goose egg on his forehead.

Minutes pass before I loose patience. Grabbing a vial of smelling salts from my pocket, I open the tiny jar and wave it back and forth near the professor's nose. His eyes snap open, and he goes to rip off the duct tape, but I wag my finger at him. He wisely stills his movement.

"What you just experienced? Fucking child's play. If I have to come back for round two? Things will get very uncomfortable for you, professor," I warn him. "Do you know what would make me come back for round two?"

He shakes his head furiously.

"If you try to fuck with Lily Grant again. You understand, professor? Lily is mine." She just doesn't know it yet.

He nods like a bobble head.

"Good. So here's what's going to happen—you're going to take the rest of the semester off to recover from your 'cycling' accident. But not before you ensure Lily's acceptance into grad school. At least, that's what's going to happen if you want to stay alive. You *do* want to stay alive, don't you, Professor Miller?"

Eyes wide, he nods again.

"Excellent. Then my work here is done. Unless you so much as look at Lily, then my work *isn't* done." I make a little gun-shooting motion with my finger and thumb before strolling out. But not before grabbing my takeout bag.

CHAPTER
Six

Lily

Spreading out our picnic blanket in the grass near the pond, Iris and I sit cross-legged as we nibble on sandwiches.

"Do I have to go with Dad today?" she wonders.

"Not today, sweetie. I'm sure he's busy with work." God, I get tired of covering for his sorry ass. If he's not busy with work, then he's busy with one of his *many* women.

"Okay," she says, not sounding too disappointed. "Time to feed the ducks," she announces dramatically, and I chuckle, opening a bag of crackers for her. She runs over to the water's edge, tossing them in one-by-one.

Grabbing my phone, I fire off a message to Harrison.

> Either be in Iris' life or don't. Your choice. But this halfway shit is getting old.

"Just a few more minutes," I warn Iris as I gather our things.

"Aww!" She goes to work tossing the crackers in big handfuls.

"A rainbow goddess feeding a duck goddess!" Darius exclaims.

"What are you doing here?" I demand.

"Perfect day for a run." He glances down to his long-sleeve tee and sweatpants, and my eyes follow. Damn the man for wearing gray sweatpants, and wearing them well.

"What duck goddess?" Iris asks, and I snap my attention to my daughter.

"Penelope. She's a duck." He makes a *quack-quack* sound.

Iris giggles. "Really?"

"Not exactly," I say. "Penelope's a goddess who was saved by ducks when she was a baby. She was later demoted from the important role of ushering in spring to that of Odysseus' wife."

"So your mama *does* like Greek mythology," he tells me with a smirk. "Who wants to go ride the carousel?"

"Me! Me!" Iris hops up and down.

I shake my head. "We need to go."

"Please, Mama?" She gives me her best puppy-dog eyes.

I sigh. "Just one ride."

"Yay!" Iris exclaims.

"I'll have to run to the car to grab some change," I tell her.

"I have it covered, milady," Darius says with another exaggerated bow, which makes Iris giggle. He squats down to her level; reaching behind her ear, he makes a dollar "appear."

"How did you do that?" Iris examines the money before reaching behind her own ear. Her little face scrunches up adorably when she doesn't find another dollar back there.

"Magic." Darius smiles, handing her the dollar. He surprises me by taking the bag from my shoulder.

"Are you Mama's boyfriend?" Iris asks Darius.

"No!" I answer quickly. Glancing over to Darius, he has an amused look on his face, like he knows something I don't.

"How old are you?" Iris asks him. Since I want to know the answer, I don't chastise her for asking.

"In dog years or people years?" Darius wonders.

She laughs, placing a hand on her head. "People years!"

He smiles. "In that case, I'm twenty-six."

"Mama, how old are you?"

"Twenty-two," I remind her.

"And I'm four, almost five," she announces proudly.

"Four, almost five, but going on sixteen," Darius comments, and I smile at his astute observation. Iris' preschool teacher has already given me the information about having Iris tested for gifted when she enters kindergarten this fall. But my smile fades when I remember this is *Diávolos* I'm dealing with here— the same *Diávolos* who threatened me in the alley; who loves offal; and who may or may not be hooked up with the mob.

"Not sixteen! Four, *almost* five," Iris says, exasperated, and I chuckle quietly.

We reach the carousel, and Iris proudly hands over her dollar to the attendant. Darius pays for the two of us, and we all climb onto the platform. Iris races to her horse. "This one!"

Darius beats me there, easily lifting Iris and placing her on a horse with a rainbow saddle. "Perfect choice for the rainbow goddess," he announces, fastening her lap belt.

"I'm not really a goddess," Iris corrects him.

"Really? Could've fooled me."

Double checking Iris' belt, I climb onto the horse beside her, with Darius standing on the outside of Iris. "You not going to ride?" I ask him. As soon as the question's out of my mouth, I can feel my cheeks heating.

"I'd definitely be up for a ride later," he tells me with another wink. Could my cheeks get any redder?

"Mama said just one ride," Iris reminds him.

"Disagree with that philosophy," he tells me, a naughty glint in his eyes.

Thankfully, the carousel begins its rotation. Iris waves at me, and I blow her a kiss. Smiling, I glance over to Darius who's looking like a man picturing a ride later. *With me.*

Yes, my cheeks can get redder.

The carousel thankfully stops spinning, but before I can even dismount, Darius has Iris off her horse. She takes his big hand with a smile, and alarm bells are blaring in my head. My daughter simply *cannot* get attached to this dangerous man.

"Come on, sweetie. Time to go," I say, pulling her away from Darius.

"I'll walk you ladies to your car," he says.

"Not necessary," I tell him, trying to grab my bag.

He smiles, holding it up to where I can't reach it.

I sigh in frustration, unable to shake him as we walk to my car. Getting Iris in her car seat, I close the door, turning to face Darius. "Look, whatever this thing is between us ends here," I declare, snatching my bag.

"Whatever you say, *aggeloudhi mou*." He shocks me by kissing the tip of my nose before turning around and sauntering off.

"Mama, you're breathing hard again," Iris points out.

"Am I?" Having a child with sharp observation skills has its drawbacks.

We return home, and I change into my lounge clothes. Needing to work on my essay, I curse when I realize my backpack is at the club.

The doorbell rings, and I walk to the front door, looking out the peephole. Opening the door, I greet the babysitter. "Hey. Oh my gosh, I forgot to text you! I've got the evening off." There's some kind of private event at the club, and I wasn't asked to be there. Probably for the best, because I'm sure extras would be involved. "But since you're here, could you watch Iris while I go run some errands?"

"No problem," she assures me.

"Great. Iris, sweetie, I'll be back in a little bit," I say, kissing the top of her head. "Love you."

"Bye, Mama. Love you," she says, her eyes glued to her favorite cartoon about a big red dog.

Driving to the club, the outside lights are turned off and it appears deserted. Hopefully that means the event hasn't started yet. I park in the employee lot and grab my phone, quickly walking to the back door and punching in the code. Entering the dressing room, I unlock my locker and grab my backpack, slipping my phone inside the exterior pocket.

That's when I hear it—a round of loud *bangs*.

Must be a car backfiring, I think as I close my locker and walk out of the dressing room. And nearly trip on something. Looking down, it takes my brain a moment to process what I'm seeing.

A body.

A dead body.

Leo's dead body.

Eyes open and glassy, his head looks like a piece of bloody Swiss cheese—with the wall behind him spattered in crimson. Horrified, I stifle a scream with my hands over my mouth; my backpack falls to the floor with a loud *thump*.

The sound of male voices are coming from the main floor, and then there's another *bang*—this one sounding closer.

Sprinting down the hall, I reach the utility closet, quietly pulling the door to and locking it. My legs give out as I slide to the floor, hugging my knees to my chest as I rock back and forth.

Oh my God. Leo's fucking dead. And if whoever killed him finds me, I'm next.

CHAPTER
Seven

Darius

I'm rapping up my solo workout at the gym, when my burner phone rings. "Darius," I answer.

"There's a problem," Sammy says.

"Agreed. Your undercut is fucking awful, but no barber's gonna be able to fix that."

"Shut the fuck up. This is serious," he snaps. "Romeo just texted me to meet him at Glitter strip club, but he knows I'm on guard duty with Valentina tonight. I think it's a setup. He was supposed to pick up a package from Matteo."

I should have killed that little shit, Matteo, when I had the chance. "On my way now."

"I'll meet you there with our crew. Wait for me before you make a move."

"Got it."

Thankfully, Lily isn't scheduled to work tonight. In fact, I was just about to drop by her house to see what the little angel was up to this evening, but my obsession will have to wait. I quickly gear up with a flak jacket and pistol. Not sure what exactly we're dealing with, I grab a variety of weapons and supplies, stashing everything in a duffle bag.

Locking up behind me, I place my bag in the hidden compartment in my trunk, making the drive to Glitter. All the while, I'm envisioning gutting Matteo like a fish. And if the redhead Amethyst is here, I'll find out about those puffer-fish lips after all. Downright giddy at the prospect, I park across the street from the club and wait. Waiting is fucking hard.

Finally, a convoy of blacked-out SUVs rolls up, with Sammy hopping out of the lead vehicle, followed by my friend Fabio carrying a battering ram. Soldiers pour out of their vehicles with various armaments; one guy's assembling a small rocket launcher.

Exiting my vehicle with my tiny bag of toys in compari-son, I tell Sammy, "While your way makes for a flashier entrance, I know the code to the backdoor." By watching Lily's lovely fingers on the keypad.

"Diversion at the front of the club while we sneak in the back," Sammy tells Fabio before barking orders in Italian to the men, and Fabio and the soldiers peel off.

Sammy and I quickly make our way to the back of the club where Romeo's SUV is parked. "Matteo is mine," he says quietly.

I grunt, making no promises.

Gunfire sounds from the front, and that's our cue. Punching in the code, I enter with my pistol drawn, Sammy at my back. I lead us down the hallway, having to step over Leo's body. A shame, as I wanted to kill the little weasel myself.

My eyes land on a pink backpack with butterflies that looks an awful lot like Lily's. Why Leo had her backpack, I don't know, but there's no time to worry about it, as we've reached the end of the hallway opening up to the main floor.

I peek around the corner. Sergio's greasy ass is hiding

behind a flipped table, along with someone I can't make out because his back is to me.

Scratch that. His back *was* to me. Sammy just put a bullet in Crazy Carlo's head, and the boss of Philly crumbles to the floor.

A bullet wizzes at me, and I duck behind the wall before popping back up and returning fire—hitting the fucker square between the eyes.

The rest of Crazy Carlo's men get popped, and Sergio's the last "man" standing. He rises from behind the table with his gun drawn, but the look on his face is priceless when nothing happens: he's out of bullets.

Sammy speaks into his earpiece, and our crew descends upon the main floor. "Clear," one of our guys announces, and Sammy and I make our way through the haze of gun smoke.

"Shit," I comment, spotting Antonio Parisi's body next to the stage.

Romeo appears from the back of the VIP room area with a smile on his face. Jesus, he looks deranged—and that's saying something coming from me.

"Shit is right," Sammy agrees.

Sergio drops his gun and holds up his hands. "Romeo, let me explain."

"By all means," Romeo says, strolling over; the calm before the storm.

Sergio reaches into his pant ankle and pulls out a knife. I raise my gun to put a bullet in the rat's head, but Sammy holds up his hand. "You kill him, and Romeo will be pissed," he tells me quietly.

Romeo's already pissed, and not wanting his ire directed at me, I lower my gun.

Sergio grunts as he lunges, but Romeo easily sidesteps him; grabbing Sergio's wrist using his right hand, Romeo gives it a good twist. The knife clatters to the floor as Sergio squeals in pain, and Romeo delivers a punishing left hook.

The blow causes the old man's head to violently snap to the side, and it's lights out for Sergio as he crumbles to the floor. Romeo pulls out his dick and pisses on the unconscious man's face. Nice touch.

Putting his dick up, Romeo kicks Sergio's head to the side —ensuring the old man doesn't choke to death, because there's no fun in that. "Luca's been shot. Sam, come with me," Romeo orders. "Darius, load up Sergio in my trunk, along with Antonio and Carlo, then torch the club," he commands, tossing me the keys to his SUV.

The men take off to the VIP rooms, and I survey the scene —the haze of gunfire lingers in the air, along with the metallic tinge of blood. It's intoxicating, but I need to focus.

Sergio's beginning to rouse, and I secure him with zip ties and drag him up the steps to the main stage. Binding him to the stripper pole, I hop down and search Carlo's body. Removing two knives and a small pistol—no need to give Sergio even a snowball's chance of escape—I drag the body out and toss Carlo's ugly mug into the trunk. Hustling back, I do the same for Antonio before dragging the former boss of Jersey out by his feet, all the while Sergio cries and pleads like a little bitch.

"Please, stop! How much is Romeo paying you? Whatever it is, I'll double it!" Sergio begs as I return inside, taking the steps two at a time.

Patting him down, I tell him, "It's called loyalty, Sergio. Something a rat like you would never understand."

"You think the family will show you *loyalty* when push comes to shove?" He sneers. "You'll never be made, no matter how much you lick Romeo's boots. You'll always be 'the Greek.'" He taunts. "The stray dog nobody in the family respects."

Having heard enough, I grab duct tape from my bag and slap a piece over his mouth before cutting him from the stripper pole and dragging him outside to Romeo's waiting trunk. Squatting down, it's difficult for me to get good grip on the rather obese man flailing about like a fish out of water. "Good God, man." I grunt, standing up with a bloody Sergio in my arms. "Would it kill you to turn down a cannoli every now and then?" Tossing him on top of the two dead bodies, I take great satisfaction in the abject terror in his eyes as I close the trunk.

Returning inside, I find Romeo carrying Luca—whose face is ghastly pale and stomach is gushing blood like a stuck pig —with Nicky following. She's wearing Romeo's shirt and is barefoot, walking on her tiptoes trying not to step on glass. Or worse.

Romeo notices his girl's situation. "Sam, carry her."

"I'm not wearing panties, remember?" Nicky says.

"Sam, don't fucking touch her," Romeo barks.

I hustle over, solving the problem by taking Luca from Romeo.

Now that his hands are free, Romeo picks up Nicky, who looks like she's bathed in a bucket of blood.

"Does this mean you two are going steady?" Sam asks me and Luca as we step outside.

"Fuck you," Luca whispers. The man's still got some fight in him if he's able to talk smack.

I place Luca in the backseat as gently as I can. "Don't die, my man," I tell him.

"I'll try my best," he says weakly, and I close the door.

Enzo nods at me before he gets behind the wheel, and they take off to the clinic.

Returning inside, I make one more sweep of the main floor, screwing on a silencer to my gun and pumping a bullet in the head of each of Carlo's men. Just in case.

After retrieving Lily's backpack and stashing it in my car, I make my way to the VIP rooms. Disappointment washes over me when I discover Matteo's dead body with a stripper heel protruding from his neck. Not as nice as me killing him, but points for creativity.

I spot a bloody corpse with a tangle of pink hair in the corner. More disappointment until I notice the lips— Amethyst has changed her hair. Squatting down, I grab my knife from my ankle strap, hovering it over her mouth. But what *if* poison oozes out from those babies when I slice them open? Deciding my morbid curiosity isn't worth the risk, I sheath my knife.

Walking to the utility closet with my bag, I jiggle the handle, but it's locked. I easily kick the door in and step inside, only to come face-to-face with an angel.

Not the angel of death, but a little angel with a blonde halo, whose hauntingly pale blue eyes are pleading with me.

CHAPTER
Eight

Lily

"Please don't kill me," I beg Darius. "I wasn't even here. I don't know anything. Please just let me go, I won't say a word!"

Before I know what's happening, he has my hands secured with zip ties. "No!" I scream, but I'm silenced when he slaps a piece of tape over my mouth.

He hoists me over his shoulder, and I struggle against him. My feet are free, and one of them connects with his rock-hard stomach.

Grunting, he grabs ahold of my ankles with his other hand, and now, my legs are bound. Muttering something in Greek, he carries me outside. An older model sedan is parked right by the door with the trunk open, and I begin thrashing and trying to scream as he carries me to it.

"Give me just a few minutes, *aggeloudhi mou*," he says, placing me inside the trunk.

My eyes wide with terror and my cries muffled by the tape, he closes the trunk, and I'm plunged into darkness.

Darius

Lily has a terrible habit of being at the wrong place at the wrong time. "Fuck!" I thunder, grabbing a chair in my way and flinging it across the room.

Taking a deep breath, I focus. First things first. I gather all the weapons, because a fire won't destroy the evidence.

Placing all the firearms—and a few knives for Sammy—in the hidden compartment under my backseat, I return inside to the utility room. I manipulate the electrical wiring and take a blowtorch, making it look like the circuit breaker over-heated. Dumping a bag of trash on the floor, I pour gasoline over the debris. It'll look like the circuit breaker sparked into the trash, causing the fire. As for the overwhelming smell of gasoline and those snitch burn patterns, that's why the fire marshal is on the family's payroll.

Stepping outside, I hop behind the wheel, moving my car a safe distance from the building before sprinting back. Noticing Lily's car in the back lot, I run over and swipe the license plate and scratch off the VIN. That's as good as I can do given my time constraints.

And now the tricky part—starting the fire without getting myself killed. Hustling to the utility closet, I strike a match and toss it on the gasoline-soaked pile of trash and run like hell.

Lily

My life has flashed before my eyes too many times to count, but my thoughts keep circling back to Iris, and what's going to happen to her when I die. I almost started to believe Darius wasn't really the devil. When am I going to learn my lesson about bad boys?

The car begins moving. Oh God, he's taking me somewhere to kill me.

We haven't traveled very far when the car comes to a stop. I don't know what's happening, but a loud *boom* rattles the trunk, and I scream; futile, because my mouth's still covered with tape.

We start moving again, and I try to keep my breathing even so I don't spiral into a full-blown panic attack. Thinking of Iris only makes things worse, and so to distract myself, I mentally count the seconds in Latin.

Having reached *octingentī duodecim*, the car lurches to a stop. Oh my God, this is it.

The trunk opens, and my killer looms over me. "*Aggeloudhi mou*," Darius says softly, scooping me out of the trunk bridal-style.

Thrashing wildly, I rear back and head butt him with all my might. Shit, that hurt.

"Σκατά," he mutters, his arms tightening around me to the point of pain. "Stop that, or I'll put you back in the trunk," he menaces. "You going to be a good girl?"

I nod furiously.

"Then you can ride up front with me," he says, opening the passenger door and placing me gently on the seat. Squatting down, he grabs a knife from his ankle, and my eyes go wide with fear. "I'm just cutting you loose," he explains, making quick work of the zip ties around my ankles and wrists.

I rip the tape off my mouth and let out a blood-curdling

scream as I scramble across the console to the driver's side door.

Darius grabs my ankle before I can get there, yanking me back to the passenger seat. "That's not being a good girl, Lily," he chastises, closing and locking my door.

He walks around the vehicle, and I desperately tug at my door handle, but it won't budge. "Help!" I scream, banging on the window.

"Why are you acting this way?" he demands as he slides behind the wheel and buckles up.

"Are you fucking serious?" I shriek. "I'm a witness to at least one murder, and pretty sure you just blew up the club because you reek of gasoline. I know too much, and you're going to kill me. I'm acting this way because I'm fucking terrified!"

"Lily, I've already told you not to be afraid of me. But yes, you do know too much, and so there's only one solution," he says solemnly.

Me dead, I think with a gulp.

"We'll get married."

"What?" My mouth falls open.

"You can't be forced to testify against me if you're my wife. We'll both keep our mouths shut about what just went down, and everything will work out," he sells it, as if it's a great idea.

"This is crazy!"

"You like the alternative?" he challenges.

"I'm not going to say anything to the cops. I swear it. Please just let me go," I beg.

He snorts. "The cops are the least of your concerns. The family finds out you were at the club tonight, I won't be able to protect you. *Unless* you're my wife."

"The family?"

"My associates."

"The mob?" I whisper with another gulp, and he slices his

head in confirmation. "What is it you do for these associates?" Besides threatening strippers and blowing up buildings.

"Nothing for you to worry about," he says in a tone indicating this line of questioning is over.

We drive in silence, my brain frantically trying to come up with a way out of this mess. Glancing over to the devil on his forearm, I blurt out, "Do you eat your victims' hearts raw?"

He snorts a laugh.

"The girls at the club hear things," I tell him defensively.

"Who says there are victims?" he challenges.

"Answer my question," I say, crossing my arms.

"Lily, I can assure you I've never eaten a raw heart."

"Did you kill Leo?" I whisper.

"No," he answers emphatically, and for some reason, I believe him.

"I heard multiple shots—"

"You didn't hear anything. You didn't see anything. If anyone asks, you weren't there. Now, no more questions." He grabs his phone, making a call in Greek as we turn onto a deserted highway.

"Where are we going?" I ask when he ends the call.

"Didn't I just tell you no more questions?" He raises an eyebrow.

"But—"

"Atlantic City. My cousin will hook us up with the marriage paperwork."

"There's got to be another way," I plead.

"You said it yourself: you know too much. If the feds don't try to get to you first, the family will," he warns.

Fuck.

"*Unless* you're under my protection. And to be under my protection, you need to be my wife. There's no other way." He locks eyes with me, and I can see the sincerity written all over his face. He truly believes the words he just spoke.

Fuck again.

Glancing at the clock, I realize how late it is. "I need to call the babysitter," I say in a rush.

Reaching behind us, he tosses me my backpack. "Not a word about this to anyone, or back in the trunk you go," he warns.

My hand shaking, I fish out my phone, seeing I've missed several calls and texts from the babysitter. Calling her back, she answers on the first ring. "Hey, I am so sorry to leave you hanging," I tell her. "Something came up." A hysterical laugh escapes my lips, and I slap my hand over my mouth.

"Are you alright?" she asks.

Feeling Darius' gaze on me, I drop my hand. "Yes, I'm fine." I try to keep my voice steady as I ask, "Is there any way you could spend the night with Iris? Of course I'll pay you double-time for the entire night."

"Awesome! I'll hang right here."

"Thanks," I say, ending the call.

"Everything alright with Iris?" Darius asks.

Narrowing my eyes at him, I say, "We need to set a few ground rules about this *marriage*."

"Do we now?" he says in an amused tone.

"Yes, we do. I'll marry you in name, but our lives need to remain separate," I tell him. "Your world is obviously dangerous, and I have Iris to protect."

He locks eyes with me—his blazing with intensity. "I'll protect you and Iris."

"You'll protect me and Iris by staying away from us. We'll be married on paper, but that's it," I tell him sternly.

He doesn't comment, instead turning on the radio to classical music.

"I wouldn't have pegged you for a classical music listener," I admit.

He smiles cruelly. "You think I'm a dumb brute."

"I didn't say that."

"Hmm."

"One other thing," I continue.

"What, more ground rules?" he mocks.

"Don't ever put me in the trunk again," I tell him, crossing my arms.

"I will do whatever it takes to keep you safe in any given situation. Any other ground rules?" he asks.

"Yes. We are *not* consummating this marriage," I say firmly.

Darius looks over to me and smiles. "Whatever you say, future wifey."

CHAPTER
Nine

Lily

We arrive in Atlantic City, making our way past the bright lights of the casinos to a less flashy residential street. Pulling into a condo complex, Darius parks the car and opens my door for me. "This is a wedding, not a funeral," he reminds me.

Funny, because it feels like both.

We walk to the front stoop, and he rings the doorbell. A pretty woman around my age answers. "Come in," she says enthusiastically, closing the door behind her. "Hi, I'm Kat," she says to me with a hint of a Greek accent. She's tall and slender, with dark features, lovely olive skin, and wild black curls flowing down her back.

"Hello. I'm Lily." I force a smile.

"Lily, it's nice to meet you. Have a seat." Kat gestures to the couch. Sniffing Darius, she makes a face. "Should I ask?"

"You shouldn't," he says matter-of-factly. "I need a shower."

"You know where the bathroom is, cousin."

"*Aggeloudhi mou*, go ahead and start on the paperwork,

and I'll be back in a few minutes," Darius tells me. He says something to Kat in Greek before disappearing down the hall.

"What Darius just called me in Greek, what does it mean?" I ask her.

"*Little angel*. So freakin' sweet." She beams at me. "How long have you and my cousin been together?"

"We're not together," I correct her.

"Oh?" She raises an eyebrow, and then glances pointedly to the marriage paperwork on the table.

"I mean we are together. It's just…" I pause, searching for the right word that won't get me killed. "Complicated."

She pats my hand. "Look at it this way: you'll never be bored with complicated."

"Are you speaking from experience?" I wonder.

"Most definitely. Red flags are my love language," she says with a laugh. "Please, sit."

I take a seat on the couch, and Kat sits cross-legged on the floor next to the coffee table as she goes through the paperwork. "How do you have all this?" I ask.

"My friend works at the Registrar's office," she explains. "There's a mandatory seventy-two hour waiting period to get a marriage license. My friend will need you and Darius to fill out the application so she can get it backdated and filed. Don't worry; we'll get the love birds all squared away."

"Great." Catching myself wringing my hands, I drop them in my lap.

Eying me with a concerned look, Kat says quietly, "Listen, I don't know what's going on here, but if you really don't want to marry him, tell me now."

Darius said not a word to anyone; besides, unloading on this woman—who seems really nice—only puts her at risk. "I'm just nervous," I answer, which isn't a lie. Accepting the application and pen, I get to work answering the questions. "So Darius is your cousin?" I ask.

"Yep. Our moms are sisters. His lives in Greece; mine here.

He got the better end of that deal." She shakes her head with a smile.

"Does he have any siblings?" I ask, feeling like that's something important I should know about the man I'm marrying.

"Only child. How about you?"

"Only child," I answer, handing her back the completed application.

Kat smiles brightly. "See, you're perfect for my cousin."

I give her a dubious look. "For *Diávolos*?"

"He's a sweetheart, once you get past the scary-as-shit exterior." She looks over the form I just filled out, signing as the witness. "Everything looks good. We'll get Darius to fill out his portion, and it's ceremony time."

"Ceremony? I thought it was just paperwork?" Paperwork feels less formal; a ceremony makes it real.

"Of course there's a ceremony. I'll have you know I'm an ordained minister," she says dramatically.

"Really?" I hear minister, I think stuffy old preacher in a suit.

"*Online* ordained," she clarifies with a chuckle. "I just officiated my friends' wedding last weekend. Yours and Darius' will be my second."

"Do we have to go though the whole 'till death do us part' bit?" I ask.

"We do," Darius answers, appearing from the hallway in a different white T-shirt and running shorts, his curly black hair wet from the shower. He's holding a bag with his crime scene clothes, and the events of the evening come crashing down on me like a baby grand piano playing the Wedding March.

"Darius, I need you to fill this out." Kat hands the application and pen to him, and he makes quick work of it. "What date do you want on the marriage license?" she asks when he returns the paperwork to her.

"Backdate it to three days ago," he instructs her, and she fills it in.

"Let's see, so that would put the application date six days ago." Kat makes a notation on a sticky note. "Now, let's talk payment. My friend will need the twenty-eight dollar filing fee, as well as a thousand dollars for her trouble. Next, my officiant fee is also a thousand dollars."

"You trying to extort me, little cousin?" Darius narrows his eyes.

"Perjurious fillings and expedited weddings are extra." Kat smiles sweetly.

He mutters something in Greek, pulling a wad of cash secured by a rubber band from his pocket. Counting out hundreds, he slaps them on the coffee table. "Two thousand, one hundred. Keep the change."

"That'll work. You two stand together over here." She points to a spot in front of the fireplace.

Oh my God, this is really happening. I stand with shaky legs, walking to my spot; Darius joins me, taking take my clammy hands in his.

"We are gathered here today to join together as one Darius Angelos and Lily Grant," Kat announces.

It feels like I'm having an out-of-body experience watching myself get married to, at best, a man I don't know, and at worst, a man I don't *want* to know.

"Lily," Kat says, jarring me from my thoughts.

"Sorry, what was that?" I whisper.

"Repeat after me," Kat says. "I, Lily Grant."

"I, Lily Grant."

"Take you, Darius Angelo."

"Take you, Darius Angelo," I repeat the words, looking at Darius. Amusement with something else flickers in his eyes.

Kat leads me through the rest of the vows, and it's Darius' turn. His intense gaze never leaves mine as he recites the words. "Till death do us part," he says with such intensity I have to avert my eyes.

"By the powers vested in me by the State of New Jersey, I now pronounce you man and wife. You may kiss the bride," Kat announces with a smile.

Man and wife.

Those words echo in my ears as Darius leans down and gives me the sweetest of kisses. I'm shocked; obviously, I knew the kiss was coming, but I didn't expect it to be so tender. He gently cups my cheeks with his big hands, angling my head to deepen the kiss.

His tongue darts out, licking the bow of my bottom lip, and I find myself opening for him. He explores my mouth with his tongue as he pulls me closer to his body—his big arms wrapped around me as his hard dick presses against my stomach. With lips as soft as pillowy clouds, he twirls his tongue around mine, and my knees feel dangerously weak.

Kat clears her throat, and I break the kiss, my face heating.

Darius smiles before kissing the tip of my nose, releasing me from his arms. "Not a word about any of this—you or your friend," he warns his cousin.

"A word about what?" Kat turns to me. "Lily, it was so nice to meet you, and congratulations! Welcome to the family," she says, hugging me.

Welcome to the family. Those words replay ominously in my mind.

CHAPTER

Ten

Lily

Feeling absolutely shell-shocked, I sneak a glance at my *husband*. Darius' face gives nothing away as he focuses on the empty stretch of road before us.

"Why are we stopping?" I finally break the uncomfortable silence when we pull into The Diamond casino.

"We're getting a room," he tells me.

Panic sets in. "But I need to get back to Iris!"

"You have a babysitter for the night," he points out. "It's late, and we're both tired."

"But—"

"We'll drive back to Newark early tomorrow morning," he promises.

"I don't have any of my things," I protest.

Parking the car, he opens my door. "We'll stop in the gift shop, and you can get what you need."

Not having any other excuses that come to mind, I take his outstretched hand—his rough bear paw practically swallows my tiny hand. He grabs my backpack before closing and locking his car, flinging my bag over one of his broad shoulders. A nervous giggle escapes my lips at the sight of this beast of man carrying my pink backpack adorned with butterflies. Iris picked it out for me; she has a matching smaller version for preschool.

"I'm secure enough in my manhood," he tells me with a wink. Based on what I felt pressed against my stomach earlier, he has reason to be secure.

I shake away that unbidden thought as we step inside the lobby and walk to the front desk. "Welcome to The Diamond," the clerk says in a flirty tone, eyeing Darius up and down. She must like what she sees, because she stands a little straighter and gives a flirty smile.

My hands have somehow balled into fists, and I force myself to relax them at my sides.

"How can I help you?" she purrs.

"My wife and I need a room for the night. Next to a stairway exit," Darius tells her.

"Let me check what we have available," she says in a much more professional tone now she knows he and I are married; *not that I care one way or the other*, I remind myself. Typing on her computer, she announces, "There's one room that fits your criteria. Price is—"

"We'll take it," Darius says, paying with cash.

He pockets the key, and leads me to the gift shop where I grab the essentials, plus some clothes. Placing the items on the counter, he joins me with some things of his own—and a mermaid doll with a *rainbow* tail.

"I know what you're doing," I say, narrowing my eyes at him.

"And what am I doing?" he challenges before handing over cash to the clerk.

Carrying the bags, he holds open the elevator door for me, and I step inside. He joins me, pressing the button.

"Darius," I start.

"Yes, wifey?"

"Don't call me that," I snap.

"What would you have me call you?"

"Stranger," I answer without hesitation.

He shakes his head with a smile. "Would a stranger know what your pretty pussy looks like? How your body shudders and arches so beautifully when you come?" he says, grabbing my chin and tilting my head so he can see my eyes. "What were you thinking of, *aggeloudhi mou*, when you touched your pink vibrator to that pretty clit of yours the other night?"

Struggling out of his hold, I say in disbelief, "Oh my God, were you watching me?"

"I'll fix your blinds," he promises.

The elevator door opens, and he silently takes my hand, leading me down the hall to the last room next to the stairwell. He's busy scanning the key card, and I take off running toward the emergency exit—because fuck yes, this is an emergency!

Cursing softly, he's already caught up to me before I can make it down the first step. "Stop that," he chastises as he picks me up and tosses me over his shoulder, giving my ass a firm smack.

I'm terrified of this psycho, and yet my pussy is tingling. My God, there is something seriously wrong with me.

He carries me inside the room and locks the door. Gripping me by the hips, he holds me up as he skims his nose along the crotch of my shorts, inhaling deeply.

I take it back; there's something seriously wrong with him!

"Now I can put a smell to the memory," he explains before placing me on my wobbly feet.

"Oh my God, this is so fucked up!" I exclaim, stumbling back from him. "How long have you been spying on me?"

"I was curious about you after I found you hiding in the alley," he admits.

"Curiosity is one thing; stalking's another," I say, crossing my arms.

He shrugs, sitting my backpack down on the coffee table. "I had to make sure you kept your mouth shut."

"If that is true, then what's the excuse for watching me alone in my bedroom?" I point out.

"It was the sexiest fucking thing I've ever seen. How could I not watch you?" he implores.

My cheeks heat, and desperately needing a distraction, I take in our accommodations. There's a sitting area with a couch and television. Bathroom with a nice shower. I peek my head in the bedroom—one bed. I return to the sitting area and remove a couch cushion, relieved to discover it has a pull-out mattress. "I'll sleep out here."

"Of course you won't," he says, like it's the silliest thing he's ever heard. "You'll take the bedroom."

"You're too big for this bed," I comment.

He grins. "I'm too big for a lot of things, *aggeloudhi mou*."

"Stop it, and stop calling me that. I'm not your little angel," I inform him crossly.

"Whatever you say, wifey," he tells me in an amused tone.

I grab my bag in frustration, marching to the bathroom and slamming the door before locking it. Gripping the vanity, I try to calm my breathing. My God, how did I wind up here? Married. To a mobbed-up man. A *crazy*, mobbed-up man who just sniffed my pussy like it was the most natural thing in the world.

Examining myself in the mirror, I look absolutely wild. Hair disheveled. Face flush. Eyes dilated. Nipples visibly hard. It's official—I'm crazy too.

Stripping out of my clothes, I take a long, hot shower—racking my brain for a way out of this mess. I give a little acrid laugh. Had I not forgotten my damn backpack at the club, none of this would be happening. Choosing the goddess of helplessness for my essay is turning out to be a self-fulfilling prophecy.

I step out of the shower and dry off, putting on my new

clothes before doing an abbreviated bedtime routine. Walking out of the bathroom, I stop short. Darius is laying on the sofa bed, shirtless, with his boxers pulled down.

Jerking his huge dick.

I try not to gasp. No wonder he's secure in his manhood—his dick is seriously bigger than my forearm. Unable to tear my eyes away, it takes me a moment to realize his anatomy looks different based on my limited experience.

"You've never seen an uncut dick?" he guesses.

I startle at being caught, and yet I'm unable to look away. Shaking my head, I say, "I've only ever been with my ex." Oh my God, why did I just tell him that?

He growls, the sound causing my nipples to pebble. "Fucker may have got there first, but I'll be there last, that I promise."

Opening my mouth to speak, I can't find the words.

"I thought I'd even the score to make you feel better. Let you watch me," he says in a husky tone. "You told me we weren't consummating this marriage, but you can't stop me from imagining it," he tells me, continuing to stroke his dick, his eyes never leaving mine. "Our first time, I'm fucking you slow and sweet. Treating you like my queen," he promises, the low timbre of his voice causing me to squeeze my legs together.

The movement catching his eye, he smiles, and continues, "The next time, *Diávolos'* is fucking you down and dirty. Treating you like his slut."

I exhale a sharp breath.

"Ah, does my little angel like that idea, being *Diávolos'* dirty little slut? I think she does."

Gasping, I run to the bedroom and close and lock the door behind me. My breath's coming out in jagged bursts as I lean against the door, listening to Darius finish in his hand.

He lets out a string of Greek before everything goes quiet.

"Night night, wifey," he calls.

CHAPTER
Eleven

Lily

"Morning," Darius tells me when I exit the bedroom. His curly black hair is damp from the shower, and the fabric of the Atlantic City T-shirt he bought last night in the gift shop is being stretched dangerously taunt by his muscular chest and arms. "How did my little angel sleep?"

"Not your little angel, and I slept great." Such bullshit. I tossed and turned all night in frustration. Sexual frustration, and frustration at myself for being turned on in the first place.

"Hmm," is all he says, reaching behind his back and producing a cup of coffee, holding it out for me.

Wasting no time, I hurry over and grab it. "Thank you." I take a sip, shifting uncomfortably when I realize I'm wearing only a thin white tank top and shorts I picked up last night in the gift shop.

"Of course." His eyes unabashedly roam over my body, and I swear it feels like I'm being touched every place his gaze lingers.

"Stop it," I snap.

"Stop what?"

"Looking at me like that!"

"Like what?" he asks softly, taking a step toward me. "Like how I'm thinking about my dick being inside this pretty little pussy of yours?" I nearly choke on a sip of coffee, taking a step back. "Or how I'm thinking about what this pretty little pussy tastes like?" he says, licking his lips as he takes another step toward me, caging me against the wall with his arms. "I already know what your pussy smells like." Leaning in, he inhales deeply against my neck, my body going ramrod straight. "So fucking sweet," he declares, his lips brushing the delicate skin behind my ear. "My new favorite smell."

"We need to go," I manage, barely above a whisper.

"Sure, wifey." Smiling, he releases me from his cage.

I cross an arm over my painfully hard nipples. "Give me five minutes." Walking briskly to the bedroom, I gather my things before hustling to the bathroom. I change into my bra and a new sundress, but now there's a problem. The gift shop didn't sell panties, so I'm left with two choices: keep on the damp pair I'm currently wearing and risk him sniffing me again, or go without panties.

Go without panties it is.

"*Είσαι ένα όραμα,*" Darius comments as I step out of the bathroom. "You are a vision."

"I look like shit," I say dismissively, walking over to stuff my dirty clothes in my backpack.

Suddenly, I'm being hauled over his shoulder. "What are you doing?" I squeak, dropping my backpack. He takes a seat on the couch, splaying me over his lap before his palm comes down hard on my ass. "Oww!"

"I will gift you with compliments, Lily, and you will accept them with your pouty little lips turned upward into a beautiful smile and say, 'Thank you, Darius.'"

"What the hell? You can't just—"

Whack.

"Spank me—"

Whack.

"Like—"

Whack.

"A—"

Whack.

"Child!"

Whack

"Stop!"

"Now, let's try this again," he says, patting my stinging ass in warning. "You are a vision. Your turn."

"'Beware of Greeks bearing gifts,'" I spit at him.

His laughter causes his entire body to shake. "Touché," he says, smacking my ass even harder, causing tears to well in my eyes. "But not the response I'm going for."

"Thank you, Darius," I grit through my teeth.

"Good girl," he purrs, massaging my ass cheek with his big hand before placing me on my feet.

"I hate you," I hiss. But more importantly, I hate my traitorous body at the moment—especially my throbbing pussy. It's official: there *is* something seriously wrong with me.

"You don't," he says, playfully flicking my nose. Grabbing my things for me, he says, "Ready, wifey?"

I answer with a death glare, marching to the door and flinging it open. Stepping out into the hallway, I eye the emergency exit.

Darius shakes his head, having caught up with me. "Don't do it." With my ass cheeks still throbbing, I heed his warning.

We catch the elevator, and I walk to the opposite side, trying to put as much distance between us as possible. "Come on now, I don't bite. Well, I do bite sometimes, but I promise you'll like it." Darius playfully snaps his teeth at me.

"Fuck off," I spit.

He *clucks* his tongue. "Don't tell me the honeymoon's already over."

Before I can come up with a scathing retort, the elevator

stops, and the door open. Two guys around my age join us, still buzzed from last night's festivities. "Hey, gorgeous. We're about to hit the bar at the pool. Want to join us?" One of the guys slurs, leaning into my personal space. The mixture of cigarettes and stale beer on his breath causes me to recoil.

Darius moves lightning-fast, now holding up both drunk guys by their necks. "She doesn't," he menaces, his eyes having gone crazy and his voice sounding completely psychotic. "But if you boys want to end up in the *bottom* of the pool, hit on my wife again."

The elevator door opens, and Darius tosses them into the hall before hitting the close-door button.

"You are insane!"

"You want me toss them in the pool instead?" he asks in all seriousness, hovering his finger over the open-door button.

"Oh my God," I say exasperated, placing a hand on my head.

"Iris does that exact move. I see where she gets it from," he comments.

"I don't want to discuss my daughter." I bristle, dropping my hand.

"What if I do want to discuss my *stepdaughter*?"

Before I can argue with him, we've reached the lobby. Darius holds open the door for me as we exit the elevator. "I need to pop in the gift shop for a second," he tells me. "You gonna be a good girl and wait right here?"

"Fine," I answer curtly.

He leans in and whispers in my ear, "You run, and I'd tear this fucking world apart to find you. So don't make me do that," he says with a flick of my nose before strolling inside the shop.

Christ. The man really is unhinged.

Grabbing my phone, I call the babysitter on speakerphone. "Hey, we were just finishing breakfast," she reports.

"Good. Just wanted to let you know I should be home in about two hours."

"That's perfect."

"Can I talk to Iris for just a minute?" I ask.

"Iris, your mom's on the phone," she calls.

"Mama!" Iris says excitedly.

"Hey, sweetie. I missed you. Did you have a fun night?"

"Yes! I had pizza and ice cream!"

"Ready to go?" Darius asks, now standing beside me.

"Is that Darius?" Iris asks excitedly.

Fuck. She remembers his name. That's not good.

"Hello, rainbow goddess," he says loudly, and I move the phone away from him.

"Is Darius coming over too?"

"Yes," he answers, and I glare at him.

"I've got to go. I'll be home in a few hours. Love you," I tell her, hanging up.

I stomp to the exit with Darius hot on my heels. "What part of *stay away* from me and Iris are you not getting?"

"The *stay away* part," he says, opening the passenger door for me. He hustles around the car and slides behind the wheel. Surprising me, he grabs my left hand and slides a ring on my ring finger. "It's the best I could do for now."

I examine the cheap mood ring, watching as the blue stone turns black.

"You're tense," he comments. "I could help you with that."

"You're the reason I'm tense!" I shout, but he just smiles.

The stone doesn't change colors the entire drive home. It appears I only have one mood around this man.

CHAPTER
Twelve

Darius

Lily's wound too fucking tight. I should take her back to my place—chain her to my bed and eat her pussy until she thinks she can't come again, and then prove her wrong. It'd help her get out of that pretty little head of hers.

She must be able to read my thoughts, because she's flushing a pretty shade of pink. "Stop it," she chastises me.

"Stop what?" I ask innocently, turning my attention back to the road.

"I need you to drop me off at the club to get my—" She stops mid-sentence. "Oh my God, did my car get destroyed last night?"

"Probably," I answer truthfully. It likely got caught up in the blast, but it's too risky to drive by the scene to check it out.

She begins to cry.

"Hey, don't do that," I say, reaching over and squeezing her thigh.

"I don't have the fucking money for a new car!" She jerks

away from me. "And now I'm going to have to find a new club to dance," she says angrily, swiping at her eyes.

"Don't worry about the money," I reassure her. "I'll get you a car."

"Why would you do that?" She eyes me suspiciously.

"Because you're mine now, and I take care of what's mine. And you're not dancing any more. Well, except for me. I wouldn't turn down a private dance." I nearly nutted on myself from the brief lap dance she gave me, until I felt eyes watching a show meant only for *me*. That's why I moved us to the VIP room; that, and I heard her stomach growl and wanted to make sure she ate something.

"You're not understanding the nature of this arrangement," she starts.

"You're not understanding the nature of this arrangement," I counter. "We're married. My associates will want to meet you, and so you need to at least *pretend* to like me."

She blows out a long breath, but doesn't argue. I'll count that as a win.

"Do you need help packing?" I ask.

"Packing?" She repeats the word like she's unsure what it means.

"You and Iris are moving in with me," I tell her what's going to happen. "Your place isn't safe."

"My place is perfectly safe," she says dismissively.

"*Safe* like how easy it was for me to watch you from your bedroom window?"

"So fix the blinds like you promised!"

"Wifey's already on my nuts about my honey-do," I say with a laugh.

Lily is not amused. Just to double check, I glance at her ring finger. *Black*. Nope, not amused.

"We need to at least ease you into Iris' life before springing this marriage on her," she finally says, rubbing her temples.

Another win. I try not to grin like an idiot. "How about this? I'm going to drop you off at your house, and then I'll be back around five to take you and Iris out to dinner."

"Iris has to ride in a car seat," she warns.

"Not a problem." I don't know the first fucking thing about a car seat, but I'll figure it out.

"Why are you doing this?" she asks warily.

"Taking you out to dinner? Because I enjoy eating dinner," I tell her playfully.

"That's not what I mean, and you know it." She narrows her beautiful eyes at me. "I hope you're not expecting something in return."

Of course I'm expecting something in return—that one day Lily will give herself to me completely. Until that day comes, I'll wait. Waiting is still fucking hard.

"Iris already has one piece of shit man in her life who lets her down. Don't ever make promises to her you can't keep," she warns.

"There might be times I'm called away for work," I answer truthfully.

Lily twirls her mood ring before looking out the window. "Should I ask about your work?"

"You shouldn't. Tell me about Iris' father."

"Harrison works long hours and tons of overtime, so I was always willing to cut him some slack, but Iris has always been an afterthought for him. His job and his women come first," she says, pain laced in her voice.

"Did he hurt you, *aggeloudhi mou*?" If she says yes, I'll be busy dismembering a body this afternoon.

"No, not like that. Not physically. I was just really young and naive when we got together," she explains. "He was a player, but I believed him when he told me he'd change. A surprise pregnancy, and Iris was born."

I do the math. "You were seventeen."

She nods. "It took me a few years after Iris was born to

discover he'd been cheating on me all along. Came home and found him fucking another woman in our bed," she says quietly. "So anyway, I learned the hard way people don't change."

What a fool, but his loss is my gain. "Is he in Iris' life?"

"When he feels like it." Lily shrugs. "He's missed the last two visits, and I haven't heard from him. I'm sure he'll turn up with some sob story. He always does."

"What's his last name?" I demand.

"Why?" She eyes me suspiciously. "So you can stalk him too?"

It's my turn to shrug.

"Please don't get involved," she begs. "It'll only make things worse for Iris. Promise me."

"I won't get involved. For now." I make no promises about the future.

Lily grabs her phone, scrolling until she gasps.

"What's wrong?" I ask.

"Nothing's wrong; I'm just surprised. One of my professors is taking a medical leave."

"Oh?" Looks like I won't have to kill Professor Miller after all.

"And the new interim professor has just given us an extension on our essay." She smiles brightly; a beautiful sight.

"What's your essay about?" I ask.

"You really want to know?" She raises an eyebrow.

"Yes, the dumb brute really wants to know."

"If you get to spank me for making disparaging remarks about myself, then I should get to spank you for the same thing." Realizing what she just said, her cheeks turn the sweetest shade of pink.

I can't help but laugh. "It'd be so damn cute watching you try."

"That wasn't supposed to be funny!" Lily huffs.

"*Aggeloudhi mou,* you can put your hands on my ass any time you want."

"Stop it," she says crossly, but her eyes have softened.

"Tell me about your essay," I encourage her.

"I'm thinking about changing my topic from the goddess of helplessness to a more empowering female figure." She considers. "Athena or Hecate. I don't know, maybe Demeter."

"How about Persephone, Demeter's daughter?" I suggest.

She scoffs. "The goddess who was kidnapped by Hades and forced into marriage? Not exactly empowering."

"Why not?" I challenge. "Gotta be pretty strong to rule as the queen of the underworld."

Lily gives me a look I can't interpret. "Actually, I like that idea." She grabs her backpack and pulls out her notebook and pen, and begins jotting down something.

And I just had an even better idea.

We arrive in Newark, and I drive us to Lily's house. Pulling into her driveway, I hop out and open the door for her. "Give this to the rainbow goddess, and I'll be back to take you ladies out to dinner."

She sighs, but takes the mermaid doll. "Okay."

"Good girl," I say, tucking a strand of her blonde hair behind her ear. Stealing a quick kiss—in and out before her busy brain can tell her to stop me—I admire her tight little ass as she disappears inside the house.

Not quite believing my good fortune, I smile the entire drive to Romeo's house. The Fates obviously fucked up, but no take backs.

Pulling up to the gate, I scan my card and continue to the end of the driveway. My boss is a smart man—lives well, but not *too* well to attract the feds' attention. And nobody wants the feds' attention. I call Romeo's head of security. "It's Darius. I'm here for Romeo's training session. Can you let me in the garage? I have some gym equipment I need to unload."

"You got it."

The garage door opens, and I pull my car into the empty spot. The older man greets me, and we unload the new cache, carrying the weapons to the basement for the time being. "Boss is in the game room."

"Thanks," I say, fist bumping him.

Walking upstairs, I find Romeo and Sammy playing a game of pool. "Boss. Sammy. How's Luca?" I ask.

"He'll be alright. Out of commission for the next few months, and he's mad as hell about it," Romeo reports, sizing up the table.

"I bet. Is he still at the clinic?"

Romeo shakes his head. "We've set up a makeshift hospital room in the guest bedroom. Nicky wants to be able to monitor him round the clock."

"Nice your girl's a doc," I comment.

"I lucked out," Romeo agrees. "Four ball, side pocket," he calls before smacking the ball into the hole.

"Can I see him?"

"Not now," he tells me, chalking up his cue. "He's asleep, and I finally talked Nicky into taking a nap. She's been up for nearly twenty-four hours."

"'Talked Nicky into taking a nap?'" Sammy snorts a laugh. "You locked her in your bedroom."

"*And* she's taking a nap. Eight ball, corner pocket," he calls before sinking the shot.

Sammy curses, throwing down a stack of hundreds.

"Any problems with the cleanup?" Romeo asks me, placing his cue stick on the rack.

"Nope. Smooth as silk." Not a lie, as Lily isn't a problem. *A challenge*? Hell yes, one I'm up for. "What's going on with Philly?"

"Sent their piece of shit boss back to them." Romeo growls.

"In pieces," Sammy adds with a devious smile. "Word is there's infighting. Carlo had no son, and his underboss and a capo are vying for the top spot."

"Burn the fucking city down for all I care, I just don't want it bleeding over into my territory," Romeo declares. Walking over to his suit jacket draped over the couch, he reaches inside the inner pocket and pulls out an envelope. "A little extra for a job well done."

"Thanks, boss," I tell him, accepting the envelope of cash and sticking it in the waistband of my shorts.

"Let's everyone take a few days to breathe before we jump back into the grind," Romeo declares. "And putting a bullet between John Davis' eyes will be the number one priority."

"On it. And while I've got your ear, I wanted to share the news: I got married a few days ago." According to the date on our marriage license.

"There's a woman crazy enough to marry your ass?" Sammy marvels.

"There is." Lily just needed a little coaxing.

"Didn't know you were serious about a woman. Congrats," Romeo says, hugging me with a hard black slap.

"Congrats, man," Sammy says, likewise giving me a half hug, half back slap.

"Thanks. I was wondering if I could ask a favor?" I put in my request.

"Done," the boss says. "Who's the lucky lady?"

"Lily Grant."

"Lily Grant," Sammy parrots the name.

"Before you go looking into my wife, she has a four-year old daughter, so don't scare them," I warn him.

"Have you vetted them?" Sammy asks.

"Yes." The only stone I haven't turned over is about Lily's piece of shit ex, but that's easy enough to remedy.

"Good," Romeo says. "Bring your wife to Sunday dinner. I know the women will want to meet her."

"God, I can already smell the estrogen," Sammy mutters.

"Might want to take a bath if the odor's that strong," I taunt.

"Already had a nice bath. With your mother." He smirks. "She likes candles and soft music."

"Fuck you," I say, cracking my knuckles.

"No thanks," Sammy says, now picking his nails with a knife—like I'm supposed to be fucking impressed. "I don't want to keep it in the family like that, if you know what I mean."

"Enough," Romeo says, bored with our back and forth. "I need to finalize Antonio's funeral arrangements."

"Sorry for your loss," I tell him. Not sorry Antonio's dead, because he was an asshole.

Romeo nods, indicating the conversation's over. "We'll see you and Lily on Sunday."

"Looking forward to it," I say.

"Tell your wife I said I'm sorry," Sammy taunts.

"For your limp dick? You can apologize to my *mamá* yourself."

"Hey, don't take the fun out of this bit," he calls after me.

CHAPTER
Thirteen

Lily

I've been a nervous wreck all afternoon, half expecting Darius to bail on us last minute. "Mama, you look pretty," Iris says, seated on my bed watching her favorite big red dog cartoon.

"She does. Your mama is a beautiful woman."

The sound of that gravely voice has me nearly dropping my lipstick. "How did you get in here?" I demand, spinning around.

"Darius!" Iris says excitedly, running over to his open arms. She stops abruptly—her sweet smile replaced by a look of terror.

"What's wrong, rainbow goddess?" Darius asks.

She returns to my side, and I squat down next to her. "What is it, sweetie?"

"He has something scary on his arm," she whispers to me.

"It's alright. Just a tattoo," I say, smoothing her hair.

"It's scary," she cries, hiding her face in the fabric of my dress.

Darius rolls the sleeve of his dress shirt down and buttons it to where his forearm is now covered. "There we go. All gone."

Iris sneaks a peek, still holding onto my dress.

He grabs his phone and types something before looking back at us. "Ladies, something just came up. I have to take care of one little thing."

"Of course you do," I say bitterly.

"Be back in a few hours, and we'll go out to dinner."

"Don't bother," I snipe.

"Not a bother." Darius either fails to notice my soured mood or chooses to ignore it. I'm not sure which one pisses me off more. He bows dramatically to Iris before walking out.

I angrily throw my makeup in my bag. "Mama, what's wrong?" Iris asks.

"Oh, nothing, sweetie," I say, taking a deep breath and calming myself. Unlike Kat, red flags are *not* my love language, and I should be grateful for the reminder. Yanking my dress over my head, I throw on a much more comfortable T-shirt and shorts.

We walk to the kitchen, and Iris spots the vase first. "Flowers!" She runs to the counter and touches a purple pedal.

"Those are irises," I tell her.

"Flowers for my name!" she says excitedly.

"And so beautiful." Damn Darius and his thoughtful gesture, only to pull a Harrison on us. "I'm going to do some work, and then how about we order pizza?" I suggest.

She pouts. "But I want to eat with Darius."

"I'm not sure if he'll be back in time for dinner," I warn her.

"He said he would."

He did. The asshole.

I get Iris set up with an educational game on her tablet while I begin outlining the new topic for my essay. *The*

Goddess Persephone: Turning Helplessness into Hopefulness. Maybe this new theme will likewise be a self-fulfilling prophecy.

The front doorbell rings, startling me. "Be right back," I call to Iris, who's still playing her game.

After checking the peephole, I step outside, closing the door behind me. "Hey, Ethan," I greet Harrison's patrol partner and best friend. A few years older than me and a few inches taller, he has fair skin dusted with freckles, with his copper-colored hair cut tight. He and Harrison could not be more different—Harrison with his outrageously good looks and swagger; Ethan, more gangly and reserved. "This is a surprise," I tell him. Also a surprise is the new black SUV parked in my driveway. Trying to wipe the shocked expression from my face, I turn my attention back to him.

"You got a new ride?" Ethan asks, also noticing.

"Yes, it's a lot safer for Iris," I vaguely respond.

"It's sharp. Must have set you back a pretty penny. How are you swinging it now that Joe's shut down?" he presses, moving his aviators to the top of his head.

"I'm sorry, is there a reason you stopped by?" I deflect. "You on patrol?" He's in uniform, with his cruiser parked across the street.

"Yeah. Sorry to just drop in on you, but I was wondering if you've spoken to Harrison lately?"

"Nope," I answer, popping the "p." "He was a no-show last weekend for his visitation with Iris. I texted him a couple times, but he never responded. Figured he got distracted by one of his badge bunnies, but eventually, he'll put his dick back in his pants and remember he has a daughter."

"Uh." Ethan rubs the back of his neck uncomfortably.

"Sorry, that was more than you needed." It's not Ethan's fault his buddy's a manwhore.

"Yeah, well, he's missing second watch with me right now.

I've been blowing his phone up, but he's ignoring me. Cruised by his house—his car's there, but he's not answering the door," Ethan admits.

"He was probably out last night and went home with a woman, and she hasn't brought him back to his place yet." I take a wild guess. "That, or he's home sleeping one off."

"You're probably right," he says. "Look, don't mention anything about this."

I snort. "To who? *Harrison*? He'd actually have to respond to any of my messages for me to do that."

"Lily, I'm really sorry about the way things went down with you two," Ethan says with an apologetic look.

"Don't be," I assure him. "I got Iris out of the deal, so I can't complain. Look, I need to get back inside."

"Sure. I'll see you around. Take care," he tells me.

"Thanks, Ethan. You too."

Same old Harrison. I shake my head, returning inside. "Screen time's up," I tell Iris, saving my work and closing my laptop.

"No," she whines, but hands over the tablet.

"What kind of pizza do you want?" I ask.

"Cheese."

"What if we do half cheese, half pineapple and ham?" I suggest.

She makes a face. "Yuck."

"Agree with the rainbow goddess. Pineapple on a pizza is a crime," Darius says, having appeared in the hallway.

"How did you do that?" Iris gasps. Clutching my hand over my heart, I'm wondering the same thing.

"Magic." He walks over to her with his tattoo covered by his sleeve; out of sight, out of mind because she doesn't get upset this time. He reaches behind her ear, producing a key fob, and she giggles with delight. "This is for your mama," he says, grabbing my keys on the console table and sliding it on my key ring. "We need to go," he tells me. "Grab an overnight bag for you and Iris."

"Why? What happened?" I ask nervously.

"Nothing happened," he assures me. "We just have a reservation."

"Darius, a word in the kitchen," I say with a tight smile.

"Of course," he says, snatching my hand and lacing our fingers together. He brings the top of my hand to his lips and places a gentle kiss.

"Are you going to kiss my mama?" Iris wonders.

"If I'm lucky," Darius says, lowering our entwined hands with a smile.

"Kitchen," I say, practically taking his arm off as I drag him into the other room. "You have got to stop—" I'm silenced when his lips crash against mine. I gasp in surprise, and he takes that as an invitation for his tongue to invade my mouth. He effortlessly picks me up by the hips and sits me on the counter.

I go to give him a little shove, but my hands seem to have a mind of their own. Latching onto his shirt, I pull him closer, letting out an embarrassing moan as he twirls his tongue around mine.

He smiles against my lips. "Lucky me—now I have a sound to go with the memory *and* the smell."

This time I do give him a shove. "I am pissed at you."

"Hold that thought until after dinner, and see if you haven't changed your mind. Now, go pack," he says, placing me on my feet.

"Darius—"

He gives my ass more than a playful smack. "*Pack.*"

I shake my head. "Not until you tell me how you got in here."

"Fixed your blinds *and* the lock on your bedroom window. Anything else on my honey-do?"

My mouth falls open, and with an amused expression, he tells me, "I'll take that as a no. Go pack, wifey."

Where do I even start with this man? Placing a hand on my head dramatically, I sigh as I walk out of the room.

"And put the red dress back on. So sexy," he calls after me.

CHAPTER
Fourteen

Lily

I enter my bedroom and sure enough, Darius has fixed the blinds. The scary part? I didn't even know the lock on the window was broken.

Grabbing my bag, I pack an assortment of clothes. If I don't bring the right outfits, it's his fault for not telling me where we're going. My hand runs over the red dress hanging in my closet before I grab it and put it back on. I tell myself I did so because we still might be going out to a restaurant; *not* because Darius said he liked it.

Finished with my packing, I walk to Iris' room and throw some of her things into her backpack. I return to the living room to find my daughter engaged in a lively discussion with Darius. "No, you can't be a dragon," Iris says, dramatically placing her hand on her head. He was right—she did get that mannerism from me.

"Ready?" I ask, sticking my computer and notebook in my

backpack—just in case there's time to squeeze in a few minutes of work.

"Ready," he says, eyeing me appreciatively as he stands and takes the bags from me. I try not to flush beneath his heavy gaze.

We step outside—me locking the door behind us—and Darius hits the key fob, making the black SUV *chirp*.

"You have a nice vehicle," I comment. Opening the back door, I inspect the car seat—it's the right size and appears to be installed correctly. Securing Iris, I walk around and climb into the passenger seat.

"*You* have a nice vehicle," he corrects me, sliding behind the wheel and backing out of my driveway. "This is yours."

"It's too much," I protest.

"What was that?" he demands.

"Thank you, Darius," I grit.

"Good girl," he says quietly, and I ignore the ridiculous tingling between my legs.

"Where are we going?" Iris calls from the backseat.

"A surprise," Darius answers.

"Yay, I love surprises!"

"Me too. Your mama, I'm guessing not so much." He glances over to me. "She likes to think she's in control."

"You don't know me," I say dismissively, even though he just hit the nail on the head.

"Hmm," is all he says.

I fidget in my seat, nerves taking over as we enter the Interstate and head out of downtown.

"It's killing you," Darius muses.

"I don't know what you're talking about," I lie. Craning my neck, I smile at Iris in the backseat, who's playing quietly with her mermaid doll.

Turning my attention back to the road, I twist my mood ring before finally pointing out, "If we're just going to dinner, then why did we need overnight bags?"

"Killing you." He chuckles. Sticking my tongue out at him is too childish, and I can't flip him off with Iris in the vehicle, so I do neither.

Darius takes an exit ramp, and we drive seemingly to the middle of nowhere until we reach a small regional airport. "Iris, see the jet?" I point out.

"Where?" she asks.

I tap my window. "Over there on the runway."

"Oh, I see it!" she exclaims.

"Are we eating at a restaurant in the airport?" I wonder. Iris will like that—she's never flown before, so this will be a fun experience for her watching the planes take off.

Darius doesn't answer my question, driving us to a gate and rolling down his window. "Evening," Darius tells the attendant, handing the man a piece of paper.

"Evening." The man writes something on the paper before handing it back to Darius. The gate opens, and the man hops in his golf cart, and we follow him down the ramp. To my utter shock, we stop near the private jet I just pointed out to Iris.

Darius opens my door for me and helps me out before hustling around the vehicle and getting Iris out of her seat. He hoists her up on his shoulders. "Look at me!" she says excitedly, holding onto his curly hair like reins.

"I see you!" So much for my daughter *not* getting attached to this dangerous man.

Darius holds out his hand for me, but I refuse to take it. Just because Iris is attached to him, that doesn't mean I have to be. Recalling my time spent in the trunk of Darius' car helps me keep things in perspective.

"You think too much, *aggeloudhi mou*," he informs me.

"Do not," I childishly reply.

We reach the steps of the jet, and Darius pulls Iris off his shoulders and places her on her feet. "Ladies first. And I whole-heartedly agree with that philosophy," he tells me with a wink.

Ignoring his sexually-laced comment, I hold Iris' hand as we walk up the steps and enter the lush private jet. The captain greets us—presenting Iris with a golden wings pin.

"Fancy seeing you here." A familiar voice has me scanning the back of the plane.

"Kat." I smile. "What a nice surprise."

"Lily, so nice to see you again. And you must be Iris." Kat smiles brightly at my daughter when we join her. "I'm Kat, Darius' favorite cousin."

"My only cousin," Darius corrects her.

"See, favorite. It's so nice to meet you, Iris. I've brought the essentials," she says, holding up a tote bag. "The three Cs. Candy. Cartoons. And coloring books."

"What kind of candy?" Iris runs over to her to check out the bag for herself.

"Kat's going to tag along and watch Iris so you can finish your essay," Darius says, motioning for me to sit down.

Iris selects a sucker and happily sits beside Kat, and I take a seat across from them, with Darius beside me. "Tag along where?" I ask him.

"'Educating the mind without educating the heart is no education at all,'" Darius says with a enigmatic smile.

"Don't quote Aristotle; answer my question!" Although whoever told this man he was a dumb brute didn't know what the hell they were talking about.

"Greece," he says.

"We're going to Greece!" Iris cheers, but then has a puzzled look on her face. "Where's Greece?"

"Let me show you." Kat pulls out her phone.

I turn to Darius, cupping his cheeks with my hands; the move surprises him. "Thank you," I tell him quietly, our eyes locking for what feels like an eternity.

"They're going to kiss. On the *lips*. He's mama's

boyfriend," I hear Iris explain to Kat. That's enough to break the trance, and I drop my hands awkwardly.

"Boyfriend?" Kat says, raising an eyebrow.

I discreetly shake my head no, and she doesn't press the subject.

The captain announces over the loudspeaker we're preparing to take off, and I make sure Iris' seat belt is good and tight before sitting back down and buckling my own.

Iris squeals in delight as the jet accelerates down the runway, her enthusiasm infectious as we hit the air.

"Her father's a damn fool," Darius leans over and tells me quietly.

"Thank you," I whisper, afraid I'm about to cry for some reason.

"Kiss her already," Kat interjects. "On the lips."

"You're no longer my favorite cousin," Darius tells her.

Clearing my throat, I grab my backpack and take out my laptop, notebook, and a pen. Iris is occupied with a coloring book, and so I put my noise-canceling earbuds in, getting lost in my research.

"Lily," Darius squeezes my thigh.

Removing an earbud, I realize the flight attendant's standing next to our seats with a drink cart. "I'm sorry. Could I get a water?" I ask.

"A woman after my own heart—'your body is a temple.'" Darius turns his attention to the flight attendant. "I'll also have water."

A loud crunch has us looking over to Kat, who's polishing off a bag of potato chips. "What? My temple, my tribute. I'll have a ginger ale," she tells the flight attendant. "See, ginger is healthy," she informs Darius.

The flight attendant goes over the dinner options, and we put in our order. It's not long before we're dining on a meal that would easily rival anything served in a five-star restaurant.

Iris' belly nice and full, she fights it for as long as she can, but it's a loosing battle. Her little head slumps over—out like a light. Darius stands and unbuckles her, picking her up gently. "Bedroom in the back," he whispers.

I follow him to the back of the plane and into a small bedroom. He lays my daughter gently down on the bed, covering her up. "Shall I tuck you in too?" he whispers.

"Not nec—" I nearly squeal with surprise when he scoops me up in his arms, laying me down just as gently as he did Iris.

Fixing the covers, he kisses the top of my head and walks out, closing the door behind him.

CHAPTER
Fifteen

Lily

In the dreamy state between sleep and wakefulness, I snuggle in closer to the strong, warm body beside me. I let out a contented sigh at the feeling of my hair being petted.

"You make the sexiest sounds when you're half asleep. I wonder what sounds you'll make when I wake you up with my tongue lapping at that sweet little pussy of yours," a gravelly voice says, making my pussy clench.

Mmm, let's find out.

Wait, no! Snapping my eyes open, I sit up in a panic. "Where's Iris?"

"In the cabin with Kat," Darius assures me, handing me a bottle of water. "We're about to land."

"Ah, okay," I say, taking a drink. Standing, I realize my nipples are visibly hard through the fabric of my dress. I cross my arms awkwardly over my chest as Darius watches with an amused expression.

He beats me to the door, opening it for me. "I'll find out

one of these days," he whispers in my ear, and I try not to shiver as I brush past him to the bathroom.

"Hey, sweetie," I say, kissing the top of Iris' head when I return to the cabin.

"Mama, they have donuts!" she says excitedly.

"I can see that," I say with a smile.

Pulling a wipe from my bag, I clean the chocolate off her face before I take a seat and buckle up.

The flight attendant appears with a tray of breakfast pastries, fruit, and other items. But more importantly, coffee.

"That's the island of Sikinos," Kat says, pointing out the window.

"Which island are we going to?" I ask Darius, blowing on my steaming cup and taking a sip.

"Naxos."

"How am I going to get any work done—there's so much to see!" I bounce with excitement in my chair, nearly spilling my coffee. "The Cortana. Portara. Apollonas Kouros. The cave of Zeus. The archaeological museum. The beaches."

"There's always next time," Darius tells me with a smile.

"As long as I'm invited," Kat pipes up.

"Let's see if you earn your keep on this trip," he quips.

She scoffs. "Wedding officiant. Nanny. Keeper of the candy. See how many hats I wear, cousin," she says smartly.

"Which hat do you wear in your day job, if you don't mind me asking?" I wonder.

"I'm a dealer at The Diamond," she answers.

"I've never gambled," I admit. "What's it like being a dealer?"

"I help people think losing money is fun," she says with a little laugh. "Dealing is actually more difficult than one would think. There are so many moving parts; payouts you have to tally quickly in your head. But it can be a lot of fun—like being the host of a lively dinner party, depending on the personalities of the gamblers and how much they've had to imbibe."

"Mama, what does 'imbibe' mean?" Iris asks.

Of course she caught that. "Adult drinks," I tell her.

Sorry, Kat mouths to me.

No problem, I mouth back. I'm sure Iris has heard much worse on the rare occasion she's spent the night at her dad's house.

"How about you?" Kat asks me.

"I'm an undergrad student. I graduate in a few weeks, and then hopefully I'll be starting up my master's program—assuming I'm accepted," I add. Professor Miller's absence from class is certainly a blessing, but the threat of him sabotaging my grad school acceptance still lingers uncertain.

"Of course you'll be accepted," Darius says as if it's a foregone conclusion.

"Congrats! What's your major?" Kat asks.

"Classical studies with a minor in Greek mythology."

"*Greek* mythology, huh. Seems you have the right 'boyfriend' for the job. Hey, Darius, does Theia know—" she begins, but then snaps her mouth shut.

"What's a Theia?" Iris pounces.

I glance over to Darius, but his face is unreadable.

The captain makes an announcement over the loudspeaker, and soon we're landing—with much excitement from Iris.

We exit the plane and step into a waiting SUV. Darius drives us on a small, winding road through picture-perfect landscape—the turquoise Aegean Sea juxtaposed against the rocky cliffs dotted with white stucco houses and villas.

We keep going until we reach a small harbor. "We're taking a boat?" I ask as Darius parks, and we exit the vehicle.

"Not exactly," he answers cryptically. A man runs over to greet us, and Darius tosses him the keys.

Following another worker down the dock, we come to a

stop in front of a yacht named *Daniella*. Now I understand what Darius meant—nothing about this vessel could be described as a mere boat.

I hold Iris' hand as we walk across the gangway, and we're greeted by a crewman who instructs us to remove our shoes before climbing aboard.

"This is amazing," I say in awe, taking in the opulence of the vessel. We're given the tour through the salon, and up to the bow of the ship with lounge pillows overlooking nothing but blue skies and turquoise water.

"Whee!" Iris runs over and jumps on a pillow, testing it out with a giggle.

We're led down a small staircase. "Here is the guest ensuite cabin with twin beds, and the master ensuite cabin for Mr. and Mrs. Angelos." The crewman points out.

"Darius, just a moment," I tell him.

"Let's go check out the snack options," Kat suggests to Iris, who's all for that plan.

Pulling him into the bedroom, I close the door, only to realize that was a really dumb move—Darius is looking at me like he's going to devour me like a *snack*.

"Yes, wifey?" he says, his hot gaze making me squirm.

"There's only one bed," I point out.

He raises an eyebrow. "And?"

"And that's a problem."

He smirks. "So you think."

"I do think!"

"Too much," he informs me.

"Darius—"

"Mr. Angelos." There's a rapping on the door.

"Yes," Darius answers.

"The captain is ready for the safety briefing when you are."

"Be up in a minute," he calls, his intense gaze never leaving mine. "Do me a favor. Just for this trip, stop living inside that pretty little head of yours," he says, splaying his big hand over my heart—at the moment, it feels dangerously close to exploding—"and live right here."

He drops his hand and opens the door for me. I'm beyond flustered as we walk up the stairs to the main deck, where the captain goes over the safety procedures before we leave the harbor.

"Time for a shower and to brush those candy-coated teeth," I tell Iris.

"No," she bemoans.

"Real quick. You won't miss anything," I promise.

"Yes I will."

"I'm going to go brush my teeth and shower," Darius tells her. "If you miss anything, that means I will too," he assures her.

"I'll keep watch to make sure no fun is had up here," Kat adds.

I practically have to drag Iris downstairs, but I get her brushed and scrubbed, and then it's my turn.

Stepping out into the hall, we bump into Darius who looks unbelievably sexy in a linen shirt and shorts, his black curly hair wet from the shower.

"Race you upstairs," he tells Iris, but lets her get there first.

"Beat you," she says proudly.

Kat sets up a game of go fish with candy used for the wagers. "Good luck," I tell Iris, kissing the top of her head. "I'm going to do some work."

"I have a feeling we're about to get hustled, cousin," Kat comments.

Stepping inside the salon, I scout out a comfy spot on the couch and set up my computer. I'd like to knock out this essay so I can enjoy the rest of this dream trip.

Once my outline is completed, I begin researching my take on the Persephone myth. Darius was right about Persephone.

She was actually a strong queen—challenging Hades by interceding on behalf of humans who were unfortunate enough to step foot in the Underworld uninvited. Her presence there also softened the notion of the feared Hades, and more importantly for the mythology, the fear of death.

"Mrs. Angelos, can I get you something?" A crewman around my age asks. It takes me a moment to realize he's addressing me. *Mrs. Angelos.*

"A sparkling water would be great. Thanks."

"Easy enough," he says with a smile, but doesn't leave right away. "What are you working on?"

"An essay that's due soon," I say politely, but really wishing he'd leave so I could get back to work.

He doesn't get the hint. "So, you're a uni student?"

"Yes."

"Smart and beautiful," he comments with another smile.

"Um, do you mind getting me that water? I'm pretty thirsty," I say uncomfortably.

"Sure thing. Be right back."

Darius

Glancing inside, I see a crewman hitting up my wife.

"Fold," I say, throwing in my cards. "Be back in a little bit."

"What does 'fold' mean?" Iris asks.

"It means more candy for us," Kat tells her as I slip inside.

Quietly entering the galley, the crewman's back is to me. "Like what you see out there?" I say menacingly.

He spins around, his eyes wide with fear. "No, sir," he stutters.

"*No*? My wife isn't beautiful?"

"I mean, yes, she is beautiful, but—"

Grabbing a knife from the butcher block, I'm now holding it to his throat. "Keep eye-fucking her, and I'll cut out your eyes and feed them to the fish. I would say while you watch, but you won't be able to watch. Because you'll have no eyes." I laugh at my little joke.

The guy has to go ruining the moment by pissing his pants.

"Get the fuck out of here. Don't show your face again for the rest of our trip." Releasing him, he scurries away with his hands clasping his throat.

I toss the knife in the dishwasher and grab Lily a bottle of water, sidestepping the puddle of urine as I walk to the salon. Watching her so engrossed in whatever it is she's reading, I can't exactly blame the guy for looking. Lily is stunningly beautiful, but there's also something sweet, almost ethereal about her. I should stay away from her and not corrupt her. Yeah, I *should*.

"Take a break," I tell her, and she startles.

Closing her computer, she accepts the water. "What's that?" She eyes the bandage on my forearm peeking from my shirt. "Are you injured?" she asks, her brows furrowed in concern.

"See for yourself."

Lily

A shocked sound escapes my lips when he peels off the bandage. "You're crazy." Darius has covered up his devil with a tattoo of a big red cartoon dog. "When did you even have time to get this?" I marvel.

"When I left your house yesterday, I went and had this inked before I came back to take you and Iris to the airport. This way, I won't scare her," he explains, turning around to walk out.

"Darius," I call.

He stops, turning back around. "Yes, wifey?"

Without a word, I run to him and pounce. He catches me as I wrap my legs around him and kiss him with everything I've got. His tongue lashes against mine, and I claw at him trying to get closer.

Growling against my mouth, he says, "Are you ready to give yourself to me?"

"Yes," I whisper without hesitation against his lips; the sweet gesture of his tattoo sealing the deal.

"Good girl," he rumbles, making my pussy ache with need. "I'm going to tell Kat we need some *do not disturb* time. Go to our room. Be naked for me when I get there."

CHAPTER
Sixteen

Lily

Feeling more nervous than I've ever been my entire life, I strip out of my clothes and lay down on the bed. I strut around practically naked when I dance, so you'd think I wouldn't be so self-conscious. But that's Pearl doing the strutting, not Lily.

Sighing in frustration, I try to get out of my head by snaking my hand down, playing with my clit.

"Naughty little angel," Darius chastises, closing and locking the door behind him. "Did I tell you to touch yourself?"

"I didn't think you'd mind. You liked watching me before," I whisper, surprising myself with my brazenness as I continue to rub my clit with the pads of my fingers.

"Fuck yes, I did." He hums. "But you don't get to steal the orgasm I'm about to give you. Drop your hand."

"Make me," I challenge, a thrill running through my body.

He laughs darkly, tugging his linen shirt over his head and tossing it to the floor. I lick my lips at the sight—he's the embodiment of a Greek god in human flesh with his hard lines and beautiful olive skin. And the man has a freakin' eight pack; I thought those were only a myth.

Next comes off his shorts and boxers, and I take in a sharp breath. Darius' huge dick stands to attention as he stalks over to me, but instead of climbing in bed, he opens the closet door. He turns back around with a robe belt, making it go taut in his hands with a *snap*.

"What are you—"

He's already bound my wrists and has me tied to the headboard with the belt before I can finish my sentence. "Bad girls get tied up," he says, a naughty glint in his eyes. A full-body shiver courses through me, and he smiles a wolfish grin. "Πανεμορφη." He looks me over from head to toe, and I'm afraid I'm going to melt into a puddle under his hot gaze. "So sweet, with a body made for sin."

I rub my thighs together, moaning. Is it possible to come from someone's words alone? I'm about to find out if he keeps talking to me like that.

"Did I give you permission to touch yourself?" Darius *tsks*. "Don't make me tie your legs."

I still my movement, and he crawls onto the bed and settles over my pussy. Lightly running his fingers through the landing pad of my Brazilian wax job, he hums. "I like this." He spreads my pussy lips open obscenely with his index and middle fingers.

"Darius," I implore.

He growls. "Fuck, this pussy is gorgeous."

"Darius, please," I beg.

"What do you need, wifey?" he coos, cupping my pussy with the palm of his hand and rubbing back and forth.

"*You*. I need you."

"And you have me," he says, dropping his hand from my pussy; the loss causes me to whimper.

He chuckles, taking his sweet time as he runs his tongue up the length of my body. Framing my face with his hands, he holds his weight off me as he captures my mouth with his— kissing me so slow and deep it makes my toes curl.

I'm a whimpering mess by the time Darius kisses and licks his way down my neck, stopping at my breasts. "So pretty." He flicks my left nipple with his tongue before sucking it into his mouth.

"Mmm," I moan, grinding my pussy against his dick to urge him along, but the man's not in any hurry.

He releases my nipple with a little *pop*, moving over to my other breast to lavish it with attention. Kissing and licking his way down my stomach, he settles between my legs. His hooded eyes watch me intently as he enters me with his middle finger, and I gasp, arching off the bed.

"What were you thinking about when you were rubbing this sweet little clit with your vibrator the other night?" He adds second finger as he flicks them rapidly in a *come here* motion.

"Oh God," I cry out, grabbing a fistful of sheets.

"Were you thinking about me fucking you?" He leans down and swipes my clit with his tongue as he continues to work me with his fingers.

"Yes," I moan, too turned on to be embarrassed by the admission.

"How did I fuck you? Did I use my fingers?" He continues to pump inside me. "My tongue?" Removing his digits, he swipes the length of my seam with his tongue, and I arch off the bed with a moan. "Or was it my dick?" Watching me with hooded eyes, he shifts his body and grabs his dick, tracing the head against my engorged clit.

"Your tongue," I pant.

"Ah," he says, scooting back down to where his head is positioned between my legs. Gripping my thighs just how I imagined he would, he gives my clit a gentle kiss. "In your fantasy, where did I eat this sweet little pussy?" He swipes me again with his tongue, and I let out a throaty moan. "Was I in your bed?"

I shake my head, teasing my bottom lip with my teeth. "We were in the VIP room. On the couch."

"Naughty angel." He smiles, looking up at me from between my legs while working my clit with his tongue in a figure eight motion. Stopping abruptly, he asks against my throbbing clit, "And did I make you come in this fantasy?"

"Yes," I moan. "So damn hard."

"Good girl." He growls against my clit, the vibration nearly sending me over the edge. "You want to come on my tongue right now?"

"Please," I beg.

"Such nice manners." He smiles, spearing my pussy with his tongue before he attacks me with quick flicks.

"Oh my God." I pant, my body writhing wildly beneath him.

He smiles, working my pussy with his skilled tongue while hitting the ridged spot deep inside me with his fingers. Just when I'm close, he backs off with his fingers and moves his tongue to a different spot. It's torture, in the best possible way.

"Fuck!" I cry out when he begins rubbing his beard over my swollen clit. My legs fall open wider—welcoming the new level of sensation.

He chuckles against my clit. "*Τόσο καλό κορίτσι.*"

"Please, Darius." I tremble and moan as he goes back to licking my pussy in long, delicious strokes—the reality so much better than any fantasy I could have imagined. Wave after wave of pleasure hits me, and my body tenses as I scream, "I'm coming!" My back arches as my orgasm hits so hard, I swear stars explode before my eyes.

He continues to lap at me soothingly until the final after-shock subsides. "Good, wifey?" Darius asks, untying me.

With my eyes half-closed and a huge smile on my face, I answer, "I'm sorry, I can't come up with a coherent thought."

"Finally," he says with a little chuckle. He braces himself over me, thrusting his tongue in my mouth. I unabashedly taste myself, flicking my tongue against his as he grinds his dick back and forth through my slick pussy lips.

Holding himself up with one hand, he lines up his dick to my entrance. "I've had a child," I warn him.

"I am well aware," he says in an amused tone, nudging me with the head.

"So I'm not as tight down there as I used to be," I whisper, shame coloring my cheeks.

He pauses, nostrils flaring. "Do I need to turn you over my knee again, Lily? This pussy is perfect, and whoever fucking told you it wasn't needs their tongue ripped out," he threatens, kissing me again—this time his kiss borders on violent as he slides inside me in one go.

We both cry out. Holy hell, it's a good thing I've had a child, because I'm not sure he would have fit otherwise.

"Παράδεισος." He rasps against my lips as he begins to move inside me. I lift my hips, wrapping my legs around him as he drops his head to my neck, panting and saying something in Greek as he fucks me slow and deep.

I gasp in shock as my body gears up for another orgasm. "This feels so good," I say on a breathy moan.

He stills, watching my face intently. "You're surprised."

"No, it's just I've never had an orgasm during actual sex," I whisper.

His *clucks* his tongue. "So I need to rip out a lying tongue *and* cut off a useless dick." My pussy flutters at his violent words, and he smirks. "Little angel likes the devil inside her.

Likes her ears filled with my bad words while her pussy's filled with my big dick."

My pussy clamps down on his dick like a vise. "Yes," I moan. God help me, I do.

"Good girl." He hums his approval, releasing another string of Greek as he falls into a slow rhythm. My God, he might be rearranging some of my internal organs with how deep he's inside me. "So good." He groans, his pelvis hitting my clit on each thrust while his dick's hitting just the right spot deep inside me.

"Yes," I pant, my body beginning to shake uncontrollably as the pressure builds. "Darius," I moan, digging my nails into his back.

"That's it," he praises, thrusting faster. "Come all over your husband's dick. Let me feel it."

"Oh, fuck!" I cry, bucking violently beneath him as my second orgasm crashes through me.

He lets out the sexiest groan before grinding out his release. Pulling out gently, he falls beside me and tucks me into his arms.

"That was," I start, my heart jackhammering and my chest heaving.

"Perfection," he answers for me, his chest rising and falling nearly as hard as mine.

"Mmm," I agree, grabbing his face and giving him a dreamy kiss. Snuggling in closer, we're both slick with exertion, and I take a moment to bask in the afterglow of the most amazing sex of my life. I trace my finger around the cobalt blue tattoo on the middle of his chest. "Why the evil eye?"

"For protection." His lips quirk. "It must not work very well, because your pretty little blue eyes have bewitched me."

Secretly beaming, I continue my exploration of his ink. "What do these mean?" I run my nails lightly over the small tattoos on his ribcage—canine teeth; three of them.

"For all the times I've escaped death by the skin of my

teeth." He playfully snaps his teeth at me before running them down the column of my neck.

"I need to take a shower, then check on Iris," I warn him, my skin breaking out in goosebumps.

"No shower."

"Why?" I look pointedly to the mess leaking down my inner thigh.

Shocking me, he gathers his cum and pushes it back inside me with his finger. "Because I want my cum dripping from your pussy for the rest of the day. I want every man on this ship smelling who you belong to."

"You're crazy," I tell him, shaking my head with a little laugh.

"When it comes to you? You have no idea." He hops up, rifling through his bag.

"What are you doing?" I wonder.

Taking a seat beside me, Darius grabs my left hand—snatching the mood ring off my finger. My eyebrow arched, he reaches behind my ear and pulls out a diamond ring. "Trade me," he says, sliding on a large, but not too ostentatious diamond ring. "Halo diamond for my little angel."

"Darius, it's beautiful," I say, my heart feeling like it's going to burst from happiness. Holding up my hand, I admire the lovely double-band ring. "But I want to keep the mood ring," I admit.

He smiles, slipping it on my right finger, and we watch the stone change from black to purple. "Ahh. Wifey just needed a good fucking to get rid of the tension."

I duck my head in embarrassment, but he lifts it with a finger underneath my chin. "You will be a thoroughly fucked woman from here on out. Get used to it." He presses his lips to mine, cementing that promise with a passionate kiss.

"I need to get a ring for you," I say a bit breathlessly when he pulls back.

"Nah, I'll get my ring finger tatted when we get back

home." Hearing him say that makes me so damn happy for some reason.

"Iris is going to ask about my new ring," I warn him, turning it back and forth, fascinated by how it sparkles in the light.

"Handle it however you think best," he tells me.

"Okay," I say, blowing out a breath. "Let's just tell her."

He grins from ear to ear. "Whatever you say."

I purse my lips. "You don't have to look so smug about it." Grabbing his wrist, I bring my lips to his forearm, placing a sweet kiss on his newly-inked skin before climbing out of bed.

"I mean it—do not clean up that pussy," he warns me.

"Fine," I tell him. "But next time, I want *Diávolos'* cum dripping from my pussy."

His nostrils flare as I smile, walking to the bathroom. Looking at myself in the mirror, he was right—a thoroughly fucked woman's reflection gazes back at me. An unfamiliar sight; Harrison was an extremely selfish lover, and that's putting it mildly.

"What did I tell you?" Darius says, now standing behind me at the sink.

"I didn't clean up my pussy; your cum's still inside me," I protest.

"About you thinking too much." He squats down, holding out my bikini bottom, and I step into it. Next, he helps me fasten my bikini top, and pulls my coverup over my head. "Take a break for the rest of the day, and let's hit the beach."

"Sounds like a plan. I've made some really great progress on my essay. Two more solid days and I should be able to knock it out."

"Good."

My hair is absolutely wild, and I grab my brush, but to my surprise, Darius snatches it out of my hand. He begins brushing my long locks, gently working out the tangles.

Placing the brush on the counter, he wraps his big arms around me.

I smile at him in the mirror, leaning back against his hard chest. For something that started out so wrong, this is starting to feel so damn right.

CHAPTER
Seventeen

Darius

"Who wants to go to the beach?" I ask when we join Kat and Iris.

"Me! Me!" Iris says, jumping up and down.

"Let's get ready," Lily says with a smile, holding out her left hand.

Iris goes to take it, but stops. "Mama, where'd you get that ring?" Lily was right—her daughter is an observant little thing.

"Darius and I are married," Lily explains.

"Okay," Iris says, but gets distracted by my new tattoo. "I want one!"

Lily shakes her head with a smile. "Maybe one day when you're older."

"Listen to your mama, rainbow goddess," I say. Flexing my forearm, I let out a little *Wolf! Wolf!* that makes Iris giggle.

"There goes your street cred," Kat taunts.

I shrug, unconcerned. At this point, I could dress up as a big red dog and still make grown men piss their pants. "You and your beautiful mama are going to move in with me when we get home," I tell her.

"How does that sound?" Lily presses.

"Does this mean I can have a cat at Darius' house?" Iris smiles.

"I love this kid," Kat says with a laugh. "You got the cards, girl. Hold em."

"Iris, we've talked about a cat, but you know I'm busy with school, and Darius is busy—"

"Managing a gym," I finish for her.

"Really?" Lily asks, surprised.

"You don't get fit sitting around all day eating chips," I say.

"Why you gotta choose violence, cousin?" Kat says, having just opened a bag of chips. She brings one to her mouth and crunches loudly. "So about this new cat Iris is getting."

"Come on, let's get ready for the beach," Lily deflects, leading Iris downstairs.

"Don't make me toss you overboard," I warn Kat.

"But then how would you and Lily have been able to consummate the marriage?" She smiles smugly.

"How do you know that?" I demand.

"Good Lord! The tension's been so thick around here you could cut it with a knife."

I grab Kat in a headlock, giving my little cousin a good old-fashioned noogie.

"*Malákas!*" She elbows me, grunting at the impact. All she accomplished was hurting her elbow, but I release her. "What did you decide about visiting—"

"Ready," Lily says, having returned with Iris now in a bathing suit and life jacket.

"You want a solo family excursion?" Kat asks.

"You're family. Of course you're coming with us," Lily answers.

"You don't have to ask me twice. Give me just a minute to fix my hair," Kat says, narrowing her eyes at me.

"Why don't I get the transfer ready," I suggest, stepping inside and relaying the plan to a different crewman than the one I threatened—seems that other guy might get to keep his eyes after all.

We're soon jetted to a small beach we have to ourselves. I set up an umbrella while Iris gets to work digging in the golden sand.

"Iris has only ever been down the shore," Lily tells me. "This is so perfect," she says, her smile brighter than the sun hanging overhead.

"Good," I tell her, stealing a quick kiss. "Walk with me, I want to show you something."

"Kat, would you mind making sure Iris keeps her life jacket on?" Lily says.

"Of course. But if it makes you feel better, I was a life-guard in high school," Kat tells me.

"Yes, that does make me feel better," Lily says. "Iris, be back in a few minutes."

"Okay," she says, busy filling her pail with sand.

I lead Lily past an outcropping of rocks until we reach a small cove. "Wow. This is amazing."

"Yes." I hum. "Completely secluded. Nowhere for my little angel to go. No one to hear her screams," I say menacingly.

"Darius?" Lily asks with a questioning look, her nipples pebbled.

Squatting down in front of her, I grab her hips and inhale deeply. It's the most intoxicating scent—our sex from earlier, combined with a twinge of Lily's fear *and* arousal.

Looking up at her, I whisper, "If I were you, I'd run."

Lily

I take off running, adrenaline coursing through my veins. My logical brain knows Darius wouldn't hurt me, but right now, he doesn't look like Darius; his eyes having gone crazy, he looks more like the man who threatened me in the alley.

"*Aggeloudhi mou*," he calls after me in a demented voice that causes my blood to chill.

I can feel him hot on my heels, but I've run out of real estate when I reach the other side of the rocky cove. There's nowhere for me to go as I spin around and face him.

He's on me in a flash, grabbing my arms and jerking them up over my head. "Red means stop. If you're unable to speak, blink fast three times if you want me to stop," he instructs me. "Understood?"

"Yes." I nod frantically with relief. It's a game. A game my pussy is more than happy to play.

With my hands over my head, he uses his free hand to untie my bikini top. My chest heaving, he smiles as he easily binds my wrists with the fabric, looping it over a branch jutting out from a tree growing from the rocks.

He smiles, and it's one of the most terrifying looks I've ever seen—causing my body to erupt in goosebumps. "Well. Well. Well. What do we have here? A sacrifice for the sea monster Cetus. Except a different monster got here first," he menaces.

"Please let me go," I whisper, a thrill running through me as I struggle against the fabric, but it's no use. The man knows how to tie a knot.

"Will you look at this dirty little whore." He chides. "So fucking sloppy. Drenched for *Diávolos*."

"No!" My pussy flutter violently at his cruel words.

"*No?*" he mocks, cupping my pussy and rubbing his palm back and forth.

I gasp when he rips off my bikini bottom at the sides— tossing the ruined material to the sand. Taking his finger, he rubs circles with the glistening evidence of my arousal dripping down my thigh. "Try again, little liar," he *tsks*, shoving his finger in my mouth. "Suck the truth off my finger."

I do as he commands, and his eyes grow heavy with desire as he fucks my mouth with his finger. "What should I do with such a filthy whore?" he muses.

He pulls his finger out, and I beg, "Please let me go. I'll do anything."

"*Anything*? Will you put those lying lips on *Diávolos'* dick?" He grabs my cheeks with one hand—forcing my lips to pucker.

Unable to speak, I bob my head up and down.

He releases me and walks over to the rocky area to my left. I can't tell what he's doing, but he turns around with a huge boulder in his arms and carries it over to me. Squatting down, he drops it at my feet with a grunt.

"What are you doing?" I ask.

"Did I ask the whore to speak?" he demands.

I'm a smart, educated woman who should be offended at this degradation—*should* being the operative word here, because I'm so turned on I can barely think straight.

He peels off his swim trunks, and I can't take my eyes off that impressive erection as he climbs on top of the boulder.

His dick is now at my mouth level, and he grabs onto my head—forcing my mouth open as he thrusts inside me. I gag as he begins to fuck my mouth with such brutal force, it makes my eyes water.

"Deep throat me," he commands in a gravely voice, my nipples painfully hard.

I open my mouth as wide as it will go, taking a deep breath through my nose as he pushes his dick impossibly deep down my throat. "That's it," he praises, tears running down my cheeks. He pulls out, only to ram back into my mouth over and over. "Such a good little slut, taking *Diávolos'* dick so deep. Are you my good little slut, Lily?"

Unable to speak because I'm being choked by his massive dick, I just nod.

He moans as he thrusts faster, grabbing a fistful of my hair and pulling hard; his other hand, he uses to massage his balls. Shoving his dick further down my throat—deeper than I thought possible—my throat constricts as I make a gagging sound.

"That's it," he praises. "Choke on my dick. Fuck, Lily, I'm about to come." Grunting, he cries out as he throws his head back—warm jets hitting the back of my throat, and I'm forced to swallow every last drop.

He pulls out when his dick stills and cups my cheeks gently. "Good, wifey?"

"Yes, but I said I wanted *Diávolos'* cum dripping from my *pussy*," I tell him, my voice hoarse from the rough fucking.

"Mouthy little angel." He playfully flicks my nose. Hopping down, he unties my wrists and scoops me up in his arms, placing a tender kiss on my forehead. "Next time. But for now, how about I make you come right here? Anyone could walk around those rocks or pass by in a boat and see how fucking desperate you are for me. Would you like that, Lily?"

"Yes," I whisper, my pussy tingling. I do like that idea.

He climbs back up on the boulder with me in his arms. Taking a seat, he positions my body to suit him—I'm now laying with my back against his hard chest, my legs sandwiched between his. He wraps his hand around my throat as he snakes his other hand down, playing with my clit. "Mmm, and I do like you splayed out, so fucking needy for me."

"Yes, so needy for you." I moan, digging my nails into his muscular thighs.

He hums his approval, entering me with his middle and ring fingers, and I moan. "Except I'd have to kill anyone who looks at you, and I don't like taking my work with me on holiday," he says with all seriousness, and my pussy absolutely seizes around his fingers. He laughs darkly against my ear. "Wifey likes that, doesn't she?"

As if he knows my body better than I do, he goes straight to my g-spot and doesn't let up, kneading it over and over with his fingertips. "Oh my God," I cry with a hoarse voice, a full-body shiver ratcheting through me.

"Likes that her husband is a bad man. Likes playing with fire." His dangerous voice mixed with his skilled fingers has worked me up into a frenzy. "You going to squirt all over my fingers? Show everyone how hard you come for me?"

Grabbing his hand around my throat, I beg, "It's too much," but he keeps hitting those bundles of nerves roughly over and over inside me.

"My dirty little slut of a wife can handle it," he rasps.

"No, I feel like I need to pee," I admit with embarrassment, the sensation overwhelming.

"Don't hold back. I don't give a fuck if you piss all over me," he reassures me, moving his fingers faster.

Deciding to take him at his word, I tweak my nipples, getting lost in the pleasure. I'm naked and completely exposed, and yet I know without a doubt I'm safe in Darius' arms; that thrilling combination has me drunk on desire.

"That's it," he praises, fucking me roughly with his fingers. "Let everyone know who this pussy belongs to."

I convulse.

I pant.

I moan.

I writhe.

I beg.

I—

"Fall apart," he commands, moving his hand faster and faster.

"Darius," I scream, the sweetest relief washing over me as my pussy absolutely gushes on his fingers—the orgasm unlike anything I've ever experienced.

I collapse into his body, my own jerking like a live-wire as he leans over and smiles at me, capturing my mouth with a sweet kiss. "Let's get you dressed," he tells me against my lips. "I'd rather not have to kill anyone today."

In a daze, all I can do is nod.

"Fuck, I need at least a week with you chained to my bed," he grumbles, sitting me upright before he hops down to retrieve my bikini. He picks me up, and I lay my head against his shoulder and close my eyes. "Uh-uh. Don't go to sleep on me." He chuckles.

Placing me on my feet, he fixes my top for me, but he frowns at the ruined bikini bottom. "Sorry about that," he says, placing it over me and tying the torn ends together as best he can.

Scooping me up in his arms, he carries me into the gentle surf. A man in a fishing boat passes, and I giggle.

"He's lucky he gets to keep his eyes." Darius glances to the boat, and then back to me. "Was I too rough?" He presses a tender kiss to my neck where moments ago his big hand wrapped around it.

"No, I loved it," I admit.

"Good girl."

"Darius?" I ask, looking into his dark eyes.

"Yes, wifey?"

Feeling like time has stopped, I blurt out the words before I can overthink them. "I love you."

Looking taken aback, he opens his mouth and then closes

it. My stomach falls as I try to jump down from his arms, but he tightens his grip. "Don't make me spank your ass right here, right now," he threatens.

"It's alright if you don't feel the same," I lie, choking down the tears.

"I don't feel the same?" Darius balks. "What I feel for you," he pauses, searching for the right words. "*Love. Mania. Obsession.* None of those words do it justice. You're under my skin, little angel, with your pretty little fingers wrapped about my heart like a vise. A lifetime with you won't nearly be enough," he declares, kissing away my tears. "But we have to start somewhere."

CHAPTER
Eighteen

Darius

Gently moving Lily's head from my chest, I slip out of bed. She stirs, but immediately returns to a deep slumber. As she should, because we were in the sun all day, and later, I made sure to wear her out in bed.

I throw on some clothes and quietly tiptoe out of our room. The Parisi family yacht is moored not too far from shore, and while I could easily swim, I'd rather not have to make a portion of my journey in wet sneakers. That's why I snag the keys to the tender and board the small boat.

Keeping the throttle low to make as little noise as possible, I approach the cove Lily and I had our little game earlier and drop anchor. I hop out of the boat and make my way to the rock outcropping. Taking a seat on the boulder where Lily squirted everywhere—the fucking sexiest thing I've ever witnessed—it feels sacrilegious to do something as mundane as put on my socks and shoes, like I'm desecrating a scared space.

I hop down and make my way to the path. Lily froze with

fear earlier, but had she really looked, there's an escape route behind the huge rock where I tied her up. Not that I'm complaining, considering how it played out.

It's a starry night, but I don't need a guide star to lead the way—I've climbed this path countless times in my youth. Reaching the top that connects with a gravel road, I begin the uphill trek, having worked up a good sweat by the time I reach my destination: *Taverna* Angelos.

The lights are off and the tavern is closed, but I easily pick the lock and slip inside. Following familiar smells to the kitchen, my *mamá* is at the stove, stirring a huge pot of something—smells like *stifado*.

"*Mamá*," I say, and she drops the spoon into the pot, going eerily still. Turning around slowly, she places her shaking hands over her mouth before opening her arms wide.

Darius, seventeen-years old

My piece of shit old man's been hitting the bottle earlier than usual, and so I sneak out the back and head down the hill to my secret cove. Climbing down the rocky path, I do a double take when I spot a huge yacht anchored in the distance. Must be fucking nice.

My envious thoughts are put on hold when something cold and sharp presses against my neck. Instinct kicks in—years of protecting myself against my old man's fists—and I move fast, throwing my head back as hard as I can.

Someone curses in Italian, dropping the blade.

Spinning around, I lunge for the knife and get there first. Stumbling back with the knife held ready to strike, I assess the situation: two guys, both around my age. The guy on my left is clearly in charge; confidence and authority radiates from him. Me having just hit a growth spurt and now over six feet tall, we're around the same height and build, but I can tell this guy has seen some shit, and would definitely fight dirty. "You just got your ass handed to you," he says with a crooked smile, addressing my attacker.

"Fucker," my attacker barks at me, his nose gushing blood. Ripping off his shirt, he uses it to stem the bleeding. This guy is not quite as big as me, but I can tell he's got enough attitude to make up for it.

"You attacked me first." I toss the knife back to him, in what I hope is a show of respect, and not a fatal move on my part.

He easily catches it by the handle and slips it into his ankle sheath. There's a Greek superstition you shouldn't hand someone a knife, or you'll never be friends; I'm not sure about tossing a knife, but I doubt me and this guy will ever be friends either way.

"Ποιο είναι το όνομά σου?" The crooked-smile man asks for my name in perfect Greek.

"Darius Angelos. Who the fuck are you?"

He curls his lips back into a smile. It's terrifying, and there's not much that terrifies me. "Romeo Parisi."

My old man was going on about Antonio Parisi—a mobster from the States he was doing business with—but I thought he was just talking shit. Apparently he wasn't. This has got to be that mobster's son. Fuck.

"This is Sam Moretti." Romeo jerks his head to his buddy.

"Sammy to you; only my friends call me Sam." He sneers at me.

"Sammy," I say in a bored tone, even though my body's screaming at me to run.

"Nice shiner, by the way," Sammy comments on my black eye, smirking.

"You should see the other guy," I lie. My old man was

railing against *Mamá*, and I intervened, taking the brunt of it. One day, when I have a wife of my own, I'll treat her like a queen—not like my *babás* treats my *mamá*.

"I bet. You've got good reflexes. How old are you?" Romeo asks.

"Old enough." I'll be eighteen soon, and I wish I could say I'm getting the hell off this island, but I can't leave *Mamá* unprotected.

"You in school?" Romeo asks.

"Nah, I help my folks with their tavern."

"Which tavern?" he presses.

"*Taverna* Angelos."

"Ah," Romeo says. "Well, Darius Angelos, it was nice to meet you. If you ever find yourself in the States and want to make some real money, look me up. I can always use muscle on my crew."

"Your crew?"

He reaches into his pocket, handing me a business card.

Parisi Construction
Newark, New Jersey

"Sorry, I don't do construction," I warn him.

"Neither do I," he says with an amused expression. "See you around, Darius." With that, he turns around and walks off.

Sammy flips me off before hurrying to catch up to his buddy, but abruptly stops. Spinning around, he flings the knife at me.

Cursing, I duck just in time as the blade sails dangerously close to my right ear. The knife hits a rock behind me and bounces off with a *clang*, landing in the sand. "Will you look at that. You do have nice reflexes. Keep the knife as a parting gift."

It's my turn to flip him off, and he chuckles as he disappears.

Holding my hands on top of my head, I laugh in disbelief. Not every day you escape death by the skin of your teeth. Or your ear.

Picking up the weapon, I examine it closer. The only knives I have experience with are found in the kitchen. This one with its razor-sharp blade made out of what looks to be black-coated steel would eat my chef's knife for breakfast.

I had every intention of working out, and now that I've got all this extra adrenaline from my little encounter with Romeo and Sammy, I place the knife down and begin my routine. First, I warm up, then move to a set of squats using a large boulder as my resistance. My goal is to one day be bigger than my old man; then he'll think twice before fucking with me and *Mamá*.

Finishing my workout, I cool off in the turquoise sea, replaying Romeo's offer in my mind. I daydreamed of going to the States when I was younger, maybe even going to uni there. Until my old man drilled into my head I'm nothing but a dumb brute. Eventually, I gave up trying in school and dropped out.

By the time I get out of the water, the sun's starting to set, and I quickly make my way to the tavern with my "parting gift" tucked into my waistband.

Giving *Mamá* a kiss on the cheek, I help her wash dishes while she mills about preparing plates. *Babás* is nowhere to be seen. Not looking a gift horse in the mouth, I don't ask about my old man.

We finish for the night, and I grab some fruit and water, sneaking to the outdoor patio for a break before tackling the cleanup.

There's a commotion coming from the kitchen, and dread fills me as I sprint inside. "This place looks like a pigsty! Are you trying to embarrass me?" *Babás* thunders, backhanding *Mamá* so hard she falls to the floor. But that's not enough—he begins kicking her over and over in the stomach.

"Παρακαλώ σταματήστε!" *Mamá* begs.

Something in me snaps, and it's like I'm watching it happen while hovering above my body. Moving silently behind *Babás* with the knife in my hand, I grip him by his curly hair, jamming the blade in the side of the neck.

He squeals, bringing his hand up to jerk the knife out, but rage coursing through my blood makes me stronger than him. I keep pressing the knife into his flesh until I hear bones splitting; that satisfying crunch fuels my bloodlust, and I laugh as he crumbles to his knees.

I squat down next to him, jerking the knife out and stabbing him again.

And again.

And again.

And again.

A wail startles me, and I realize that sound's coming from me as I continue hacking at the lifeless body—blood covering me like a second skin.

"Darius, stop!" *Mamá* shouts; or maybe she's been shouting this entire time.

My chest heaving, I drop the knife. The figs and water I consumed earlier come back up in a violent rush, and I puke everywhere.

"What do we have here?"

I look up to see a man dressed in an Italian suit who's obviously Romeo's father—same build, same face, same frown—surrounded by muscled-up men.

"Antonio, that's Darius. He's my new associate," Romeo says, appearing next to his father, along with Sammy.

"I see," the elder Parisi says, tenting his fingers. "The problem is this new associate of yours just butchered *my* new associate." Eyeing my father's lifeless body, he adds, "And created quite the mess."

"Whatever business you had with my husband, I can handle," *Mamá* says, now standing beside me, grasping my bloody hand. Her right eye's starting to swell shut, and she's clutching her stomach with her free hand.

"And Sammy and I can help with the cleanup," Romeo offers.

"Maria, isn't it?" Mr. Parisi addresses *Mamá*.

"Yes, sir."

"You really think you can handle your husband's business interests?" Mr. Parisi questions.

"I've run this restaurant without his help for years, so yes, I know I can," she answers without hesitation.

Mr. Parisi silently weighs my fate. Finally, he says, "Very well. Come with me, Maria. We have much to discuss."

"No!" I shout.

Shut the fuck up, Romeo mouths at me.

"*No*?" Mr. Parisi raises an eyebrow in challenge.

"I mean, I'd like to come with her," I say quickly.

"No harm will come to your mother, you have my word. Boys, I'd suggest you get started on the cleanup." He turns to his son, narrowing his eyes. "Romeo, it'll be your ass if this turns into a problem for us later."

"There won't be a problem," he assures his father. Romeo looks to me, and I slice my head in agreement—not going to be a problem.

"*Μη στεναχωριέσα. Ολα θα πάνε καλά*," *Mamá* assures me, squeezing my hand before letting go. She tries to hide her injuries as she walks out with her head held high.

"First kill, huh?" Sammy asks, glancing at the puddle of vomit. "It gets easier."

I answer by puking again.

Darius

"Why didn't you tell me you were coming? I would have made you something special!" *Mamá* chastises me.

"It was a spur-of-the-moment decision. How's business?" *Mamá* runs drugs for the Parisi family out of the tavern.

"Busy with the summer holiday crowd. Let me heat you up something," she tells me.

Knowing better than to argue with her, I say, "Please." We're standing in a different kitchen than the one where I killed my old man; that kitchen burned in a "grease fire" all those years ago, along with that piece of shit excuse for a human.

Mamá ladles me a big helping of the stew before fixing *choriatiki* with a piece of feta larger than my hand. She places the bowls before me, and I dig in. "*Λατρεύω τη μαγειρική σου*," I tell her.

"Who feeds you at home?" she worries. "You need a wife to take care of you."

"I am capable of feeding myself," I tell her, taking a bite of the piping hot stew. "But I have a wife."

"What?" she says excitedly, placing her hands on her heart.

I grab my phone from my pocket, proudly showing her a picture of Lily and Iris I snapped at the beach earlier today.

"*Ftou. Ftou. Ftou.*" She spits, making a sign of the cross.

"*Mamá*," I chide, wiping my phone on my shorts. "That's my wife, Lily, and my stepdaughter, Iris. They're not going to curse you." Blue-eyed people are especially adept at doling out the evil eye, or so the superstition goes.

"Not me. *You*." She points to me. "This woman will be the death of you, mark my words."

I shrug, unconcerned. *Mamá* fancies herself a seer, but I've always taken her pronouncements with a grain of salt. "I've gotta go out someway."

"Don't tempt the Fates," she chastises me.

"I'm not." But I will strangle the Fates with their own weaving thread if they dare try and take Lily from me.

CHAPTER
Nineteen

Lily

It's our last day, and I'm so sad this Grecian dream is coming to an end. The good news is I'm almost finished with my essay, though. Yay!

"Wifey." Darius returns to our cabin with a breakfast tray.

"Thank you," I say, giving him a kiss before closing my laptop and placing it on the nightstand. I look over the selection of pastries, breakfast meats, and fruit—my eyes landing on a bowl of pomegranate. "You wouldn't be trying to pull a Hades?" I tease. "Trick me so I'll return to you always?"

"Your beauty puts Persephone's to shame," he says, popping an aril into his mouth as he takes a seat next to me.

"You didn't answer my question," I remind him.

Darius yanks me into his lap to where I'm straddling him. Kissing me, he thrusts his tongue into my mouth—transferring the ruby red seed to mine.

Pulling back from him, I make a show of chewing and swallowing. Smiling, he feeds me another aril, and I accept his offering. "I'm not going anywhere," I say, cupping his face and kissing him again—this time moving the aril to his mouth with my tongue.

His eyes darkening, he tugs my hair gently to where I'm nose-to-nose with him. It's his turn to chew and swallow. "And I'm not going anywhere," he declares. "Where would I go, when heaven is right here?" He yanks on the ends of my tied belt robe, and it parts like a curtain.

I shrug out of it, and Darius' eyes travel to my bare tits, looking at me like I'm the most delicious thing he's ever seen. My confidence soaring, I give my nipples a little tweak; God, this man makes me feel like the sexiest woman on earth.

"Naughty angel." He chastises, his nostrils flaring. "You know what happens to bad girls, don't you Lily?"

Mmm, I do. But before he can follow through with that yummy threat, Iris knocks on the door. "Mama! Darius!"

"To be continued," Darius promises, pulling my robe back on and tying it for me.

I hop out of bed and open the door, and Iris comes whirling into our room like a tiny tornado. "Morning, sweetie," I say, picking her up and kissing her.

"Who's ready to go explore?" Darius asks.

"Me!" Iris says, bouncing in my arms.

"I knew I could count on the rainbow goddess," Darius says, and she beams. "I've got a big day planned for us, and then we'll visit my *mamá*."

"Really?" I ask, feeling nervous at the prospect.

He nods. "She's excited to meet you. Both of you," he says to Iris.

"Darius, a word," I tell him.

"Are you in trouble?" Iris wonders.

"Probably," he tells her with a wink. "Let's go find Kat."

Iris hops down from my arms without protest and takes Darius' big hand as he leads her out.

I finish my coffee and a few bites of pastry, and throw on a casual sundress and comfy sandals. Walking to the bathroom,

I'm putting the finishing touches on my makeup when Darius returns.

"Yes, wifey?" he watches me in the mirror with an amused expression.

"What's our story?" I ask, placing my makeup in my bag.

"What do you mean?"

"How did we meet? In case anyone asks." I can't exactly say I was walking into a strip club where I dance, when I accidentally overheard Darius threaten another dancer.

"The park," he answers smoothly. "I was running. You and Iris were there, and you couldn't keep those pretty little eyes off me. Or my dick," he says smugly.

My cheeks heat at being caught. "You're not allowed to wear gray sweatpants in public."

Darius laughs.

"That wasn't supposed to be funny!" I huff.

"Look at you getting all jealous. So cute." He nips playfully at my downturned bottom lip. "We met at the park, and the rest is history."

"I like that," I tell him, standing on my tiptoes and giving him a kiss. "I'm ready to go. But I mean it about the sweatpants."

"Wifey's already on my nuts about my wardrobe," he jokes. Not his nuts, but his dick I'm concerned about—and other women ogling it.

He grabs my bag, and we walk upstairs to find Kat entertaining Iris. We're greeted by a crewman, and Darius helps us aboard the small boat to be ferried to the mainland. I haven't seen as much as a glimpse of the crewman who was being a little too friendly with me. Honestly, it's for the best, because I'd be afraid of what Darius would do to the guy.

"What's that smile for?" Kat asks me.

"Oh, nothing." Just that red flags are turning out to be my love language after all.

We reach the mainland, and Kat parts ways with us to

meet up with some childhood friends. Darius, Iris, and I explore Portara.

"This is amazing!" I'm in awe of the magnificence of Apollo's door and the stunning view the islet offers. "What do you think?" I ask Iris.

"It's a big door," she says, clearly unimpressed, and Darius chuckles.

"That hurts my heart," I say dramatically, but I guess an eighty-ton, 6th century BC archeological ruin isn't a four-year old's thing.

Our next stop is Naxo Town. We're strolling through the charming stone streets, when Iris spots an ice cream shop—definitely a four-year old's thing. "We haven't had lunch yet," I warn her.

"It's a tradition in Naxos to have ice cream after visiting the Portara, as tribute to Apollo."

"Really?" I say, narrowing my eyes at him.

"Trust the local." Darius winks at me. "What flavor, rainbow goddess?" he asks Iris.

"Chocolate!"

"Lily?"

I give him a dubious look, but concede defeat. "Pistachio."

He pops into the shop, and Iris asks me, "Is Darius my dad now?"

I pause, considering the best way to explain this. "Darius is your stepdad—like an extra bonus dad," I tell her. "But your dad will always be your dad."

"I want Darius to be my dad," she tells me. "He likes me more than Dad does."

Picking her up, I give her a big hug. "I'm sorry your dad's so busy with work." God, I hate covering for that piece of shit Harrison. I've turned my cell service off while we're out of the country, so I don't know if he ever texted me back; I can't wait to hear his excuse this time. "I want you to know your dad loves you." That's only halfway true. A man like

Harrison is too self-centered to love anyone other than himself. "But hey, now you have two dads. That's pretty cool, huh?"

"I guess."

Darius returns holding two cones. "Chocolate for the rainbow goddess," he announces.

"Thank you!" She hops down from my arms, grabbing the cone.

"My pleasure. And pistachio."

"Thank you. You don't want any?" I ask him.

"Nah, I don't eat many sweets. Well, there is one sweet thing I *love* to eat—"

I shove the cone at his mouth to shut him up.

His big smile is now covered in green ice cream. "Wifey, you're going to pay for that."

Of course, Iris takes that as an invitation to shove the chocolate cone in her face with a delighted squeal. "Oh, no! I've started a bad thing." I laugh, pulling wipes from my bag.

"Just another Naxos tradition," Darius declares.

"Uh-huh. Trust the local," I say with a wry smile, wiping chocolate off Iris' face. "You next," I tell Darius. He playfully snaps his teeth at me, and Iris giggles. "Behave," I tell him, wiping the ice cream from his face and part of his beard.

"Not me; him." Darius flexes his dog tattoo and barks, causing Iris to break out in a fit of giggles.

Finishing our cones, we continue our leisurely exploration. A shop catches my eye, and we step inside. "Lots of pretty things, but please don't touch," I tell Iris, as there's pottery and other breakable souvenirs as far as the eye can see.

Darius scoops her up and places her on his shoulders. "There. Just don't touch the ceiling," he warns Iris, who's grinning from ear to ear.

I explore the shop, my eyes landing on a small Hades and

Persephone statue set. "Handmade with an alabaster cast," the shopkeeper calls to me.

"We'll take them," Darius says, now standing beside me with Iris perched on his shoulders.

I stand on my tiptoes, giving him a proper thank you.

"They kiss a lot," Iris informs the shopkeeper, much to my embarrassment.

"Ah, Eros. To be young again." The old man smiles, carrying the statutes over to the counter and wrapping them in bubble wrap before bagging them.

Darius says something in Greek, and the man returns something before reaching behind the counter—handing Darius a large evil eye charm.

Darius passes it to Iris, and she asks, "What is it? It looks like my eyeball!" She holds the cobalt blue glass charm up to her eye.

"*Mati.* A good luck charm," Darius tells her, handing the man some Euros. Feeling pretty lucky myself, I say a silent prayer of thanks to the Fates for bringing this crazy, wonderful man into mine and Iris' lives.

We make one more stop in a jewelry store, where Darius picks out for me a dainty evil eye charm made of diamonds and gemstones on a gold chain. He pays, and we step outside.

Taking the necklace out of the bag, I turn around for him and hold up my hair as he fastens it around my neck. "I love it. Thank you," I swoon, giving him one more kiss. "Now that we have all this good luck, where to?"

"Let's visit my *mamá* before our flight home," he announces.

"What about your dad?" I wonder.

"He's no longer with us."

"I'm sorry," I tell him.

"I'm not," he answers bluntly, and so I don't push him on it. "It's a pretty good clip up some steep hills, so I've rented us a car. With a car seat," he assures me.

We walk to the car rental company, and soon we're off—making our way out of town on a narrow, winding road. I grip the armrest for dear life, trying to ignore the terrifying drop-off on my side.

"Relax, Lily," Darius tells me. "I know these roads like the back of my hand."

"Why did you leave here? It's beautiful," I comment, trying to distract myself.

"I received an offer to move to Jersey I couldn't pass up."

An offer with the mob. I don't ask any more questions.

We reach *Taverna* Angelos, and Darius pulls into the gravel parking lot. "This is your family's place?"

"Yes."

He opens the door for me, and gets Lily out of the car seat. Taking our hands, he leads us to the restaurant's outdoor patio. A group of local men speaking in Greek falls silent; one look at Darius has them hopping up and scurrying away.

"They must not like dogs," Darius comments.

We take a seat at a cute table with mismatched chairs underneath the pergola. "This is so beautiful," I comment, taking in the surrounding flowering trees swaying in the breeze, the stunning valley below us.

"*Είσαι τόσο όμορφη,*" he tells me.

Before I can ask for a translation, Kat appears with a pretty Greek woman around our age. "Hey." Kat waves, and she and her companion join us. "This is my friend, Zoe. Zoe, of course you know Darius, and this is his wife, Lily, and his stepdaughter, Iris."

Darius stands, and he and Zoe greet each other in Greek before exchanging a hug.

My jaw clenching, I now regret choosing Latin as my language requirement for my degree instead of Greek. I take a deep breath, trying not to be so triggered—just because Harrison was a cheating asshole, that doesn't mean Darius will be.

"Hello," I say, standing and offering Zoe my hand.

Wondering if I've made a cultural mistake when she just looks at it, she says something in Greek to Darius before taking my hand and finally addressing me. "Nice to meet you," she says in perfect English.

Feeling extremely self-conscious as the woman continues her unabashed appraisal of me, I take a seat.

"Darius, Kat told me you were back. And *married*. I had to see for my own eyes," Zoe exclaims.

"Happily married," Darius takes a seat beside me, grabbing my hand and giving it a squeeze. "What have you been up to, Zoe?"

"I'm on break from uni. How fabulous we're all here on holiday together!" I play with my evil eye charm on my necklace, not sharing in her enthusiasm.

"Lily's also a university student," Darius comments.

"Oh," she says, feigning interest.

"I go to Miss Mary's," Iris adds proudly.

"Sorry?" Zoe asks.

"It's a preschool," I explain.

"How nice," she says dismissively. Turning her attention back to Darius, she says, "Is this the first time you've been back, since you up and left your *girlfriend* without so much as a goodbye?" So she's the ex-girlfriend—clearly upset about the *ex* part.

"You can't be Darius' girlfriend. He's married to my mama," Iris informs Zoe, and it takes all my willpower not to high five my daughter.

"Right you are, rainbow goddess." Darius winks at Iris, bringing our hands up and kissing the top of mine.

"Zoe, it was so nice to catch up. Thanks for dropping me off," Kat hints.

"Of course." Zoe eyes Darius and my interlocked hands before giving Kat a hug. Turning to Darius, Zoe says something in Greek, and he replies.

"Be right back, ladies," Darius says in English, releasing my hand and following a smiling Zoe. I suddenly feel like I'm going to throw up. So much for *not* being triggered.

"Sorry about that. Zoe offered to drop me off, but I didn't know she was going to be weird about it," Kat explains.

"Not your fault. Is there a restroom?" I ask, feeling like I'm about to break down in tears, and would rather do so out of my daughter's presence.

"Inside, and go straight back past the kitchen," Kat tells me.

"Be back in a little bit," I say, stepping inside.

I'm passing the kitchen, when a beautiful Greek woman in her mid-forties wearing an apron appears in the doorway. "You must be Lily."

"Hello. You must be Darius' mom. It's nice to meet—"

"Do you love my son?" she demands.

"Yes," I answer, taken aback by her bluntness.

She pins me with her gaze, crossing her arms. "Then if you love him, you'll let him go."

"I'm sorry?"

She says something in Greek, switching over to English. "You're no good for him. *Ftou. Ftou. Ftou.*" My eyes go wide with shock as she spits on the ground near my feet.

"I'm sorry you feel that way. Excuse me," I say, running to the bathroom and shutting and locking the door as I break down into tears.

CHAPTER
Twenty

Darius

We board the Parisi family jet, and Lily immediately puts in earbuds and grabs her laptop, getting to work. She's been distant ever since lunch, and I don't fucking like it.

Hours pass of her ignoring my existence. She finally has to take a break, and I wait for her right outside the bathroom. Lily opens the door, jumping in surprise when she nearly runs into me. "Sorry, all yours," she says, trying to squeeze past me.

I grab her, tossing her over my shoulder and carrying her to the small bedroom. "Darius, what are you doing?" she asks as I close and lock the door.

"I'm not letting you out until you tell me what's wrong," I warn her.

"Nothing's wrong," she says in a clipped tone.

Taking a seat on the foot of the bed, I splay her petite body over my lap. My dick becomes rock-hard when I hike up her dress and palm her pretty little ass cheek in my hand. Ducking my head, I slowly pull her thong down and off with my teeth—obsessed with the way her skin pebbles before my eyes. I focus, giving her ass a firm smack.

"What the hell?" She hisses.

"Let's try this again," I say, giving her ass a warning pat. "What's wrong?"

"Don't fucking touch me." Lily tries to squirm out of my lap, but she's not going anywhere.

I give her ass another smack, this one harder. "Lily, tell me what's wrong, or it's going to be a long, uncomfortable flight for you," I warn her.

"*What's wrong*? What's wrong is you left me for a quickie with your ex, and then your mother insulted me *and* spit at me!"

I smack her ass again. "That was for the first part of that statement, which is fucking ridiculous. I didn't have sex with Zoe."

"Did *she* have sex with you?" Lily demands.

"What? No."

"Not sex then, but did you hook up in any way? Oral? Hand job? Fingering? Kissing?"

"Lily, of course not. Why would you say that?"

"I just thought..." She trails off as her body begins to tremble.

I sit her up so I can see her face. "Hey, don't do that," I say, taking my thumb and wiping away her tears.

"Why did you go with her, then?" she asks quietly.

"Because Zoe asked me to take a look at the check engine light on her rental." The check engine light wasn't even on; she just wanted an excuse to hit me up. Probably because she heard from bigmouth Kat how successful I am now. Zoe was always an uppity social climber, even as a teenager. I don't fucking feel bad about skipping town on her all those years ago.

"Oh," Lily says quietly.

Slipping off my shoes, I remove Lily's sandals and walk us

around to the bed. "*Aggeloudhi mou*, I'm not your ex." I gently lay her down before climbing in bed beside her. "He was a fool." She's stopped crying, and I take that as a good sign as I continue, "I am many things, but a fool isn't one of them. What we've got is too damn good; there's no way I'd fuck it up like that, I promise you." Cupping her cheeks, I tell her unequivocally, "I've never been a cheater, and I'm not going to start by cheating on the woman of my dreams. *Αφοσίωση*."

"I don't know what that means." She sniffs.

"*Loyalty*. You have mine."

"I'm scared this is too good to be true," she whispers.

"Then give me time to prove to you just how good this can be," I tell her, running my hand through her long waves.

"Okay," she says quietly.

"Good girl." I move on to the next issue. "Now, what about this thing with my *mamá*?" I introduced them at the table after I got back from dealing with Zoe's bullshit. Lily seemed tense, but I just thought it was because she was nervous about meeting my mother.

"I ran into her on the way to the bathroom. Your mom told me I'm no good for you," Lily admits. "That I should let you go, and then she spit."

"The spitting is to fend off the evil eye. It's silly, and I'm sorry she treated you that way."

"Why would she think I'm no good for you? She doesn't know me. Unless she knows I'm a dancer?" Lily worries.

I shake my head. "She doesn't know you *used* to be a dancer." Past tense as far as I'm concerned. "My *mamá* believes in old superstitions, that's all." I don't want to tell Lily about my *mamá's* "prophesy." I'm not putting that in Lily's head and giving her something else to fret over. "Now, quit thinking so fucking much, and come sit on my face." Pulling her upright, I roll over onto my back.

"What?" She takes in a sharp breath.

"That sounds like thinking," I chide, tugging at the hem of

her dress; she helps by shifting to her knees and lifting her arms, and I pull the dress over her head, tossing it across the room.

Next off is her bra, freeing those beautiful tits. "So perfect. You are every wet dream I've ever had come to life, little angel." I help guide her into kneeling position—with that beautiful pussy of hers hovering over my face.

"Darius, I'm not sure—"

I spread her pussy lips open wide with my fingers, taking a deep inhale. *Ah, so sweet.* Gathering saliva in my mouth, I spit.

"Darius!" She gasps in shock.

"That wasn't for the evil eye; that's just because my wife's such a filthy little slut for *Diávolos*," I say, rubbing my saliva around her pretty clit.

"Yes." She throws her head back on a moan.

"I told you to sit." I grab her by the hips, slamming her down to where her pussy's plastered over my mouth. There, better.

The tip of my tongue swipes at her seam before I spear her. Lily makes the most beautiful throaty sound, and I encourage her to ride by face by grabbing her hips and moving her back and forth.

"Mmm." She arches her back on a whimper, swaying her hips.

"That's it. Ride my face like a good little slut." I hold her off me enough to encourage her, before yanking her pussy back down and spearing her with my tongue.

"Oh God, this feels so good!" She grabs onto the head-board for leverage, grinding her pussy against my face.

Fuck, she's so damn wet—her juices are running down my chin and neck. "Squirt all over me, little whore. Paint my lips and beard with your cum," I instruct her, holding her up by her ass cheeks. "Show me how hard good girls come when they're tongue fucked by the devil."

"Yes," she moans, her body shaking as I jerk her back down and relentlessly fuck her with my tongue. My little angel pants and moans, her movements becoming sloppy. "Oh my fucking God!"

Almost there. I spread Lily's ass cheeks and take my index finger, circling her tight hole. Her ass tenses, but her pussy absolutely throbs against my tongue, and I hum my approval. My little angel will give me all her pretty holes in due time. The thought makes my dick so hard, I might embarrass myself and come before she does.

Resolved not to let that happen, I move my tongue just to the left of her clit—what I'm learning is wifey's sweet spot— and I don't let up. She's riding my face so damn hard, she's going to have beard burns all over her inner thighs; damn, that's a sexy thought.

"Darius! Oh, I'm coming!" She throws her head back in ecstasy as her pussy gushes all over my face.

I eagerly drink in Lily's cum—hell, I'd bathe in it if I could —licking and sucking as I gently bring her down from her high. Pulling her off my face before she collapses, I tuck her into my arms. "Good, wifey?"

She mutters something incoherent, and I chuckle, kissing the top of her head. "Nothing or no one is ever going to take you away from me; and that includes *you.* The next time you're upset about something, I want you to come talk to me instead of shutting me out. Okay?"

"Okay," Lily whispers against my chest.

"Good girl." Lifting her chin so she's looking at me, I command, "Φίλα με. Kiss me. Taste your perfection on my tongue." She does so without hesitation, smiling against my lips.

It's going to take time to prove to my little angel just how much I worship her. I'm up for the challenge.

CHAPTER
Twenty~One

Lily

"I've got so much to do," I comment as Darius drives us home from the airport. Grabbing a notebook and pen out of my backpack, I start a list. "First, I need to contact my landlord to see if I can get out of my lease." Unlikely, as the man's a complete asshole.

"Give me his name. I'll handle it," Darius says.

"How?"

He raises an eyebrow.

"Never mind." There are some things about my husband's "work" I really don't need to know. I give him the name, and that taken care of, I move on to the next items on my list—scheduling the electricity, water, internet, and streaming service to be shut off. "Where should I have my mail forwarded?"

He rattles off an address, and I write it down. "That's my gym. Don't give out our home address to anyone. Ever." Another reality of my husband's "work."

We reach my house, and Darius parks on the street—only because a Parisi Construction truck is blocking the driveway, with men carrying out Iris' bedroom dresser. My mouth falls open, and Darius takes his finger and closes it with an amused expression. "How did they even get in?" I wonder.

"I told you your place wasn't safe." He hops out and opens my door before getting Iris out of her car seat.

"Darius, a word," I say sharply.

"You get in trouble a lot," Iris tells Darius, and he throws his head back with laughter.

"Sweetie, why don't you play outside," I tell her, escorting her to the backyard and opening the gate, closing it behind us.

She takes off for her rickety swing set, and I turn to Darius. "I don't like—"

"Not being in control over this process?" He finishes for me. "I know."

"That's not what I was going to say!"

"Then what don't you like?" he challenges

Not being in control over this process!

He smiles, knowing he's right. "Come on," he says, taking my hand.

We step inside through the back door, finding several burly men speaking to each other in Italian. They fist bump Darius, who likewise says something in Italian. I need to up my foreign language game around my husband.

"This is my wife, Lily," Darius says proudly, introducing me to the movers.

"Hello," I say.

"Ma'am," one of the men says. "We've already packed up everything from your daughter's room. Tell us what else you would like moved?"

"Everything in my office, please. The rest of my things, I need some time to sort through." The thought of these men pawing through my stripper outfits in my closet has me breaking out in a cold sweat.

"Not a problem." They take off down the hall.

Walking to my bedroom, I raise the blinds so I can keep an eye on Iris, who's swinging.

Darius joins me carrying several boxes, and I get to work, going through my closet and boxing up my clothes.

"Darius, we're gone," a worker says from the doorway, and I shove a black pleaser behind my back before turning around; the move causes Darius to chuckle quietly.

"Thanks, man," Darius answers.

"No problem. Mrs. Angelo, just let us know if you need help moving anything else."

"Thank you so much," I say.

They leave, and Darius turns to me. "My naughty angel is wearing those shoes for me later tonight," he says in a low timbre that causes my nipples to pebble.

Before I can answer, his phone vibrates, and he fishes it out of his pocket. I take it back—not a phone, but a *pager*. "I've never seen a pager in real life. I thought those were extinct," I marvel. "Why do you need that?"

"Work," he responds.

"Oh," I say nervously. He may have covered up his tattoo, but he's still *Diávolos*.

"Nothing for you to worry about, *aggeloudhi mou*," he assures me.

"How can I not worry after what I've s—" I stop mid-sentence, catching myself. "I didn't see anything," I whisper.

"There's my good girl." Darius hums. Wrapping his big arms around me, he tells me, "Finish packing, and I'll be back later to pick you and Iris up." Lifting my chin, he looks into my eyes. "Alright?" He places his lips gently to mine, and I melt into his arms.

"Alright," I say on a sigh when he pulls back.

"Don't forget to pack the heels for tonight. And this," he

says with a naughty smile, reaching in a box and holding by his finger a shear red thong—twirling it round and round.

"Stop it!" I snatch the thong from him.

Chuckling, he reaches in his pocket, handing me another dinosaur of a gadget—a phone that looks older than me. "Burner phone. I've programmed my cell and pager in there. Only use this to call or text me." He gives me one final kiss before walking out. "I'm going to send Iris inside," he calls.

I grab my phone—not the clandestine one I have to use to communicate with my husband—and pull up a playlist. Realizing I've forgotten to switch service back on, I do so now. *Ping* after *ping* after *ping* sounds as I'm flooded with messages.

"Mama, all my stuff is gone!" Iris shouts.

I walk to her room, stopping at the door and smiling. "Yep. The movers are taking everything to our new house with Darius. Let's say goodbye to this house."

"Bye, house," Iris says, hugging the wall.

I get her set up with an educational game on her tablet before getting back to packing. Trash pile. Donate pile. Need to pack pile. There is a method to my madness, even though it looks like a disaster zone.

The doorbell rings, and I walk to the front of the house, thinking Darius must have forgot something. Glancing out the peephole, I find an older man in a suit; the vehicle parked in my driveway looks like an unmarked police car.

Taking a deep breath, I mentally go over my story. I wasn't at the club the other night; I don't know anything. "Hi, there. Can I help you?" I ask when I open the door.

"Ms. Grant?"

"Yes."

"I'm Detective Regan," he says, flashing his badge. "I need to speak to you."

"Sure, let me step on the porch," I say, closing the door. *I wasn't at the club; I don't know anything.* "My daughter's inside, so I can only chat for a minute."

"Iris, right? Officer Harrison's kid," he says.

"Yes, that's right."

"When's the last time you spoke to him?" Detective Regan asks.

"We don't really speak," I correct him. "Just exchange texts about Iris now and then."

"So it's a contentious relationship," he challenges.

"No, I didn't say that. I'm sorry, but what is that about?" I ask, confused.

"Officer Harrison was found dead in his home last night."

"Oh my God," I say, my legs feeling wobbly as I grab onto the porch railing.

"You didn't know?" he questions.

"No," I say, placing a hand over my heart. "How did he die?"

"Gunshot wound."

"Suicide?" I gasp.

"No. A homicide," he answers gruffly, but doesn't elaborate. "I'm just trying to piece together his last days. When was the last time you exchanged texts?"

"Harrison was supposed to have a visit with Iris last weekend. He was a no-show at the park—our exchange point. I texted him a couple of times wondering where he was. He never responded."

"And you didn't think that odd?" he asks, the question dripping with judgment.

"No," I say defensively. "The man flakes on his daughter all the time. That's just Harrison."

"And you were angry about it?" he says, putting words in my mouth.

"What? No. I mean, sure, I was annoyed, but mostly feeling bad for my daughter. She doesn't deserve to be treated like that."

"Where have you been these past forty-eight hours?" His eyes land on my diamond ring.

"You come here, spring the news on me my child's father is dead, and now you're what? *Accusing me*? It's beyond ridiculous, and I'm done with this conversation," I say, clasping my hands together so he won't notice them shaking.

"I can just as easily take you downtown to finish answering my questions," he threatens.

Squaring my chin, I say, "You can't. Not unless you're arresting me." I learned at least that much from Harrison. "Am I under arrest, detective?" I challenge.

He doesn't answer.

"Then that's a no. Please remove yourself from my property."

"If that's how you want to play it," he says in a threatening tone. "I'll be in touch, Ms. Grant."

CHAPTER
Twenty~Two

Darius

It pains me to leave Lily and Iris at their old house by themselves, but when I get a lead on John Davis, I have to follow it.

Turning on a true crime podcast—Nonna got me hooked on them—I roll my eyes. Forgetting the knife at the crime scene; the motherfucker deserved to be caught.

On the road for around two hours, I arrive in AC. I'm not holding my breath John Davis will still be here, but that's assuming it was really him sighted to begin with.

I do a slow drive-by of Ace's Wild Boxing Club before parking the next street over. Grabbing my file, I look over the man's photo one more time. *Know thine enemy*. The fact that I don't know this one—that no one does—makes me uneasy.

I was able to pull a better image of John Davis from The Diamond's pool security feed, and I now owe Kat another favor. The guy was dumb enough to approach Romeo's girl at the rooftop pool—a fatal mistake on John's part, and I'm sure a nearly a fatal mistake on her bodyguard's part.

In the photo, John's wearing a hat and sunglasses—not

exactly helpful—but the edge of a red tattoo peeks out from beneath the left sleeve of his T-shirt. He'd better not have a big red dog tattoo like mine, or I'll turn the guy over to Sammy; fucker prides himself on skinning men alive.

I exit my car and sling my backpack over my shoulder, strolling to the alley beside the gym. Watching the front door, I bide my time.

Finally the door opens, and I inwardly curse. Sneaking up behind the woman who just left, I place a hand over her mouth and drag her to the alley. "What the fuck, Darius!" Kat smacks me with her gym bag when I release her. "Are you trying to give me a heart attack?"

"What the fuck are you doing here?" I growl.

"Uh, I live in this city, in case you forgot."

"What are you doing at this *gym*?"

"I started working out," she tells me. "Boxing with a trainer. My friend recommended this place—she loves it."

"Since when do you work out?" I ask, eyebrow raised.

"Since I got back from our trip and realized how freaking out of shape I am! Those damn hills nearly killed me. And you'll be happy to learn I've quit smoking, so you can get off my back about that." She points at me. "But I'm not giving up chips, I don't give a fuck what anyone says."

"Let me inside," I command. "I got a tip about a guy who fits John Davis' description."

"Jesus, you're going to get me blacklisted on my first freakin' day!"

I shrug.

She hands me her key card. "Keep it. I'll tell them I lost my card and get another one. But seriously, don't get me blacklisted."

I grunt, making no promises.

"Tell Lily and Iris I said hi."

"Will do," I tell her. "Now get the hell out of here."

I hang back in the alley as a few other gym-goers exit.

Glancing at my watch, I wait until one minute before the posted closing time. Strolling to the front door, I scan Kat's card. The door *beeps* green, and I pocket the card as I step inside the empty gym.

"Hey man, can I help you?" A guy around my age sticks his head out of an office to my left. He's short and stocky; not my target.

"Hey there, what's your name?" I ask.

"I'm Russell Jackson. This is my club. What's your name?" he asks in a friendly tone.

"John Davis," I fish.

Either the man's a professional poker player, or John Davis uses an alias around this gym, because Russell doesn't so much as bat an eye. "Nice to meet you. Are you looking for a boxing club?"

"Yes."

"Awesome. You look pretty fit. You already work out?" he asks.

"Yeah, I do my own thing, but I'm looking to get into a more structured routine," I tell him.

"I hear you. I was just about to close up for the evening, but let me give you a quick tour," he suggests.

"Excellent."

"Training rings. Bags. Weights in the corner." Russell points everything out.

"Nice," I comment, following him to the back.

He holds open a door. "Men's locker room." Glancing to the end of the hall, there's a closed door with a hand-sensor entry system; so that's where I need to be. We step inside the locker room, and he continues with the tour. "Lockers. I recommend you supply your own lock."

"Good to know," I say.

"Right this way to the showers and sauna." He holds open another door for me, and I step inside first. I glance in the mirror above the sinks to watch my back—a good thing, because Russell's pulling a 9MM from his waistband.

Adrenaline floods my body as I grab my own pistol from my waistband—spinning around and pulling the trigger as I dive to the floor. The sound of gunfire reverberates in my ears, and it takes me a second to realize I've been shot. *That motherfucker.* It appears to be just a graze on my left tricep, but my body's too keyed up to feel any pain.

Pulling myself up off the floor, I walk over to Russell's lifeless body. There's a bullet hole in the center of his forehead, but I add another for good measure.

My ears ringing, I run to the back, kicking the sensor-entry door several times, but it's reinforced with steel and won't budge. Cursing, I sprint back to the locker room. "I need a hand," I tell Russell as I slip on gloves and a slicker from my backpack. Grabbing the large hunting knife I packed just in case, I work it back and forth against his wrist with effort. Dripping with sweat, I finally cut through the last of bone and tendons.

Returning to the locked door, I press Russell's severed hand to the sensor, and the door opens. I hustle down a set of stairs, entering a large gambling setup in the basement with poker tables and a bar. "Will you look at that?" I say, wagging Russell's finger. John Davis and his now deceased buddy, Russell, were trying to undercut the family's gambling racket.

Exiting another door, I walk down a hallway past bathrooms, to a room marked *Private*. I position Russell's hand to the sensor, gaining entry, and whistle. It's a command center rivaling a top-dollar casino's, with multiple security feeds and a heavy-duty safe built into the wall.

Returning upstairs, I toss the severed hand onto Russel's face; it lands with a wet *smack*. I peel off my glove, sending a message to Fabio's encrypted pager.

> Need someone to move gym equipment
> ASAP. Ace's Wild Boxing Club.

Fabio's taken over the rat Sergio's AC rackets, and so hopefully, he can get a crew over here quick. Romeo will want to go through the security footage, and I need to focus on the more pressing issue—making Russell disappear.

"Let's do this," I announce, giving Russell's hand a high five with his severed one before I begin the tedious task of dismembering his body.

Where's Sammy when I need him? He enjoys this kind of thing.

Lily

"Lily." Darius' deep voice rouses me.

Sitting up in my bed, I look around, confused; Iris is sound asleep beside me. "What time is it?"

"Almost eight in the evening."

"What? I meant for us just to take a little nap." I hop up and grab Darius' hand, leading him to the hall. "I tried calling you earlier," I whisper.

"I'm sorry. My phone was turned off," he tells me, smoothing my hair. "You ready to go?"

"Yes, but I need to talk to you. A detective stopped by—"

"*Και οι τοίχοι έχουν αυτιά.*" He holds his finger to my mouth, silencing me. "Wait until we get to my place. I don't know if your house has been bugged," he whispers in my ear.

"I didn't finish packing," I say when he drops his finger, my chin trembling; I'm dangerously close to losing it. God, it is so fucked up the cops think I killed my daughter's father!

"Hey, it's alright. You don't have to get it all finished today," Darius says, wrapping his big arms around me. "Grab what you need for tonight, and I'll carry Iris to the car," he says, kissing the top of my head.

Nodding, I follow him into the bedroom. Iris doesn't so much as make a peep when Darius picks her up and carries her out. I quickly grab our things, locking up behind me.

Once in the SUV, I buckle up as Darius pulls out of my driveway. Glancing back at the still sleeping Iris, I spot Detective Regan's car behind us. "Darius, the detective's following us," I whisper in alarm.

Darius slams on the brakes, pressing the emergency lights button. Before I know what's happening, he hops out of my vehicle and stalks over to Detective Regan's, knocking on his window.

Darius

Cop or not—this motherfucker harassing Lily is about to learn a lesson in manners.

I knock on the tinted window, and a familiar face appears when it rolls down. Love it when the Fates smile down on me. "Evening, Detective Regan."

"Darius," he says, surprised. "Didn't know that was you."

"In the flesh. There a reason you're stalking my wife?" I menace.

"I didn't know she was your wife," he's quick to answer. "I was just following up on a case."

"What case?" I demand, and he fills me in about Iris' dad.

"I promise you it won't happen again," Detective Regan adds.

"It better fucking not. I'd hate for that video from the Jersey Motor Inn to come to light." Cops aren't the only ones who can set up a sting, and lucky for the family, the detective loves to visit male prostitutes. "You're what, just a few years from retirement?"

"Two," he answers tightly.

"In the home stretch," I comment. "Well, see you around, detective. Kiss your wife and kids for me."

CHAPTER
Twenty-Three

Lily

The men exchange a few words before Darius returns, flipping off the emergency lights as we continue driving.

"What just happened?" I ask quietly.

"He won't bother you anymore," he assures me.

"Just like that?" I say in shock.

"Just like that."

"Darius?"

He looks over to me. "Yes, wifey?"

"Never mind." I don't even know what I was going to say, so I just close my eyes, leaning my head back against the seat. Except my brain won't stop screaming: *Harrison is dead!* Remembering I have a mountain of messages to go through—now I know why—I grab my phone.

Three messages from Harrison's partner. Pressing play on the first one, I listen to Ethan's choked up voice relaying the news. God, I feel awful—Ethan thought something was wrong with Harrison, and I downplayed his concerns.

I search the local news, finding an article about Harrison's death.

Police are investigating a homicide that appears to have stemmed from a home burglary. The victim was pronounced dead at the scene. Anyone with information is asked to call Newark Police Department Homicide Detectives.

Finding Ethan's contact, I send him a message.

> Got your messages about Harrison. I haven't broken the news to Iris yet, but please keep me posted about funeral arrangements.

> Where the hell have you been? I've been calling you and stopped by your place like five times.

Not knowing how I should respond, I ignore him for the time being.

I listen to two other voicemails—both from Detective Regan. The more I think about it, the madder it makes me. Like I would really kill my daughter's father! I get the detective was only doing his job, but it's still absurd.

Checking my email, I hold my breath as I open a message from the Chair of The Department of Classical Studies. "I've been accepted to grad school!"

"Congratulations. I'm so proud of you," Darius tells me with a big grin.

"Thank you," I say, smiling, but that celebratory feeling is short-lived when the guilt kicks in. I just found out my child's father is dead, after all, and it feels wrong to be so happy.

Iris wakes up disoriented and begins crying, and I turn around and squeeze her leg. "Hey, sweetie. It's okay. We're in the car driving to Darius' house."

"And I have a big surprise for the rainbow goddess," Darius says.

"What is it?" Iris asks, rubbing her eyes.

"Now you sound like your mama." He chuckles. "If I told you, it wouldn't be a surprise."

We make our way out of downtown, turning into a nice, understated neighborhood. "You live in the burbs?" I ask, surprised.

"You got a problem with the burbs?" he teases.

"No, it's just I would have guessed you lived downtown, maybe in a high-rise."

"I used to live downtown. Not in a high-rise, but an apartment above my gym."

"When did you move?" I wonder.

"Today," he informs me.

"What?"

"Iris needs more room to play. Plus, she'll be zoned for some really good schools, and the commute for you isn't that much longer to campus than what you were doing."

"Darius," I say, tears welling in my eyes. "I love you."

"Love you too," he says, squeezing my thigh.

"Are you going to kiss? *Again*?" Iris pipes up from the back.

"I will kiss your beautiful mama every chance I get," Darius answers, winking at me before turning his attention back to the road.

We reach a cute two-story colonial on the end of a cul-de-sac. Pressing a garage button now clipped on my visor, we pull inside and park next to his car. Following him inside to the sweet little kitchen I can picture us enjoying as a family, my heart feels so full it might burst.

"What's that?" Iris asks. I hear it too—a tiny crying sound.

"Go see for yourself," Darius says.

Iris takes off to the living room, and I chase after her—discovering the source. "A cat!" Iris exclaims.

"Your cat, as you so expertly negotiated," Darius tells her.

"I can't believe it!" Iris jumps up and down.

"Darius—"

"A word?" He finishes for me. "I know, I should have talked to you about it first—"

"Thank you," I say, standing on my tiptoes and giving him a kiss.

"They do that a lot, Lucky," Iris tells her cat—who I guess is now named Lucky.

"Lucky. I like it. Where'd you come up with the name?" I ask.

"Her eyes are blue like the good luck charm Darius gave me," Iris explains.

"Wait, are we sure it's a she?" I ask Darius.

"It's a she," he confirms. "Lucky's around a year old. Already litter box trained," he assures me.

Squatting down, I give the gray-and-white striped cat with bright blue eyes a little scratch under her chin. "Hey, Lucky," I tell the cat, who's purring like an engine. "I've never seen a cat with eyes like this," I comment to Darius.

"Ojos Azules is the breed. They're supposed to be good with kids," he tells me.

Lucky demonstrates that trait by allowing Iris to pick her up. "Be soft. Don't squish her tummy too hard," I warn my daughter.

"This is the best day of my life!" Iris exclaims.

"I'm so glad to hear it. But it gets better. Let me show you to your new room," Darius says with a sly smile.

We follow him down the hall and up the stairs. "Your office," Darius tells me, flipping on the light to the first room we reach.

I take in the cozy space with my desk and bookcase—the Hades and Persephone statues prominently displayed on the top shelf. There's also cushioned window seat—the perfect place to snuggle under a blanket with a cup of coffee and a good book. "I love this so much," I swoon.

"Good," he says, flipping off the light and continuing down the hall. "And Iris, this is your room."

We enter a bedroom with all of Iris' things, plus a cute little reading nook with a bean bag and bookcase. Behind it painted on the wall is a beautiful pastel rainbow mural. Iris squeals in delight, and Lucky hops down as my daughter runs over to explore her new room.

"Enough. You're getting lucky later," I whisper to Darius, and he laughs.

We manage to talk Iris into checking out the rest of the house, and after a mouthwatering dinner of takeout—the same Italian food Darius got us on our first "date" back at the VIP room of Glitter—we tuck Iris into bed. Deciding today has been so perfect, I'll wait to tell her about Harrison tomorrow.

"But I want Lucky to sleep in my room," Iris begs as we tuck her into bed.

"I'm sorry," I say, shaking my head. "Sometimes cats like to play at night, and it's already way past your bedtime," I explain.

"Please, Darius," Iris begs with puppy dog eyes, already trying to work over her stepdad.

"Mama knows best," he says. "Lucky will be nice and cozy in her cat condo, and when you wake up, she'll be ready to play," he assures her, kissing the top of her head. If the man wasn't already getting lucky, his backing me up would seal the deal.

We give Iris a hug and kiss goodnight, flipping off her light and closing the door.

Following Darius downstairs, I ask him, "Do you have any wine?" I could use a glass after the events of today.

He shakes his head. "I'm sorry, I don't drink alcohol."

"Ever?" I wonder.

"Nah, my old man was a piece of shit alcoholic. So whatever he did in his pathetic life, I make a point to do the opposite."

"You're a good man," I tell him.

"I'm many things, little angel, but good isn't one of them," he corrects me.

"Don't make me spank your ass," I warn him, and he laughs.

My playful mood sobers when I remember why I asked for the wine. "I found out earlier today Iris' dad passed away. I don't know the details, but he was shot in what appears to be a robbery at his house."

"That's why the detective came to see you," Darius guesses.

I nod. "He acted like I was involved in Harrison's death."

He snorts. "That's the dumbest fucking thing I've ever heard."

"Thank you," I say, blowing out a breath.

"Does Iris know about her dad?"

"No, I'm going to tell her tomorrow. One big change at a time."

"Alright," he says, squeezing my hand. "I have some calls to make. Why don't you go on to bed?"

"Yeah," I say, exhaustion hitting me over the head like a ton of bricks even though I slept the afternoon away.

Walking to Darius' bedroom—*our* bedroom, I correct myself—I grab my things and go to the bathroom, taking a nice, long bath. I climb out of the tub and dry off before putting on a tank top and panties. Giving my hair a quick brush, I halfway dry it with my hair dryer, too tired to finish.

Darius walks in and grabs his toothbrush—the two of us sharing space like it's the most natural thing in the world. I break down into tears.

He spits and places his toothbrush down before scooping me up in his arms and carrying me to bed. "I'm feeling a lot of guilt for being this happy when Harrison just died," I explain, dabbing my eyes.

"Lily, you and Iris both deserve the world, no matter what. You hear me?" he says, shrugging out of his shirt.

My eyes land on the small bandage covering part of his ribcage. "Did you add another tooth?" *He barely escaped death today while I was asleep?* The thought nearly sends me over the edge.

"Breathe for me," he commands, and I take in a deep, slow breath before releasing it. He smooths the worry lines on my forehead with the pads of his fingers. "I have thirty-two teeth —so twenty-eight lives left," he assures me.

"I don't think it works that way. And this one?" I ask, touching the edge of a bandage on his left tricep.

"Just a little scrape."

"Let me see," I insist.

He peels off the bandage, and I gasp. There's a bloody divot in his skin about an inch wide and two inches long. "What happened?"

"Just a graze."

"As in a *bullet* graze?" My voice sounds hysterical to my own ears. "Oh my God, you have to go to the hospital!"

"We're going to the Parisi family dinner tomorrow night," he says, reapplying the bandages. "My boss' girl, Nicky, is a doc. She can take a look at it then."

"Darius—"

He silences me by thrusting his tongue inside my mouth. Kissing me until I'm breathless, he pulls back—resting his forehead against mine. "I'm fine, but if it makes you feel better, I'll have Nicky look at it tomorrow. Now, stop thinking so fucking much and lay back," he commands, pushing me onto the bed with his big hand. "I'm eating this sweet little pussy until you pass out."

And he makes good on that promise.

CHAPTER
Twenty~Four

Lily

Waking with a start, I sit up in bed and glance at the clock—way too early for me to be up.

"Go back to sleep," Darius rumbles with his eyes closed, pulling me back down.

Admiring my sexy husband in the early morning sun, I run my nails through his prickly beard. His eyes remain closed even though I know he's awake, and I smile as I pull down the covers to find his dick is also awake.

Climbing on top of him, I lick and kiss his neck, savoring the taste of his salty skin as I work my way down to his hard pecs. He told me the old adage "your body is a temple," and this man's body is absolutely a temple—one I'll happily worship at this Sunday morning.

I continue my journey south, kissing and licking his happy trail until I get to his massive erection. As I open my mouth wide to take him in, he grabs my hair, giving it a tug. "If you put those pretty little lips on my dick, I'll come too soon," he says in a guttural tone, his eyes now open. "I want you to ride me."

I eagerly crawl up his body, holding onto his chest as grind my pussy against his shaft. "Put my dick inside you," he says in that gravely tone of his I love so much.

Shaking my head with a smile, I continue to slide my pussy lips against his length, dry humping him—except I'm already so wet, there's nothing *dry* about it.

"Such a fucking tease," he chides. "Pussy dripping on my dick like a little whore."

Mmm, I'm getting Diávolos this morning. "You made me this way," I tell him.

"I did," he readily agrees. "Don't ever forget, little angel, the devil owns this pussy." He grabs me by the hips with one hand and holds his dick with the other, slamming me down hard on him.

"Oh, God! You're too big," I whimper. He's a snug fit anyway, but with me on top, it's an overwhelming feeling of fullness, bordering on painful.

"My dirty little slut will stretch." Darius gently thumps his dick inside me, but otherwise remains still—giving me time to adjust to his size. I take a deep breath, relaxing my body. "That's it. Like a fucking glove," he praises in a choked tone, a look of ecstasy on his face. "This pussy was made for me. Now, ride," he commands, moving me back and forth with his hands bruising into my hips.

I lean back, bracing my hands on his muscular thighs as I move on his velvety-smooth dick. "This feels so good." I moan, my clit hitting his bunched up foreskin on each forward motion.

"Heaven," he rasps in agreement. Releasing one of my hips, he holds up his thumb over his pelvis.

When I propel myself forward on the next thrust of my hips, I find out why. "Oh, fuck," I cry, my clit hitting the pad of his thumb. I speed up my movement, chasing after the orgasm that's oh so close.

He smirks. "Look at my greedy little whore, so desperate to squirt all over *Diávolos'* dick."

"Yes," I pant.

That now familiar tug deep in my pelvis causes me to become sloppy with my movement. He takes control, grunting as he moves my hips faster with his hands. "My little slut's good for one thing, isn't that right?"

His cruel, dirty words send a thrill down my spine. "No," I argue.

"No?" He runs his hand underneath where we're connected, the damning evidence glistening on his fingertips.

Before he can command me, I grab his hand and lick his fingers clean—one-by-one.

His nostrils flare. "Such a filthy whore. *Diávolos'* little fucktoy."

"I'm not," I lie, moving my hips faster as my pleasure builds and builds.

He reaches behind me, and before I know what's happening, he shoves my discarded panties from last night into my mouth. "*Diávolos* has heard enough lies from the little slut. Mouth stuffed with your panties; pussy's about to be stuffed full of my cum," he threatens. "You're nothing but the devil's pretty little plaything."

His eyes wild and dangerous, he thrusts up into me hard —over and over. "Yes, fuck me harder," I moan, the word sounding like nonsense with the panties still wadded in my mouth.

"Who owns this pussy?" He bounces me on his dick while rubbing my clit back and forth with the palm of his hand.

Wave after wave of pleasure courses through my body as I barrel over the edge. "*Diávolos!*" I try to scream. My orgasm's so intense, the only reason I'm upright is because he's holding me there.

"Fuck, Lily!" Darius' hands squeeze my hips hard as he

grinds out his release; that warm feeling of his cum spurting inside me causes me nearly to orgasm again.

He pulls me off him and into his arms, a big dreamy smile plastered on my face as he removes the panties from my mouth.

"Such a good girl." He hums his approval, petting my hair with his bear paw of a hand, and I snuggle in closer to the delicious warmth of his body.

"Σ' αγαπώ," I try to pronounce as best I can the Greek phrase: *I love you.*

"Λατρεία μου." His eyes soften. "Είσαι στην καρδιά μου." I don't know what that means, but it sounds lovely.

There's a pitter-pattering of little feet in the hall, and Iris calls through the door, "Mom! Darius! Can I get up now and play with Lucky?"

"You're already up," I call through the door with a little laugh. "So yes."

"Yay!" she says excitedly before taking off down the hall.

I sigh. What I've put off for tomorrow has turned into today's problem.

"Let's shower, and you can break the news to Iris about her dad," Darius tells me, reading my mind.

"That would require me to move," I point out.

Standing, Darius scoops me up in his arms and tosses me over his shoulder.

I squeal in surprise. "You shouldn't be carrying me with your injured arm."

He answers by playfully nipping at my ass.

We shower, and I help him wash and rinse—trying my best to keep his wound and new tattoo as dry as possible. "If anyone asks where I was these past few days, what should I tell them?" I wonder.

"The truth. You were on your honeymoon," Darius says, kissing the tip of my nose.

"Won't it look suspicious I just got married?" I worry.

"Anybody hassles you—about this, or *anything* else—you tell them to fucking come talk to me," he tells me in a very *Diávolos* tone.

That settled, he turns off the water, and we step out of the shower. Wrapping a towel around myself, I say, "Alright. I'm going to call Harrison's partner to see about funeral arrangements, and then I'm going to tell Iris."

"You want me to be there when you break the news to her?" he asks.

"Let me talk to her alone first," I decide, blotting my hair dry with another towel.

He nods, giving me a peck before walking out.

Quickly getting ready, I walk to the bedroom and throw on some clothes before grabbing my phone and calling Ethan; he answers on the first ring. "Lily."

"Hey, Ethan. How are you holding up?" I ask gently.

"It still seems unreal at this point," he says in a dazed tone.

"Yeah, it does," I agree. "I read a report about a break-in at Harrison's place. Have you heard anything else?"

"Just a bunch of whispers and hearsay. One bullshit rumor about Harrison being mixed up with drugs."

"What?" I say in disbelief.

"Agreed. People need to keep their fucking mouths shut," he says angrily before pausing. "Sorry about my language."

"Don't apologize. You have every right to be upset," I assure him. "What about funeral arrangements?"

"You know Harrison and his old man were estranged, but suddenly his pops shows up acting like the bereaved father of the year," he says with a snort. "Anyway, the funeral is tomorrow at two at Saint Peters Church. It wasn't a line-of duty death, so it'll be smaller scale—but everyone from our patrol unit will be there," he explains.

"And Iris and I will be there," I add.

"Good. Now, are you going to tell me where the hell

you've been? Detective Regan's been looking for you; I didn't know what to tell him."

"Mama!" Iris calls, running into the bedroom holding Lucky in one hand, a fishing pole toy in the other.

"Ethan, I'm sorry, but I have to go. I promise we'll talk tomorrow," I say, ending the call. "Hey, sweetie," I tell Iris.

"Mama, watch this!" She sits Lucky down and moves the feather on the fishing line; the cat swats at it a few times before rolling over on her back, trying a different angle.

"How fun," I comment. "Iris, I need to talk to you about something important. Come sit with me," I say, patting the foot of the bed.

She climbs up beside me, and there's no easy way to say this, so I jump right in. "Your dad died, sweetie. Do you know what 'died' means?"

"Like Princess Peacock's dad," she says, bouncing the fishing pole.

"That's right, like in your book. Your dad's in heaven now, so we won't be able to see him anymore," I explain.

She doesn't say anything, continuing to dangle the feather as Lucky rolls back over and swipes at it; her claw gets stuck this time.

Helping Lucky untangle herself, I tell Iris, "Can we wait on playing for just a second?" I smooth a blonde wisp of hair framing Iris' face before taking the fishing pole from her. Laying it on the bed, I continue, "I want you to understand your dad won't be coming back, but we can always love and remember him in our hearts," I say, touching mine.

"Okay," is all she says.

"It's alright to be sad if you need to be," I gently tell her. "We'll go to the funeral tomorrow afternoon. It's a time to remember your dad. Some people might be upset and crying, and that's okay."

"I know what a funeral is. My friend went to her grand-ma's funeral," she tells me matter-of-factly.

"Ah, alright."

"I'm hungry," she announces.

"Then let's go see about breakfast," I tell her, worried what I just told her didn't register.

Walking downstairs—with Iris carrying Lucky—we follow the delicious smell to the kitchen, where Darius is behind the stove.

"Who wants pancakes?" he asks.

"Me!" Iris says excitedly; Lucky startles, hopping down.

"Wash your hands, please," I tell Iris as I pour myself a cup of coffee.

She does so, and takes a seat at the table. Darius plates a stack of pancakes with a side of bacon and strawberries, presenting it to her. "How much maple syrup?" he asks, holding up the bottle.

"A lot!" Iris exclaims.

He smiles, drizzling the amber-covered sweetness over her stack.

"Are you going to die like my dad?" Iris asks Darius. Damn if that doesn't gut me.

"I don't plan on it any time soon," he answers reassuringly. "So we'll just focus on today. And today is going to be amazing! Kat's coming to play with you while your mama and I go to dinner."

I almost forgot. Sunday dinner. With Darius' "boss." I'm nervous just thinking about it.

"Yay! I want to show her my cat! And my room!"

"She'll be excited." Darius smiles. "You want some pancakes, wifey?" he asks me, sipping on what looks like a protein shake.

"I actually want to try some of your protein shake." If he's going to be Mr. Healthy, it wouldn't hurt me to do the same for Iris' sake.

He grabs the blender and pours me a glass.

"Thank you." Taking a sip, I make a face. "*No* thank you. I'll take those pancakes."

He chuckles, swapping me out.

We finish breakfast, and I tell Iris, "Sweetie, let's get ready. I have to run to the library for about an hour this morning to finish my bibliography for my essay. You can play a game on your tablet while I'm working."

"How about this? Iris and I will drop you off at the library, and we'll play at the park until you're finished," Darius offers.

"Yes! Park!" Iris chimes in.

"An even better plan." I stand on my tiptoes and give him a kiss.

"Again?" Iris groans, and I giggle against Darius' lips.

CHAPTER
Twenty-Five

Lily

Having returned home from the library, I'm now standing in my underwear with several outfits strewn across the bed. I'm not familiar with Italian Sunday dinner customs, which does nothing to help my jagged nerves.

Darius exits the bathroom, and I smile. "You look so handsome." He's traded his casual look for a white dress shirt, dress pants, and loafers.

"Wifey approves? I've been forbidden from leaving the house in gray sweatpants," he teases.

"I approve, and yes, you have," I inform him, crossing my arms.

He chuckles, stalking over with a naughty gleam in his eyes.

"Don't get any ideas," I warn him.

"Then don't tempt me," he retorts, his voice dropping in timbre.

"I'm not! I don't know what to wear; help!"

Darius looks over the choices on the bed before selecting

my new sundress I picked up in Greece. "My little angel should wear this one."

He holds up the white dress, and I take it, pulling it over my head. I check myself out in the mirror. "What do you think? Not too casual?"

"Perfection."

"Thank you, Darius," I tell him, having learned my lesson about accepting gifts from this Greek.

"Such a good girl," he purrs.

"Stop it," I tell him, my cheeks heating as I walk inside the closet, grabbing my stiletto sandals.

"I want to show you something," Darius says, scooting past me. He squats down and moves his shoe rack, and my mouth gapes when he lifts up a large wooden plank—revealing a safe built into the floor. "Combination is your birthday; inside is our emergency bag with passports, cash, and a burner phone," he explains. "In case we need to get out of here in a hurry, I want you to know where it is."

"Will we ever need to use this bag?" I ask, my voice sounding small.

Darius stands, wrapping his arms around me. "Lily, I don't want you to worry." He tilts my chin so I'm looking up at him. "It's just like having insurance: we hope we won't have to use it, but it's nice to have just in case."

The doorbell rings, and he pulls out a different phone from his pocket; Christ, how many phones does this man have? "That's Kat," he announces, putting everything back into place. Grabbing my hand, he leads me out of the closet and closes the door.

"Give me a few minutes to finish getting ready," I tell him, needing a moment to compose myself.

"Sure." He presses a kiss to my lips before walking out.

Looking in the mirror, I give myself a little pep talk. I can do this—dinner with a mob boss. *Why not?* I can handle emergency bags, and funerals for exes, and homicide investigations, and anything else the Fates throw my way.

Fastening my evil eye necklace, I follow the sound of laughter to find Kat and Iris on the living room floor playing with Lucky. "Hey, Lily. You look amazing," Kat says.

"Thank you. Could I speak to you in the kitchen before we go?"

"Sure thing," she says.

"Now Kat's in trouble?" Iris marvels.

"Trouble is my middle name," Kat announces.

"That's a weird middle name," Iris decides, and Kat chuckles.

"No one's in trouble, sweetie. Just adult talk."

"Phew, you heard her." Kat winks at Iris, following me to the kitchen.

"Did Darius fill you in about Iris' dad?" I ask Kat when we're out of earshot.

She nods. "Yeah, he said the guy passed away. I'm sorry."

"Thanks. Iris seems to be handling it well, but if she acts out or becomes upset, that's probably why."

"Hey, don't worry. I'll take good care of her," Kat assures me.

"Thank you."

"Lily, we need to go," Darius calls.

We return to the living room, and I give Iris a hug and kiss. "Bye, sweetie. Love you."

"Love you," she says, busy playing with Lucky.

"Have fun, rainbow goddess." Darius kisses the top of Iris' head before ushering me out the door.

"I'm worried Iris took the news about her dad a little too well," I comment as we back out of the garage.

"Everyone processes things differently," Darius says. "But from what I'm getting, she wasn't very close to the guy. Maybe it's a normal reaction," he suggests.

"Maybe. I just hate leaving her for a second time today," I admit, guilt washing over me.

"Iris seemed fine at the park. Besides, Kat is great with her," he reassures me.

"Yeah, she is," I agree. "So tell me again who's going to be at dinner?" I ask, nerves replacing the guilt.

"Romeo and his fiancée, Nicky. Romeo's little sister, Valentina, and his grandma—who we all call Nonna. Sammy; also goes by Sam. He's usually a dickhead, so don't take it personal if he's rude. And Luca, though he probably won't be there because he's recovering from an injury."

"What kind of injury?" I wonder.

He shrugs. "Work-related."

"Like your 'little scrape?'" I ask, but he doesn't answer. And I have my answer.

We enter the wealthiest suburb of Newark, with the homes getting more and more extravagant by the second. Darius turns onto an unmarked road, until I realize it's *not* a road, but a private driveway.

We pull up to a gate with a man in a guard booth. "Afternoon, Mr. Angelo. Mrs. Angelo."

"Afternoon," Darius answers as the man walks around our SUV with a German Shepard on a leash.

The guard returns to Darius' window. "I need to scan all electronics, please."

"Hand me your phones, Lily," Darius tells me, and I do as instructed. Darius hands them to the guard, who runs a wand-looking thing over them before returning them. I try not to let my mouth fall open when Darius hands over four phones, a radio of some sort, and two pagers.

"All clear," the guard says, handing back all of my husband's electronics. He returns to the booth, opening the gate for us.

"Is this type of security the norm?" I wonder.

"The norm for now," Darius says, whatever that means.

We continue down a seemingly endless driveway until we reach a mansion plucked straight from the Amalfi Coast. "Wow, this is something. It's a good thing Iris isn't with us; she'd already be splashing in the fountain."

He chuckles. "Understandable."

Opening my door for me, Darius helps me out and escorts me to the front door. As soon as he rings the doorbell, an older woman with white hair and a weathered face appears. Dressed in a black tracksuit and sneakers, she says something lively in Italian to Darius, who returns something with a laugh.

"Nonna, this is my wife, Lily." Darius introduces us.

"Hello," I say.

"*Ciao*." She pulls me in for a double cheek kiss. "You bring your daughter next time," she tells me excitedly.

"Thank you." Let's see how terrifying this experience is before I commit to that.

"Come. Come. I've left Valentina in the kitchen." She mutters something in Italian as we follow her inside the palatial home.

We reach the family room, where a man with downturned lips is speaking on the phone. Ending his call, his cold, hard eyes land on me as he rises, joining us. Darius must sense my nerves, because he gives my hand a reassuring squeeze before letting go. The two men fist bump. "Boss, this is my wife, Lily," Darius says, his hand now resting on my lower back.

"Hello, Lily. I'm Romeo Parisi. Welcome." He extends his hand.

"Thank you," I manage, shaking his big hand with my clammy one.

A raven-haired beauty radiating confidence glides into the room. She looks familiar, but I can't put my finger on where I've seen her before.

Romeo watches the woman like a hawk, and I'm borderline concerned for her safety. She apparently is *not*, as she greets him with a kiss. Turning to me, she says, "Hi, there. I'm Nicky. You must be Lily. It's so nice to meet you," she says, extending her hand without batting an eye.

I, on the other hand, am having trouble keeping my eyes from bugging out of my head—it's Candy from Joe's Cabaret! "Hi," I manage, shaking her hand.

"Darius, nice to see you again," Nicky says. She leans back against Romeo, who drapes his arms around her. I try not to marvel—it's like watching a woman stick her head in the mouth of a lion, yet somehow not being ripped to shreds.

"You too, Nicky. How's Luca?" Darius asks.

Nicky *clucks* her tongue. "A terrible patient. Nearly as bad as this one," she says, jerking her head behind her toward Romeo. "But Luca is doing much better."

Speaking of patients, I say, "Nicky, do you mind taking a look at Darius' arm? He has a little 'scrape.'" If Darius thought I'd forget about it, he's sorely mistaken.

"Let me see," Nicky orders.

Darius grumbles something in Italian as he unbuttons his shirt, and Romeo smirks, saying something back to him in Italian.

"I caught that." Nicky narrows her eyes at the men before turning her attention to me. "I'm taking Italian lessons so I know what these *stronzia* are saying."

"*Stronzi*," Romeo corrects her.

"*Stronzia*," Nicky fires back at Romeo.

Darius chuckles, shrugging out of his dress shirt and peeling off the bandage on his tricep. It looks just as bad as last night, if not worse.

Nicky walks over to take a closer look, raising an eyebrow. "By scrape, you mean bullet graze. I wouldn't recommend sutures—the wound's too shallow. Can someone grab my medical bag from the car while I wash up? Lily, come chat with me," Nicky commands.

CHAPTER
Twenty-Six

Lily

I follow Nicky down the hall, and she ushers me inside the bathroom and closes the door. "Thanks for playing it cool back there," she says, turning on the water as she soaps up her hands, giving them a wash. "Romeo knows I used to dance while I was in school, but not everyone in the family does. I'd like to keep it that way."

"Not a problem," I tell her. "Darius knows I used to dance, but only a few others do. I also want to keep it that way."

"Deal." She smiles, drying her hands. "I'm so happy for you and Darius. I always liked you, and Darius is like a brother to Romeo."

"Thank you. But I've got to admit, your fiancé is intimidating."

"That's just Romeo. You'll get used to him. Could you get the door for me?" She holds up her hands—I guess to keep them clean.

I do so, and follow Nicky back to the family room. She puts on gloves from a large black bag laid open on the coffee table, before walking over to Darius. "May I touch your wound?"

He nods, and she runs her finger along the divot in his flesh. "Does that hurt?"

"Maybe if you poured some salt in the wound first before poking it," Darius jokes.

"Don't give her any ideas," Romeo advises.

"Luckily for you, I don't have any salt in my bag," Nicky says smartly. "But I also don't have antibiotic cream; are you allergic to honey?"

"No," he says, surprised by the question.

She likewise surprises me by pulling out a jar of honey and a swab. "All is well when the honey—"

"Is sweet," Darius finishes for her. "Greek proverb," he explains to me.

Nicky gives Romeo a little smile before turning her attention back to Darius. "Natural antibiotic," she explains. Dabbing the sticky honey on the wound, she applies a bandage. "There you go. Keep it dry for at least twenty-four hours. If the skin around it becomes hot or an angry shade of red, call me. Another tip—try not to get shot next time," she says, shaking her head. "I need to wash up again. Be right back," she tells me, walking out.

"Excellent tips," Darius calls after her, buttoning up his shirt.

Romeo says something to Darius in Italian, and he replies. They continue their conversation, with Romeo's hard eyes on me, and I try not to squirm.

"Glad to see no one was shot while I was gone," Nicky announces, and I'm grateful the lion tamer is back.

"Odds increase when Sammy arrives," Darius tells her.

"In that case, I'm off the clock," Nicky says with a laugh. Turning to me, she smiles. "I'm not sure I told you congratulations!"

"Thank you. And I hear congratulations are in order for you as well."

"Yes, thank you. Five months until the big day," she tells me. "Just to warn you, Valentina is going to be mad she didn't get to plan your wedding."

"My cousin, Kat, married us at her place," Darius explains.

"Very informal," I add. And *coerced*, but I keep that last part to myself.

"Plead your case to Valentina," Nicky tells me.

"What case?" A pretty young woman with a red-spattered apron appears, and it's a day of double takes for me—it's the barista from the coffee shop.

"Oh my gosh, Lily! I remember you, but I didn't know you were Darius' Lily!" She removes her apron before giving me a double cheek kiss. "Ha, and you told me you weren't getting married anytime soon."

"Valentina and I met at the coffee shop while I was studying," I explain to Darius, whose eyebrows are raised in question. "Turns out I was wrong," I tell Valentina with a soft smile.

"Aww. I *love* love stories. So spill, I want to hear how you two met."

"At the park," Darius and I both say at the same time, and I'm grateful for us getting our stories straight.

"I have a four-year old daughter, and she and I visit the park quite a bit." Grabbing my phone, I pull up a picture of Iris, holding it up proudly.

"Adorable," Nicky comments.

"Oh my God, sooooo cute," Valentina agrees.

"*Sooooo* cute." A man mocks Valentina, having joined us.

"Look what the cat dragged in." Valentina scowls at the attractive Italian man.

He smirks. "What can I say? Pussy loves me."

Valentina makes a gagging sound.

Romeo barks something in Italian, switching over to English. "Apologize for speaking to my baby sister that way," he orders.

"Ugh, I'm not a freakin' baby!" Valentina huffs.

"Sorry," the man mutters.

"You know how to make a first impression," Darius tells the man, shaking his head. "Sammy, this is my wife, Lily." So this is the dickhead Darius warned me about. Sammy's playing the part well thus far.

Sammy grabs my hand, giving it a kiss. Darius growls, and Sammy smiles against my skin—prolonging the uncomfortable moment. "Lily, a pleasure. Can't believe you married this *stronzia*." He jerks his head toward Darius.

"Nice to meet you." I remove my hand from his and glance over to Darius, who now has that look—the *Diávolos* crazy-eye look.

"Darius, if you kill Sammy, pretty please with sugar on top let me watch," Valentina begs.

"Nobody's getting shot today—I just want to enjoy dinner," Nicky warns everyone.

"Who said anything about a gun? There's more than one way to skin a cat," Darius says in a menacing tone.

Sammy laughs, a knife somehow appearing in his hand. He tosses it in the air, and I hold my breath as it falls, but he expertly catches it by the handle.

"Enough," Romeo says in a bored tone.

"Seriously, put that thing away," Valentina tells Sammy, exasperated. "Sorry, we can't take him anywhere," she tells me.

Nonna appears in the doorway, announcing something in Italian. "Come, come. Let's eat."

Nicky whispers to me, "Do not, under any circumstances, tell Nonna you're full. Trust me."

"Alright," I say, confused.

We enter the dining room, where Darius pulls out my

chair for me. Food's passed around the table, and I try my best to keep up with the lively conversation that switches between Italian and English.

"Nonna, you and Valentina are moving in with me and Nicky," Romeo declares.

"I just got out of Antonio's prison, and now you're trying to put me in yours!" Valentina crosses her arms. "No fucking way."

"Language," Nonna chastises her granddaughter.

"You can take the pool house if you need more privacy," Romeo offers. "Renovate it however you wish."

She considers, finally saying, "I'll think about it."

"There's nothing to think about," Romeo corrects her. "Nonna?"

"Kitchen not big enough," she says dismissively.

"I'll build a bigger kitchen," Romeo tells her.

Nonna smiles. "Give me *pronipoti*, then we talk."

I don't know what that means, but Nicky must, because she throws back her wine glass.

The dessert course is served, and while I'm beyond full, I heed Nicky's warning.

"We have some business to discuss," Romeo declares, kissing Nicky before standing.

"Always business," Nonna chastises, waving him away.

"Be back in a little bit," Darius whispers to me, giving me a kiss on the top of my head.

"Don't miss me while I'm gone," Sammy tells Nonna, and she shoos him away with a smile.

Valentina rolls her eyes so hard I'm afraid they'll get lost in the back of her head. When the men leave the room, she turns to me with narrowed eyes. "Explain to me how I didn't get to plan your wedding?" Valentina crosses her arms, and Nicky quietly chuckles.

"There was no planning; it was a very spontaneous thing." Now there's an understatement.

"Fine, but that means I get to throw you and Darius a little reception." She rubs her hands together with excitement.

"That would be so nice," I tell her.

"Be careful what you sign up for," Nicky warns me with a wry smile, pouring herself another glass of wine before topping off my glass.

"Excuse me, but the 'it' wedding of the year doesn't just happen," Valentina says, exasperated. "Speaking of—"

"No more wedding planning. Not tonight," Nicky pleads.

"Fine." Valentina pulls out her phone. "When do you want to schedule our next sit-down?"

"I don't know. It really depends on Luca's progress," Nicky says.

Valentina narrows her eyes at her future sister-in-law. "You don't get to use your husband's bodyguard as a freakin' human shield against me."

"Isn't that the purpose of a bodyguard?" Nicky retorts.

I giggle, the second glass of wine having gone to my head.

"I call Father Ferrera over tonight, and Romeo and Nicky married. *Ecco*. Problem solved," Nonna interjects.

"Don't you dare," Valentina says, pointing to her grandmother.

"Why not?" Nonna demands. "Then they get to work faster on my *pronipote*."

Nicky mutters something under her breath before knocking back her wine.

"Great grandchild," Valentina translates for me.

Darius

I follow the men to the billiard room. Romeo breaks open a box of cigars, but I decline.

"Nobody likes a fucking health nut," Sammy chides, grabbing a cigar.

He goes to set his whiskey glass down, and I fling at him the knife he "gifted" me all those years ago. It slices off half of the cigar in his hand, the knife landing with a reverberating *thunk* in the center of the dart board behind him.

"Thanks, man. No need to cut my cigar now," he says, lighting the now-short stogie and taking a puff.

Romeo chuckles, lighting his cigar. "Darius let you off too easily," he informs Sammy. "Put your lips on any part of my woman, and I'd fucking slice them off your face."

Damn, now that really makes me regret not slicing off Amethyst's lips.

"Nobody around here can take a fucking joke," Sammy mutters.

"Maybe it's just you're not funny," I inform him.

He smirks. "Your mom disagrees."

"Does she laugh at that limp dick of yours?" I mock. "I bet that is funny."

"No, but she is really ticklish, especially when I do that one thing with my—"

"Give me an update on the security feed from the boxing club," Romeo says, cutting the bullshit and getting to business.

"Fabio's crew is watching the surveillance videos from Ace's Wild round the clock. There's months' worth of footage, so it's going to take some time to wade through it," Sammy reports. "Darius, Fabio is to let you know ASAP if his crew finds something helpful with your job." My job being to put a bullet between John Davis' eyes.

"Good," I say, sipping on my sparkling water as I take a seat on a leather couch. "Boss, I noticed you added extra security."

Romeo takes a puff of his cigar, making a smoke O ring. "Thanks to John Davis and his confetti bomb 'gifts.' Fucker sent one the morning of Antonio's wake while you were in Greece. Everything and everyone now stepping foot on this property gets additional screening."

"Guy must have a death wish," I comment.

"He does, so let's help him out," Romeo tells me in an ice-cold tone. "I want you camped out in AC until this problem is dealt with."

"Boss, my stepdaughter's dad passed away." I fill them in on everything.

Romeo takes another puff, considering. "I'll give you forty-eight hours to get your house in order. But after that, I expect results."

CHAPTER
Twenty-Seven

Lily

"You look beautiful," Darius comments, leaning against the door jamb of the bathroom. I chose a demure black dress and my evil eye pendant for this somber event.

"Thank you, Darius," I tell him, closing my lip gloss before walking over and giving him a quick kiss. Grabbing my clutch from the bed, I toss both my phones inside.

"You sure you don't want me to go with you?" he asks as we walk downstairs.

I shake my head. "Thanks, but it would just raise too many questions."

"Lily, what have I told you?" he chides.

"I know, I just think it'd be better if Iris and I went to Harrison's funeral by ourselves," I tell him gently. "Iris, sweetie, it's time to go," I call.

She emerges from her room holding Lucky. "Bye, Lucky." Iris kisses her cat on the top of the head before letting her down.

"Where's my hug?" Darius asks.

Iris smiles, running over to him. He scoops her up and twirls her around before giving her a big bear hug. "Bye, rainbow goddess. You and your mama be careful, alright?"

"We will," I assure him.

Darius helps me get Iris buckled, and I give him one last kiss before backing out of the driveway. I flip on Iris' favorite music as we drive to the church; she's uncharacteristically quiet on the car ride.

Parking, I get her out of the SUV, reminding her, "It's alright to be sad today if you need to be."

"Okay," is all she says.

I take her little hand in mine, and we step inside the church lobby. Several people are waiting to sign the guest book, and Iris and I get in line. Reaching the front, I sign my name and give the pen to Iris, because she wants to write her own name.

"Good job," I tell her. She took up half the page writing her name in all caps, but she's Harrison's daughter, so if she wants to take up the entire guest book, I'm not going to say anything.

Entering the sanctuary, we're greeted by a man who hands us a program, and I scan the crowd. Ethan's in his uniform with a row of patrolmen seated near the middle of the church. He cranes his neck and spots us, waving us over.

We make our way down the aisle until we reach him, and all the officers slide down the pew to make room. "Hey, Lily. Iris. Please." Ethan gestures to the seat next to him.

"Thank you." I take a seat, with Iris crawling into my lap.

Ethan introduces us to the officers, and I smile politely, while Iris fiddles with the program.

"That's Harrison's old man on the right front row," Ethan leans over and whispers to me.

"This is the first time I've ever laid eyes on the man, but I can see the resemblance," I whisper back.

"Maybe he thinks he'll be coming into some money. Don't know why else he's here," Ethan speculates.

I can't imagine there's much money to go around, considering Harrison never seemed to have any to support his daughter, but I bite my tongue.

"What's that?" Iris asks, pointing to the front of the church.

"That's the casket." Thank God it's a closed one. "It's what your dad's body will be buried in. But he's in heaven now, so we don't have to worry," I assure her.

The service begins, and Iris wriggles in my lap. She's bored, not that I can blame her—the preacher is especially long-winded. We stand to join in a hymn, except Iris doesn't want to stand; instead, she plops down on the floor, taking off her shoes.

Sighing, I squat down and pick her up—her bare feet now dangling from my hip. Ethan gives us a little smile before his eyes land on my ring. His eyebrows shoot up in question, but the song ends, and we're instructed to have a seat.

"Excuse me," Ethan says quietly, slipping out of the pew and walking to the podium. He gives a touching eulogy about his fallen partner. Regardless of any personal animosity I harbor toward Harrison, it's nice to hear someone speak highly of Iris' dad.

The officers file out of the pew on the other side, helping Ethan carry the casket out of the church. The service comes to a conclusion, and I help Iris with her shoes before walking to the car. Getting us situated, I maneuver my SUV in the funeral procession, following everyone to the cemetery. "There's more?" Iris wonders.

"Yes. This is the cemetery. It's a place where we can come any time you want and remember your dad."

"I already remember him," Iris says matter-of-factly.

"I know you do, sweetie." Hopefully, a few of those memories of her dad are happy ones; I fear they aren't.

Reaching the gravesite, the preacher proves he's still just as long-winded here as he was at the church. Finally, everyone's invited to toss a flower onto the casket. I accept a rose and hand it to Iris, explaining to her what to do. Holding her in my arms, I walk us to the casket. She tosses the rose, her expression giving nothing away.

The graveside service comes to a conclusion, and Iris and I mill about in the back, waiting to speak to Ethan. I wave at him, but before we can make our way through the crowd, Harrison's dad appears. "Hey, Lily. We've never met. I'm Harrison's old man. And this pretty young lady must be Iris. I'm your grandpa," he addresses her, and I mentally cringe. My daughter's been through enough for one day without a new family member popping out of the woodwork.

"No you're not," Iris says, and I have to choke down a laugh. From the mouth of babes.

"I am," he assures her. "Lily, I was wondering if I could follow you to Harrison's house. I'd like to keep a few personal mementos to remember my son."

"I'm sorry, but I don't have access to Harrison's house," I tell him. Had this man been in his son's life, he would have known Harrison and I weren't together.

"Who do you think would?" he presses.

"I'm not sure. If you'll excuse us," I say, walking off. It's rude, yes, but my bullshit meter is running low at the moment.

Tracking down Ethan, I tell him quietly, "You might be right about a certain individual's motives."

He glances over my shoulder at Harrison's dad, then back to me. "What I figured. Hey, I just learned Harrison's house has been cleared, so I can let you in. I still have a spare key," he tells me.

"Cleared?" I ask.

"The C-R-I-M-E scene," he spells.

"Sweetie, why don't you play a game while Ethan and I

talk," I tell Iris, leading her to the front row of folding chairs and pulling up a game on my phone.

Returning to Ethan now that Iris is out of earshot, I admit, "I'm not sure if I feel comfortable going through Harrison's things."

"Iris is his next of kin, so whatever possessions of Harrison's are hers now," he points out.

"I haven't even thought that far ahead," I admit, toying with my evil eye pendant.

Ethan nods. "You'll also want to apply for social security for Iris, and there's a compensation fund for surviving dependents of police officers. I can get you the paperwork and help with anything else you need. But you might want to hire a lawyer for the probate stuff."

"Ethan, that would be amazing. Thank you," I say.

"Of course. I've got time now, if you want to follow me over to his house," he offers.

"You said the crime scene has been cleared. Is there…" I trail off. "*Blood*?"

He shakes his head. "Me and some buddies hired a company that cleaned up the scene," he assures me. "It's safe to come inside."

"That was really thoughtful," I tell him.

He shrugs away the compliment. "Do you have time now?"

"Sure, we'll meet you there. I'd really like to find a rainbow charm Iris made Harrison for Father's Day," I explain. Maybe it'll be something to help her with those happy memories.

"Then we'll look for it," he says, walking us to the parking lot.

I get Iris situated in her car seat before sliding behind the wheel. Sending a text to Darius, I pull out behind Ethan—following him to Harrison's house. By the time we make our way across the city, Darius has already beaten us there, parked across the street.

I park in front of the house, and Ethan smiles as he approaches, but stops short when he spots Darius hustling over to my SUV. "Thank you," I tell my husband, giving him a quick kiss when he helps me out of the vehicle. "I didn't want to leave Iris by herself while Ethan and I go through the house, in case it upsets her being here," I quietly explain.

"Not a problem," Darius assures me.

A car pulls up behind me. "Oh, no," I say wearily.

"What?" he asks.

"That's Harrison's dad. He was acting sketchy at the funeral; I guess he thinks he's coming into an inheritance. Made me really uncomfortable telling Iris he's her grandpa, considering we'd never laid eyes on the man until today."

Without a word, Darius marches to the car and knocks on the driver side window. Harrison's dad rolls it down, and there's a back and forth, but I can't hear what's being said. *Whatever* was said, the man backs up, turning around and driving off.

Darius returns, and I quip, "Just like that?"

He playfully flicks my nose. "Just like that."

CHAPTER
Twenty-Eight

Lily

We join Ethan on the sidewalk, with Iris perched on Darius' shoulders. "Hey, I don't think we've met. I'm Ethan McGregor," he says, extending his hand. "Officer Harrison's former partner."

"I'm Darius Angelos, Lily's husband. It's nice to meet you. Sorry for your loss," Darius says politely.

"Thanks." The two men shake, and Ethan turns to me. "Ready to take a look?"

I nod. "Darius is going to hang out with Iris while we're inside."

"Take your time," Darius tells me. Placing Iris on her feet, he reaches behind her ear, making a bubble wand "appear." She jumps up and down, eagerly grabbing it.

I smile at the two of them before following Ethan up the steps to the front door. He uses his key, and we step inside the eerily quiet house. Flipping on the light, I take a look around the living room that screams bachelor pad. A huge gaming system with a leather couch takes up the entirety of the space, with not a single picture of Harrison's daughter to be found.

"Lily, what have you gotten yourself mixed up with?" Ethan demands, suddenly in my face.

Taken aback, I say, "I'm sorry, but I don't know what you're talking about."

"That's fucking Darius Angelos!" he says, rubbing the back of his neck. "Do you know who you married?"

"Yes, I know who I married." I square my chin and cross my arms. "A good man who loves me and Iris."

"A good man?" he parrots incredulously. "For Chrissake, Lily, he's connected to the mob. Everybody knows it!" He grabs me by the shoulders and gives me a little shake.

"Just a bunch of whispers and hearsay," I throw his words back at him as I shrug out of his hold. "Like the bullshit rumors about Harrison. You of all people should know not to believe everything you hear."

"That's different," he argues.

Holding up my hand, I say, "I'm going to start in the bedroom looking for Iris' rainbow charm. How about you start with Harrison's car, and then the living room?" I don't wait for Ethan to answer, taking off down the hall.

Stepping into Harrison's bedroom, the noxious smell of bleach lingers in the air, and I try not to think about why—or why the bed's missing for that matter. What's left of the room has been ransacked, but I go through the mess anyway, not finding the rainbow charm. I do find several discarded thongs, a box of condoms and lube, and various plugs and cock rings—none of which you could get me to touch with a ten-foot pole.

Opening the closet, I check the pockets of Harrison's pants and his jackets, but no luck.

Walking across the hall to the spare bedroom that served as Iris' room the few times she spent the night, I search the room in vain. I peek inside the small closet—some toys, plus a few of Iris' outfits that were missing after visitation. Harrison swore up and down he sent the clothes back with her.

There's a large plastic dollhouse in the corner; underneath it, the cheap carpet tiles are pulling away from the floor. I wonder if maybe Iris played back there and used it as a hidey spot? Squatting down, I move the dollhouse pull one of the tile pieces off the floor.

Trying not to gasp, I find a safe built into the floor with an electronic number lock. Knowing why Darius has one in our house, I'm struggling to understand why a cop would need one in his. Maybe Harrison used it to store his gun collection? He was robbed, so clearly this isn't the safest neighborhood. Or maybe some of the "bullshit rumors" about Harrison are more than just rumors?

Giving Iris' birth date a try, the safe *beeps* red. Maybe it's a four-digit code instead of six? I punch in just her birth date and month, but again, it *beeps* red. Trying the same numbers in reverse; *red*. What would a man like Harrison use as his combination? Punching in his birthday; *red*. I cringe, typing in 6-9-6-9. *Red*. Harrison always wanted to receive head without having to return the favor, so it makes sense that's not the code.

Grasping at straws, I try 1-2-3-4. *Red*.

"Lily," Ethan calls.

Covering up the safe—if Harrison was into anything shady, it'd upset Ethan far more than it would me—I stick my head out of the bedroom. "Did you find Lily's rainbow charm?" I ask.

"No, but I found Harrison's birth certificate and social security card," he says, holding up a file. "You'll need these to fill out the paperwork I was telling you about. I didn't see a will. My guess is he didn't have one."

"Thank you. Well, maybe the charm will turn up," I comment.

We walk down the hall, and he hands me the file folder,

but doesn't let go. "At least consider what I said about Darius. Trust me, Lily, you don't know your husband like you think you do."

"Ethan, thanks for your concern," I say, trying to see this from his perspective: a cop's perspective. "You've always cared more than Harrison in a lot of ways." Which sadly is true.

His face softens. "I just worry about you and Iris."

"And I appreciate it. Truly. But I know what I'm doing, and I would never endanger my daughter," I assure him.

Ethan clearly doesn't like my answer, but he releases the file, and we walk out of the house. On the porch, Iris is blowing bubbles, with Darius trying to pop them with his teeth. I place my hand on my head with a sigh, but I can't help but laugh.

Darius flexes his forearm and gives the big red dog a little *wolf.*

Iris giggles. "He's silly," she informs Ethan.

Ethan clears his throat. "Well, I need to get to work. Lily, I'll make a copy of the key and drop it by your place, along with the paperwork," he tells me.

"Why don't you just go ahead and give Lily the key now, since you won't need it anymore. Everything else, you can drop off at my gym," Darius interjects, giving him the address.

"Uh, yeah, alright," Ethan fumbles, obviously not expecting that response. He hands me the key. "Lily, Iris, it was good to see you both. Darius, nice to meet you."

"You too," Darius says politely.

Darius

Ethan's eyes lingered on my wife just a little too long, and the urge to chase after him and gouge out those offending orbs with the bubble wand is strong, but I rein in my impulse. "Who wants to grab a bite to eat?" I ask, tightening the cap on the bubbles.

"Me!" Iris says.

"Sure, we can stop somewhere. I'm just not very hungry," Lily admits.

"How about Corner Caffè?" I suggest. "We'll just grab a snack."

"Perfect," Lily says with a smile, but it doesn't reach her eyes.

I follow them in my car, and we arrive at the coffee shop. Holding the door open for them, we step inside my boss' shop, placing our order.

We snag a table in the back, and Valentina waves at us, bounding over. "Hey!"

"Valentina, it's so nice to see you. This is my daughter, Iris," Lily says.

"Hello, Iris. It's so nice to meet you. I'm going to send over a special cookie with your name on it," Valentina tells her with a big smile.

"Thank you," Iris tells her politely.

"Hey, Valentina. Romeo here?" I ask.

Valentina shakes her head. "I came in after school; if he was here earlier, I missed him."

She plops down in the chair beside Lily. "So let's talk reception." She pulls out her phone. "We need to nail down a date."

I raise my eyebrow in question; Lily just shakes her head. "Now's really not the best time," Lily gently tells her. "Finals are coming up for me, then graduation."

Valentina perks up. "Oooh, let's talk about the graduation party, then."

"We'd be happy to come to your graduation party," Lily says.

"Not my party." Valentina rolls her eyes. "That's been planned for months now, and of *course* you're coming. I'm talking about yours," she corrects Lily.

"Oh, my parents are already planning on hosting a party," Lily says, surprising me. This is the first time she's brought up her family.

"Fine, but you're not off the hook about the reception. I'm like an elephant—I never forget." Valentina taps her temple. "Gotta get back to work. My boss is a real tyrant," she jokes, flittering off.

A different barista delivers our order, and Iris goes to town on a cookie bigger than my hand. "How was the service?" I ask Lily.

"It was fine," she says, picking at a much more reasonably-sized amaretti cookie. "Ethan gave a very nice eulogy."

"I need to potty," Iris announces.

"Sure, sweetie," Lily says, standing and taking her daughter's hand. "Be right back," she tells me.

My burner phone goes off; I check the message, gritting my teeth. Lily and Iris return a few minutes later, and I tell them, "I've gotta go to the gym for a little bit. I'll meet you at home."

"Alright," Lily says, sounding tired.

"I'll grab dinner. What would the rainbow goddess like?" I ask.

"Pizza!"

"Extra pineapple, right?" I tease.

"No!" Iris dramatically places her hand on her head.

"Pepperoni for you; Pineapple and ham for wifey." Winking at Iris, I lean over and give Lily a kiss before walking out.

Driving to the sketchiest part of town—my car gets stolen, I'm gonna be pissed—I enter the office of the Jersey Motor Inn.

"I'm here to see Big Benny," I tell the methhead desk clerk who's seated behind a bullet-resistant partition. I call it resistant and not bullet proof, because I guarantee the projectile from the gun I'm packing could bust a hole through it.

"He ain't here," she says with a mouthful of rotten teeth, flicking her cigarette.

Grabbing a twenty from my pocket, I wave it in the air; that gets her attention. She opens the deal tray, and I drop the cash inside. "Be right back," she says, pocketing the cash before taking off through the back.

Looking around the office, the only furniture on this side of the partition is a rust-colored chair—then again, that just could be a blood stain—and I decide it's best to remain standing.

Big Benny appears, unlocking the door for me, and I follow him through the back to his office. He gestures for me to sit; I don't fucking want to, but at least this chair looks marginally cleaner. "You got a lead for me?" I cut to the chase.

"You got my money?" he counters.

I reach into my pocket, pulling out some cash and slapping two hundred on his desk. "Let's hear what you've got before I decide if it's worth more," I warn him.

Big Benny smiles as he accepts the cash; not a methhead smile, but nevertheless grotesque with his teeth stained yellow, his face coated in a sheen of grease, and the folds of his chin creasing uncomfortably upon themselves. "This your guy?" he asks, sliding over a photo.

I examine a pic of a man exiting one of the motel rooms. He likely has European ancestry, but that doesn't necessarily help me narrow things down. The guy could be anywhere from mid-twenties to early thirties. He's fit, dressed in a white tank top and shorts, with a large flaming-red Phoenix tattoo covering the entirety of his right shoulder. Lucky for him, he didn't go with a big red dog. Pulling out my phone and comparing the pool security pic of John Davis to this one, I smile. Same build; same facial features; tattoos even line up.

Counting out an additional three hundred bucks, I slide the cash across the table. "Tell me everything you know about this guy."

"One step ahead of you." He accepts the cash before handing me a file folder, and I open it to find a copy of a driver's license. "That's the ID he used to check in for the first time, about a month ago. Before I knew you were looking for him," Big Benny's quick to add.

"Andrew Wang." A fake or stolen ID, considering the picture is of an Asian man, and John Davis clearly isn't.

"He was here for about an hour today; I texted you as soon as I caught wind," he tells me. I don't comment, flipping to the next page. "That's the picture I snapped of his license plate," he explains.

The plates are likely stolen, but still won't hurt to check them out. "Did he meet anyone?"

"That, I don't know," he admits. "I didn't want to hang around too long and scare him off."

"You did right," I tell him, closing the file. "This guy's next stay, make sure he's given the Jersey Delight room." And now to dangle the carrot. "Tip me off in time, and a nice finder's fee will be coming your way."

Big Benny narrows his eyes. "How nice?"

"Twenty grand nice." I'm not fucking around anymore.

He flashes a disgusting grin; I can tell he's already spent the money in his head.

CHAPTER
Twenty-Nine

Darius

My eyes snap open; a faint sound coming from the hallway has me rolling out of bed. Placing my finger on the sensor of the small gun safe mounted to the back of the headboard—added it for Iris' safety—it opens, and I grab my pistol.

Lily's fast asleep, and I tiptoe quietly out of the bedroom. It's dark, but I can make out a set of glowing eyes at the other end of the hallway. "Lucky, you nearly lost a life," I whisper to the cat.

Unconcerned, she saunters off.

Since I'm now wide awake, I do a quick sweep of the house just in case. All clear.

Securing my gun and crawling back into bed, the morning sun's peeking through the curtains, and the way the light hits Lily's blonde hair—Jesus, she really does look like an angel. Gently tugging down the covers, my mouth waters at the sight. Beautiful creamy skin. Perky tits just the right size for her petite frame. Pussy bare, inviting me to steal just a little taste.

Invitation accepted.

I nestle myself over her, running my tongue along her seam. Lily makes the sexiest little sound I've ever heard—a combination between a sigh and a mewl. She's still asleep, and I lick the outer part of her lips, needing to devour every single inch of her pussy.

Her hands find my head as she moans, her eyes still closed.

Spreading her pussy lips with my fingers, I get to work with the flat of my tongue, lavishing her with slow, long laps.

"Darius," she moans. Her eyes opening—heavy with sleep *and* desire—she holds onto my head tighter as she writhes beneath me.

"Morning, *aggeloudhi mou*. Just as I suspected. You *do* make the sweetest little sounds when I'm lapping your pussy while you're still half asleep." I press a gentle kiss to her engorged clit.

"Please don't stop," she begs.

"Like the nice manners." Rubbing my beard back and forth over her slick pussy, she nearly jerks off the bed.

"Oh, God!"

"Wrong answer," I say, continuing to tickle between her thighs with my scruff. "Try again, little angel. Who owns this pussy?"

"*Diávolos*." She moans.

I hum my approval. "That's right. The devil's stealing a little taste of heaven." Swiping Lily's clit over and over with my tongue, her entire body trembles. "You going to be a good girl and squirt all over my tongue this morning?"

"Yes," she moans, digging her nails into my scalp as her thighs fall open wider.

"Let's see it," I challenge. Moving my tongue to her favorite spot, I get back to business. Lily nearly flies off the bed when I add a finger to the mix, and I chuckle against her clit, eating and fingering her in a nice rhythm. Using the pad of my finger to find that little ridged spot deep inside her, I rub it over and over until she's worked up into a frenzy.

"Right there," she cries, gripping my hair to the point of pain.

"Δε σε χορταίνω. This perfect μουνι." I groan, going back to eating her pussy like a man addicted; maybe I am. But not having any vices in my life, I'm more than happy to surrender to this addiction.

Her entire body shaking, she screams, "Fuck, I'm—"

Coming. And coming. And coming. I might have to add another tooth tattoo, because I nearly died by drowning.

Moving up to my spot in bed, I pull her limp body into my arms. Lily has a satisfied smile on her face, and I never tire of seeing it, and knowing I'm the man responsible for it. "Good, wifey?"

"Better than good," she practically purrs, burrowing into the crook of my arm. Just then, music blares from her phone. No," she groans. "Is it six o'clock already?"

"Is that a problem?"

"I need to get to campus early today," she says apologetically, grabbing her phone and turning off the alarm.

"Why don't you get ready, and I'll make coffee?"

"But what about you?" She asks, eyeing my bulging hard-on.

"Next time," I tell her, getting up and pulling on my boxers and a pair of running shorts.

"I'm so sorry," she says, hopping out of bed.

"For what? Don't ever apologize for turning me on."

Lily runs over and pounces, and I catch her as she wraps her arms and legs around me, pressing her sweet lips to mine on a sigh.

"You're not helping, aggeloudhi mou." I growl, nipping her bottom lip. Holding her up by her bare ass, I carry her to the bathroom and place her on her feet, turning on the shower for her. "Now, stop temping me." Giving her ass a playful smack, I walk out.

Willing my erection to stand down, I round the corner, nearly stepping in a puddle of cat puke. That'll do the trick.

After cleaning up the mess—Lucky is wisely ducking me—I turn on the coffee pot before downing a glass of water and blending my protein shake.

Lily joins me in the kitchen, and I hand her a cup of coffee in a travel mug. She smiles brightly. "You spoil me."

"As I should. You look beautiful." She does look beautiful with her face still flush from pleasure; blonde hair piled on top of her head in a messy bun. Her tight little body's displayed in a short sundress; while I love she's more comfortable now that her piece of shit professor is out of the way, the flip side is every motherfucker on campus gets a better look at what's mine.

"Thank you, Darius," she says sweetly.

Such a good girl. I'd love to push her to her knees, let her show me just how good of a girl she is by wrapping those pretty lips around my dick. My fantasy's put on hold when Iris comes running into the kitchen.

"Morning, sweetie," Lily says, walking over and kissing her daughter.

"There's the rainbow goddess. Orange juice or coffee?" I tease.

"Orange juice!" Iris says exasperated, and Lily chuckles.

Iris takes a seat at the table, and I pour a glass and present it to her. "Milady," I say with a dramatic bow, and she giggles.

"Let's grab a quick bite. How about some cereal?" Lily asks Iris. "I need to leave early so I can stop by the library before class."

"You go on," I tell Lily. "I can take Iris to school. I've got to be at the gym, but I'm not in any hurry."

"If you're sure you don't mind," Lily says.

"Not at all."

"I don't want to go to school." Iris whines.

"Why not?" Lily asks.

Iris pouts. "I just don't."

"That's not a reason. Tell me why you don't want to go," Lily gently asks.

"Some of the girls are mean to me," Iris admits.

"Who?" I demand. Lily cuts me a warning look, one that I ignore. "Who, rainbow goddess?"

"Megan and Harper," she tells me.

"How are they mean?" Lily asks. "What do they say?"

"They call me dumb," Iris admits, and my blood fucking boils.

"Sweetie, you know that's not true. You are so smart, and they're just saying that because someone was probably mean to them and told them that, okay?" Lily soothes her daughter's hair.

"What else do they say?" I press. Lily shoots me another look, one I likewise ignore.

"That I'm poor, and I don't have a dad," Iris admits.

"None of that is true, either," Lily says. "Just tell your teacher the next time they're being mean."

Nah, we don't snitch. I have a better way to handle it, one that I keep to myself as I pour Iris a bowl of cereal. "Go on to class. Me and the rainbow goddess can handle it from here."

"Okay." Lily nods, but doesn't look sure. "Her school uniform's laid out on her dresser, and she likes to wear her hair in a ponytail, and you'll have to pack her lunch and two snacks, and don't forget her water bottle and backpack, and—"

"Wifey, I've got it. Now go." I grab Lily and kiss her senseless so she'll stop fretting.

"Bye, rainbow goddess," I tell Iris, squatting down and hugging her.

"Bye," she tells me, walking hesitantly inside her classroom.

After introducing myself to Iris' teacher, I exit the building. A group of moms is hanging out near the entrance, and I pause, pretending to check my phone.

One of the moms takes the bait, strutting over. She has a water bottle in one hand, a coffee cup in the other—and a bag around her waist I don't care what anyone fucking says, is a fanny pack. "Hey, I've never seen you before at drop-off." She eyes me up and down. "I'm Becca, Megan's mom."

How fortuitous. "Hello, I'm Darius. Iris' stepdad," I say with a friendly smile.

"Oh, I didn't know Lily was married." I think she just tried to arch an eyebrow; hard to tell with all the botulism she's injected into her face. "I always felt sorry for the poor thing, having to juggle it all by herself. We all wondered how she managed—in school while struggling to pay the private tuition here," she stage-whispers.

I envision the best way to kill this woman. I'd start by stringing her up and ripping off her fake fingernails, followed by her real fingernails. Jesus, I'd have to tape her mouth shut; I couldn't stand to listen to her nasally voice.

"What is it you do for a living?" she asks, sizing me up.

"Personal trainer," I tell her.

"I bet," she purrs. "You look like you're in good shape." Her eyes take an entitled stroll down my body, glancing at my arm before landing on my dick. "My, what a big *tattoo* you have."

Her eyes meet mine, and I curl my lips back, baring my teeth. "All the better to rip you to fucking shreds, my dear."

A nervous sound—somewhere between a gasp and a giggle—escapes her lips. "What?"

"You heard me. Your kid and her friend want to tell *my*

kid she's dumb, poor, and doesn't have a dad, I'll ensure the no dad part is true for Megan and Harper. Once that happens, the poor part will take care of itself." No way this woman does anything for a living other than stir up shit.

Her mouth gapes like a fish, and before she regains the ability to speak, I tell her, "See you around, Becca." I snap my teeth before turning around and walking off.

CHAPTER
Thirty

Darius

Pulling out of the parking lot, my burner phone rings. "Darius," I answer.

"Change of plans. We're training at my house this morning," Romeo tells me.

"On my way," I say, hanging up and turning my car around.

Flipping on a new episode of a true crime podcast, I'm all worked up all over again by the time I reach Romeo's house —leaving bloody footprints at the scene will get you every damn time.

Arriving at Romeo's, I clear security and walk to the front door, ringing the bell. The housekeeper greets me, escorting me to Romeo's office. Thanking the woman, I knock on the door, and Romeo calls, "Enter."

The boss is sitting behind his desk when I step inside. "We not lifting today?" I ask. He's dressed in a sharp Italian suit.

"Ace's Wild surveillance." Frowning, he turns his computer monitor to where I can view the screen. It's a video from the basement poker room, showing a full house with games in progress. A dealer steps into view, and I do a double take. My eyes must be playing tricks on me, but sadly, they're not.

He stands. "Follow me upstairs."

"Romeo—"

He silences me with a withering look.

We walk upstairs, entering the guest bedroom. Luca's out of the hospital bed, seated in a chair next to a table with a laptop and various equipment and cords; across from him is Kat, hooked up to all those cords.

"Darius, I swear to God I didn't know John Davis was running the poker room!" Kat says in a panic. "I was told it was a party, and they just needed an extra dealer."

"Save it for the test," Romeo says in a bored tone.

"Test?" She gulps.

"Lie detector test," Luca explains.

"Just let me have a crack at it the old-fashioned way," Sammy says, weaving a knife between his fingers. "Torture her until she *cracks*."

"Fuck you," I spit, stalking over to him.

Romeo holds up his hand, and I halt. "Both of you. Out," he barks.

"Thanks a lot," Sammy grumbles.

"Your fucking fault," I tell him as we exit the room.

"Come on, let's go work out," Sammy says, slapping my back.

We walk to the basement, and I try not to think about what's happening upstairs as I get my weights set up. "She telling the truth?" Sammy asks.

"If she's not telling the truth, it'll gut me; Kat's more like a little sister to me than a cousin," I admit.

"If she's not telling the truth, I will have to *gut* her," Sammy warns.

"We'll cross that bridge if we get to it," I decide.

Putting in earbuds—I need the distraction from the

thoughts swirling in my head—I hit the treadmill, warming up before doing some interval sprints. I'm drenched with sweat by the time I turn off the machine and move over to weights. Just as I'm wrapping up my workout, the house-keeper calls for us.

We walk upstairs and knock on the bedroom door; Romeo beckons us to enter. Luca's in bed, with Nicky giving him up the road. "If you're well enough to get out of this bed and terrorize a woman, you're well enough to start physical thera-py," she says, hands on hips.

"Where's Kat?" I interrupt, trying not to panic at her absence.

"*Tesoro*, we need to talk business," Romeo tells Nicky.

"Fine, but I'll be back later," she warns Luca. Giving Romeo a quick kiss, she walks out, closing the door behind her.

"Thanks for saving me." Luca chuckles.

"And Kat, does she need saving?" I ask.

"Enzo's delivering her to AC," Romeo answers my question.

"In good condition?"

"For now," he tells me, and I suppress my sigh of relief. "Kat's been instructed to secure another invitation to deal. You've taken out Russel, but I suspect John will continue with business as usual."

"Some of that 'business as usual' is being conducted in Newark." I report what I've learned from Big Benny, pulling the file from my gym bag and handing it over.

Flipping through it, Romeo passes the file to Sammy. "Put Fabio and his crew on watch in AC. Darius, I want you to hang tight in case you need to visit the motel again," Romeo instructs me.

"Will do." Works out perfectly for me, because I didn't want to be away from Lily and Iris for that long.

"Darius, come with me," Romeo commands.

"Glad to see you up and at it," I tell Luca, fist bumping him.

"Don't tell Nicky that." Luca shakes his head.

"Sammy," I nod before following the boss to his office. He slides behind his desk, and I take a seat across from him.

He pins me to my chair with his hard gaze. "What if Kat knows more than she's letting on? She passed the polygraph, but that test isn't one hundred percent accurate. Are you with blood, or are you with the family?"

"I'm not really *with* the family, now am I?" I challenge.

"You're family as far as I'm concerned," Romeo tells me, leaning back in his chair.

"But I'll never be made." It might be petty, but I air the grievance I've been carrying around for years; my insecurity Sergio tried to capitalize on.

"Don't I treat you like you're made?" Romeo counters.

"Not the same," I tell him.

He waves his hand. "What do you need? More money? Name your price."

"It's not about the money; it's about the respect."

"Matteo was made. Did I fucking respect him?" he demands.

"No," I admit.

"There are some old ways even I can't change," Romeo tells me. "Greek blood runs through your veins and Italian through mine, but we're family as far as I'm concerned." Retrieving his knife, he pricks the palm of his hand.

Turning the knife handle-side out, he hands it to me. I likewise prick my palm, returning the weapon.

"You have my *imprimatur* as boss of this family." He rises behind his desk, extending his hand. I stand, and we shake on a blood oath. He narrows his eyes at me as he takes a seat. "Now, if you're wanting a fucking hug, go find Sam."

I chuckle, taking a seat. "Only if I'm wearing spiked armor."

"Everything settled with your family situation?"

"Yeah, I think so."

"I don't want any problems," he warns.

"Me neither, boss."

Romeo kicks up his feet on his desk. "Every time someone calls me that, for a split second I have the urge to look around the room for Antonio," he admits.

"You're already more of a boss than your old man ever was," I assure him.

He smirks. "No need to ass-kiss. You've already been given my seal of approval."

"Not ass-kissing, but fact. Now, if you're ready for me to kick your *ass*, change and meet me downstairs," I taunt.

"Give me about ten minutes." He narrows his eyes. "Do *not* tell Nicky."

"Man, don't bring me into that war," I say with a laugh. "I'll be downstairs."

I walk out of his office and run into Nicky in the hallway. "Glad I caught you. Here's a list of physical therapy exercises for Romeo's shoulder." She hands me the printout with a smile before sauntering off.

CHAPTER
Thirty~One

Lily

Having finished with my morning class, I arrive home. Darius isn't here; I guess he's still at the gym, or wherever he goes for "work."

"Hi, Lucky," I greet the cat, giving her a scratch behind her ear. Changing into leggings and an old tee, I grab the cleaning supplies. Darius doesn't trust a housekeeper, but honestly, I enjoy cleaning. I'm a borderline neat freak, and thankfully, my husband's pretty tidy himself.

I give our bathroom a good scrubbing before moving to dusting and vacuuming the bedroom. Opening the walk-in closet, I turn the vacuum to low setting, running it over the hardwood.

Curiosity gets the better of me, and I turn the vacuum off before moving the shoe rack and lifting the floorboard— revealing the safe. I punch in my birth month, day, and year. The safe *beeps* green, and I open it, removing a gym bag. Unzipping it, I find the passports Darius was telling me about on top of stacks of hundreds. There's also a prepaid credit card, some Euros, and a piece of paper with numbers written on it; likely an account of some sort.

Flipping through the passports with our aliases, I've freaked myself out enough for one day, and so I toss them in the bag. As I'm going to put everything back, I notice a black sachet in the bottom of the safe; it blends in so well I nearly missed it.

I grab the small bag and open it, finding a picture from Darius' childhood. I'd guess him around Iris' age; he's flashing a playful grin while being wrapped in his mother's arms. Even though the woman isn't my biggest fan, I can't deny she's a beauty.

The bag still feeling heavy, I dump it upside down. "No," I whisper in horror when I see what's landed on the floor.

Darius

Returning home, Lily's SUV is parked in the garage. "Wifey," I call when I open the door, tossing my keys and phones on the table.

The house is eerily silent. "Rainbow goddess," I call, but nothing. "Hey, Lucky. Where are my girls?" I ask the cat, but she just looks at me.

That's when I see it on the coffee table.

Darius, a few weeks ago

Parking down the street, I make my way under the cover of darkness to Lily's house. Having staked out the property after I left Leo's office, I hop over the gate in the backyard, sneaking to Lily's bedroom window. The light's on even though it's late, or early, depending on how you look at it; either way, she should be asleep. And when I peek inside, I discover why she's not asleep.

Fuuuuck.

I have too many enemies to be caught with my pants around my ankles—that's the only reason I haven't pulled my dick out and jerked off to the hottest show in the world. Lily should really add curtains to her bedroom window, not that I'm complaining.

My face plastered to the window, I watch through a small opening in the askew blinds as she moves a pink wand around her pretty clit. I stifle a groan as her legs fall open—she must have found a spot she likes. Damn, I wish I could hear her throaty little moans of pleasure.

Arching off the bed, Lily closes her eyes as she continues to run the vibrator over her clit. "Move it inside that sweet little pussy," I instruct her quietly, even though she can't hear me.

Her mouth falls open in a perfect O as she pushes the vibrator inside her.

"Good girl," I praise her.

Watching as her hot little body convulses, I turn around and walk off. It's that, or shoot a load in my pants.

Oh little angel, you're playing with fire tempting the devil.

My pager vibrates, and I wait until I'm in my car before retrieving it. This night just keeps getting better when I learn the identity of my new "training client."

Dropping by a Parisi Construction warehouse, I switch out the plates on my car, continuing on to my client's house. I park two streets over and approach the older shotgun house. My target has a security system, one I easily disable before using his spare key and unlocking his back door. You'd think a cop would be smarter than to leave a key under the welcome mat.

Taking a seat at the kitchen table, I screw on the silencer to my gun and wait. I'm a sight in coveralls, shoe coverings, and a hair covering, but hey, Luca isn't the only obsessive motherfucker in this crew.

The front door opens, and I inwardly curse when I hear Tommy's brought home a companion. "You going to use those hand-cuffs on me?" the woman asks in a flirty tone.

"Consider yourself under arrest," he says, and I try not to snort. What a fucking cheeseball.

Listening to the bed squeak for about ten minutes before things go quiet—pathetic; I bet he didn't even bother to get the woman off —I hear soft footsteps and the sound of the front door opening and closing.

I wait until the woman's long gone before I creep up the stairs.

"Baby, I want to see you, but I'm working tonight," Tommy lies to someone on the phone; I'm sure a different woman than the one he halfway fucked moments ago. "Next time," he says, and is quiet. "Yeah, I miss you too. Bye."

Finally.

Slipping into his bedroom, Tommy looks up in shock. "Darius. What the fuck?" He dives for his nightstand housing his gun, but I'm faster on the draw. A soft pop, and a bullet's now lodged between Tommy's eyes; he falls over like a sack of potatoes.

I make quick work ransacking his bedroom before swiping the cash and credit cards from his wallet, along with his cell and burner phones, tablet, and laptop. Placing those items in a signal-blocking bag, I go to make my escape when something in the top drawer of his dresser catches my eye—a small rainbow charm made out of beads. I don't know why, but I pocket it.

Performing one last sweep, I kick in the backdoor to make it look like a burglary.

My next stop—a Parisi Construction worksite, where I watch

the foreman pour concrete over the bag of electronics that could tie
me and the family back to Officer Tommy Harrison.

Never get caught holding the bag.

The rainbow charm is laid out on the coffee table beside a note. Grabbing the piece of paper with trembling hands, I read it three times, hoping it'll say something different.

How could you? Wait, I know the answer.
Because you're the devil. People don't change, and
you proved that for me yet again. Don't come
looking for us.

"Lily!" I thunder.

Sprinting to our bedroom, I panic when I spot her cell-phones, her wedding ring, and her mood ring on the dresser. I fling the closet door open so hard it nearly flies off the hinges, finding the safe empty. "Fuck!"

I've been caught holding the bag, and Lily's skipped town with the emergency bag.

CHAPTER
Thirty~Two

Lily
A few days later…

Now that the adrenaline's worn off, I don't have a fucking clue what to do next. A life on the run is no place for my daughter. God, how did things go from heaven to a living hell?

"Mama, I want to see Darius. And Lucky." Iris pouts.

"I know, sweetie." I've thought about lying and telling her Darius is dead, but that seems too cruel for a child who's already lost her dad. "Darius is busy with work and wanted us to have fun on our girls trip—just the two of us. He'll take good care of Lucky while we're gone." I hated leaving Lucky, but a cross-country road trip with a kitty would have made things even more difficult than they already are. "Why don't we go to the beach?" I suggest. We spent the first two days just trying to get as far away from Jersey as possible. After we catch our breath here in South Carolina, I need to figure out a plan.

"Yay! Beach!" Iris says excitedly.

We spend the day frolicking in the sun and surf. She does, anyway. I plaster on a happy face and try not to have an emotional breakdown.

Returning to our villa—I didn't want to spend this much, but we arrived late, and this was the only thing available at the first hotel we came across—we clean up before I turn on a show for Iris so I can strategize.

I unfold a United States map I purchased at a gas station. *Where should we go?* Maybe Louisiana? I've always wanted to visit New Orleans. Then again, Iris and I have those fake passports, so we're not limited to the United States. Paris, perhaps? I speak conversational French, and Iris is smart; she'd pick up the language in no time.

A knock on the door has me jumping. My heart racing, I walk over to check the peephole—pizza delivery.

After dinner, I tuck Iris into bed and return to my map. Charleston is closer, but Atlanta has a bigger airport—and I'm guessing better flight options—so I plan on us driving to Georgia tomorrow. Paris, here we come.

I step into the master bedroom, flipping on the overhead light and closing the door.

"Hello, wifey," Darius menaces, appearing from the bathroom.

Slapping a hand over my mouth so I don't scream, I go to run, but he's already on me, pinning me against the wall. "I told you I'd tear up the fucking world to find you, and yet you made me do it." He grits, his chest heaving. "Bad girls get punished, Lily."

"I'm not playing your sick games anymore, Darius," I whisper furiously. "You killed Iris' dad!"

"And you're both better off he's gone. Admit it!"

Shoving down the guilt—I've had that exact thought he just verbalized—I tell him, "You're crazy."

He laughs; the sound sends a chill down my spine. "Oh,

Lily. You have no idea how fucking crazy I'll get if you ever run from me again." Banding his hand around my wrists, he pins them over my head as he uses his free hand to rip my panties off.

"No!"

"Beg all you want. No one can save you from *Diávolos*," he says in a demented voice, moving a hand down to free his dick from his shorts.

"Red!" I shout in a panic.

He backs off, dropping my wrists. Holding his head in his hands, he flings his arms down with a growl, spinning around and punching a hole in the wall opposite me.

"Darius, stop!"

He jerks his hand out of the wall—a plume of dust and a large hole left in his wake. "You want me to splay my chest open and rip out my heart for you?" He pounds his chest with his plaster-covered fist. "Just say the fucking word."

"No, what I want is for you *not* to have killed Iris' dad!"

"Lily, the deed's done! I can't go back and change it."

"Did you get him out of the way so you could take his place?" I ask, angrily swiping at the tears.

"No," he shakes his head emphatically. "It was business. I swear to you, I didn't know your connection to Tommy at the time."

"Like I could ever believe a fucking word that comes out of your mouth," I spit.

"Don't be that way," he begs. "I've always been honest with you—as much as my job allows."

"More fucking lies." I point to the door. "Get out. We're finished here."

He stalks over to me, gripping me hard by my chin. I swallow nervously, but before I know what's happening, something sharp pricks my neck. Looking down in horror, I see he's holding a hypodermic needle with his other hand.

"I'm sorry, little angel, but we'll never be finished," he

tells me quietly.

My eyes growing heavy with whatever's coursing through my veins, I'm no longer able to hold my head upright. Slumping into his arms, everything goes black.

Darius

Gently placing Lily on the bed, I dress her before buckling her sandals. Giving my little angel a kiss on the forehead, I scoop her up and open the door.

"Darius!" Iris says excitedly, running to me. She stops abruptly when she notices her mama unconscious in my arms.

"Rainbow goddess! Shhh," I warn her. "Your mama's asleep. I'm going to put her in the car so she can rest on the trip. Can you grab the things you want to take? It's time to go home. I've missed you, and Lucky has too." It's a dirty move bringing up the cat, but there's nothing I won't say or do to get my family back.

Iris looks unsure about what's happening—kid's too damn smart for her own good—but she nods, taking off to her room.

I carry Lily to the car, buckling up her limp body. Her head droops at an awkward angle, and I try to right it, but it immediately slumps back over. Not much I can do about it, so I lock the door behind me, hustling inside to grab the emergency bag. I stick my head inside Iris' room. Her tiny body trembling, she's clutching her rainbow mermaid. "You ready?" I ask her gently.

She nods, and I walk over to her and pick her up—hugging her tight as we walk out of the villa. Getting her bucked in, I toss the bag in the trunk before running around and sliding behind the driver's seat. The urge to high tail it out of here is strong, but I obey the speed limit—no need to add the complication of explaining to the local yokel cops why my wife's incapacitated.

"I heard you and Mama fighting," Iris tells me from the backseat, hugging her mermaid doll that has a tracker sewn inside the tail. Honestly, I put it in there in the event she ever lost her favorite stuffie—never imagining I'd have to use that tracker to find my *lost* wife and stepdaughter.

"Just a little misunderstanding. We'll work it out." That's more an assurance to myself than to her.

"It's my fault Dad died," she whispers so quietly, I'm not sure if I heard her correctly. "I didn't want to see him anymore."

"Iris, it is *not* your fault he died," I tell her firmly, wanting to nip that idea in the bud. "He was a cop, and that's a dangerous job. Listen," I tell her, locking eyes with her in the rearview, "I don't want you to worry. Everything's going to be alright."

"Do you have a dangerous job?" she asks.

"At the gym? Nah, not unless I drop a weight on my toe. Ooof! Now that would hurt," I tell her, and she smiles. "It's late. Why don't you close your eyes for me, and go to sleep?"

"But I'm not tired," she protests, only to yawn loudly. "Why is Mama so tired?"

Unable to answer her, I flip on classical music, and it's only a matter of minutes before she's out for the count.

Driving to the airport, I pull up to the tarmac—the Parisi family jet waiting there for us. Carrying Iris first, I run back down the steps and scoop Lily into my arms. She doesn't stir. I start to panic, but feeling her pulse—still beating strong—I sigh a breath of relief.

I told Iris her mama and I would work it out, but I don't have a fucking clue how to make that happen.

CHAPTER
Thirty~Three

Lily

Feeling like I've got the mother of all hangovers, I bring my hands to my forehead, only to realize I'm now wearing my wedding ring on my left ring finger, my mood ring on my right. Dread fills me as I slowly open my eyes to find I'm in the private jet, with Darius seated in a chair across from the bed. "Hey, wifey," he says softly.

"Don't call me that." My voice sounds like I've got a mouthful of gravel.

He walks over to me, taking a seat on the edge of the bed as he offers me a bottle of water. I can't help but notice his new ink—a wedding band tattoo on his ring finger.

"What would you have me call you?" he asks gently.

"Stranger." And this time when I say it, I mean it with every fiber of my being. "Is this safe to drink, or is it drugged too?"

"I'm sorry, *aggeloudhi* mou," he says, guilt written all over his face. "I didn't want to, but I knew you would have fought me, and that would only have traumatized Iris."

"Oh my fucking God, you don't get to act like you care about my daughter after what you've done!"

"That is such bullshit." He spits. "You know I love Iris like she's my own flesh and blood."

I snort an acrid laugh. "Thankfully, Darius, your tainted blood doesn't run through her veins. Your father was right: you're nothing but a dumb brute."

He flinches like I've slapped him across the face. Nodding, he silently places the water on the table as he walks out, closing the door behind him.

It's what I wanted to happen, and yet I still break down in tears.

We arrive home late, with Iris asleep, and me ignoring Darius. He carries my daughter inside and puts her to bed, and I give Lucky a scratch before silently walking to the bedroom. Locking him out, I get ready for bed, going through the motions like a zombie.

Opening the bathroom door, I nearly run into Darius; of course a lock doesn't keep the devil out. He goes to open his mouth, but I hold up my hand, brushing past him. "There's nothing else that needs to be said."

"There's a hell of a lot more that needs to be said." He growls, grabbing my hand and jerking me around to where I'm facing him. "Tommy Harrison was on the take."

"What?" I say, my legs feeling wobbly.

"Tommy was on the family's payroll. He was a dirty cop." Darius spells out for me. "He must have fucked up along the way; I don't know the details, but there was a hit out on him. I was just doing my job."

"Your job," I whisper.

"*My job*," he confirms.

I had my suspicions, but there it is—I'm married to a mob hitman. Feeling like I'm going to pass out, it doesn't help my situation when Darius reaches up his sleeve, now brandishing a knife. My eyes wide with fear, I stammer, "What are you—"

He answers by pricking the palm of his hand with the blade.

"Darius, stop!"

Fisting his cut hand, red droplets land on the hardwood with a *plop*. "Lily, I swear by my blood—*tainted* as it is—I didn't know you and Iris were connected to Tommy until after our wedding. When you spoke about him, you called him Harrison; he always went by his first name with me and the family."

"When did you find out?" I demand.

"When I confronted Detective Regan for following us," he admits. "After we got back from our honeymoon."

"So you found out after we were married. The point is you *did* find out; you were just never going to tell me the truth," I say, crossing my arms.

"Remember I told you I would do anything to protect you in any given situation? You're right; I was never going to tell you," Darius agrees.

I narrow my eyes at him. "That's not protecting me; that's protecting yourself."

"No, it's protecting *you*. Knowing too much about my world is dangerous; you already know too much as is." He paces back and forth, finally saying, "Is it better knowing I killed him?"

"No," I whisper. "But now that I do know, how can we go back?"

"We just go back. Things were so good between us, weren't they?" he asks, his dark eyes pleading.

"They were, but now I know everything was built on a lie," I tell him sadly.

"Not a damn thing was built on a lie," he says adamantly. "I swore to you 'till death do us part.' That wasn't a lie. I love Iris like my own; that's not a lie. You have my heart; that's not a fucking lie. Give me time to prove it to you," he begs.

"What choice do I have?" I shout. "You've already demonstrated I can't escape from you!" And how he found us, I still don't know. I was so damn careful, ditching my phones, and even renting a car because I was afraid my SUV might have a tracker. *Is this what I get for tempting the Fates with the pomegranate*?

"You can't," he readily agrees.

"Till death do us part," I say bitterly. "Well, *husband*, you got it. Look forward to a lifetime of celibacy, because we'll never share a marital bed again."

"Careful, wifey," he warns. "I don't want you to choke on those words when you have to eat them; if you're choking on anything, it's going to be my dick."

"Fucking dream on." I stomp over to the door, unlocking it and flinging it open. "The couch has your name on it."

"Very well," he says, but walks over to the dresser. Opening the top drawer, he grabs my vibrator and sticks it in his pocket. "I don't get to touch your pussy, neither does this." With that, saunters to the door.

"I don't need a vibrator to get off," I grit.

Darius cranes his neck, giving me a cruel smile. "No, little angel just needs to think about her bad husband to get off. My hands can get dirty while you get to keep your wings nice and clean."

"Fuck you." I seethe.

"You can live in that ivory tower if you want, Lily, but it'll be lonely as hell up there. When you're ready to climb down, you know where to find me." With that, he closes the door behind him.

CHAPTER
Thirty~Four

Lily

After a terrible night's sleep, I enter Iris' room to wake her for school, but the bed's empty. Following the smell of coffee and maple syrup to the kitchen, any hopes of not having to interact with Darius go out the window.

"Morning, wifey," he says, extending a travel mug of coffee.

Ignoring him, I walk over to Iris and kiss her on the top of the head. "Hey, sweetie. Finish up, please. We need to get going."

"Darius made pancakes!" She smiles, her mouth and teeth stained from the blueberries.

"I can see that." I smile back tightly. "Come on, let's brush teeth. We need to go."

"I want Darius to take me to school," Iris says.

"I'm taking you," I tell her firmly. "Come on, let's wash up."

"Listen to your mama," he says, opening a bottle of pomegranate juice and taking a swig. Either the Fates are fucking with me or Darius is. "Maybe I can take you another day this week," he tells Iris.

"You can't," I say tersely. "Let's go, Iris," I say, practically dragging her up the stairs to her bathroom.

"Mama, what's wrong?"

"Nothing, sweetie. I just have a final, and I need to get to school early."

"What's a final?" Iris asks.

"A test."

"What's a test?"

What I'm being subjected to right now, I think with a sigh. "Let's get ready, and we can talk about it in the car, okay?" Helping her wash up and brush her teeth, I say, "Put your uniform on, please."

Of all the mornings, she chooses this one to slow-walk getting ready. "Why can't Darius take me?"

"Sweetie, please get your clothes on," I tell her.

"But I want to ride with Darius." She pouts.

My left eye feels like it's about to twitch, and I slap a hand over it. "Please just get ready for me."

She finally puts her clothes on, and I have to go through three different ponytail attempts before she's satisfied with the finished look. "Let's go," I say, ushering her out of the room.

"Wait, I need to tell Lucky bye."

"We're going to be late," I call, but she's already taken off.

I walk to the kitchen, where Darius extends the coffee yet again, along with Iris' lunch box he's already packed.

"Just stop," I tell him, exasperated.

"Stop what?" he asks innocently.

Stop acting so fucking perfect, because I should have known it was too good to be true. "Iris, let's go!" I shout.

She runs into the kitchen; Darius opens his arms, and she practically jumps into them. He picks her up and spins her around.

"Bye, rainbow goddess. Have a good day." He kisses the top of her head before sitting her down. "Good luck on your exam," he tells me.

"Thanks," I say cooly, taking the coffee and lunchbox. He beats me to the garage door, helping Iris into her car seat. He looks like he wants to say more, but I close my door and hit the garage opener, backing out of the driveway.

"Mama, why are you mad at Darius?"

"I'm not mad at Darius, sweetie." Honestly, I'm more mad at myself for letting my guard down. I did, and look what happened? I fell in love with the mob hitman who whacked my daughter's father. *Is whacked even what they call it?* I'm sure Darius knows the proper terminology, but I'll be damned if I ask him.

We pull into Miss Mary's parking lot with about two minutes to spare. I hurry Iris out of the car and to the front door. The mom clique is hanging out, but I don't have time for their bullshit as I race Iris inside. Hugging my daughter bye, I walk back outside and give a wave to the moms.

"Lily, wait up," Becca calls, chasing after me.

"Hey, Becca. I'm in a bit of a hurry trying to get to class," I tell her as I keep walking.

Unfortunately, she doesn't get the hint. "I'll be brief. This is about that rabid dog of a husband of yours."

"Excuse me?"

"I'm sure this will come as a shock to you, but the man *threatened* me," she whispers the last part.

"What do you mean?" I say, stopping in my tracks.

"When he dropped Iris off the other morning. It was all out of the blue, quite unprovoked," she says dramatically.

"What did he say?"

"I'm not sure how much you're ready to hear," she says, giving me a patronizing smile. "But your husband hit on me." Even though things between me and Darius have gone to shit, I don't believe a word out of Becca's mouth. "I turned him down, of course," she continues, "as you know how I adore my husband." Sure, the husband she cheats on with the pool boy, the tennis instructor, and the yoga instructor. "Well, that set him off. He threatened my family. My husband, specifically. *Physical violence*."

I try not to laugh. "Becca, I have a final exam; I really have to go."

"Of course, and like I said, I hate to be the bearer of bad news."

"I know you do. Thanks for letting me know." Somehow I managed to say that with a straight face as I hurry to my car.

Driving to campus, I replay my encounter with Becca. I take it back—I do believe a few words out of her mouth. There's no doubt Darius threatened her husband; his attempt to help Iris with the bullying problem. Christ, how many bodies does my husband leave in his wake? The bigger question is why it felt so damn good when she told me about the threat.

Maybe my wings aren't as nice and clean as I'd like to believe.

Answering the last essay question, I give my exam a once-over before walking to the front and turning it in. My interim professor smiles at me, and I smile back at her before exiting the classroom.

Driving to Harrison's house, I park and walk up the steps. Using the key, I let myself in—marching straight to the guest room closet. Removing the tile carpeting, I eye the safe. Having researched this particular model, I know it requires a four-digit code. Grabbing my notebook, I turn to the page with potential number combinations I've come up with. I go through each and every combo without luck.

The last on my list: *Iris,* but her name as a number cipher based on the alphabet. Punching in 9-18-9-19, the safe *beeps* green. My eyes wide with shock, I mutter, "Holy shit, it worked." I open the safe to find stack after stack of wrapped hundreds. This only confirms what Darius told me—Harrison was on the take.

Grabbing the cash, I count a stack; one thousand dollars. I mentally tally the number of stacks as I fill up my backpack. My hand shaking, I close the safe and move the carpet back into place. Locking up behind me, I turn around and nearly have a heart attack when I spot Ethan at the bottom of the steps.

"Hey, Lily. I was driving by on my patrol and saw your car," he tells me.

"Ethan, hey. I just finished class." I shift my backpack as I walk toward him. *A backpack filled with three hundred grand in cash, if not more.* "I wanted to give the house one more sweep for Iris' rainbow charm."

"Any luck?"

"No." I shake my head, trying to play it cool.

"Have you thought any more about what we talked about?" he asks. "About your husband?"

"I'm sorry, I don't have time to get into it now; I've got to get back to class," I lie. I'm finished for the day, but he doesn't know that. "Finals."

"Okay, but I'm serious, Lily. If you need help, I'm here for you," he tells me.

Need help? This poor guy has no idea.

His radio goes off, and a dispatcher says something. He responds, "10-4." Turning his attention back to me, he says with an apologetic look, "I have to go."

"Sure, I'll talk to you later." I hurry to my car, trying not to look suspect.

Ethan takes off in his patrol car, and I turn in the opposite direction, driving until I find a parking lot to pull over. Searching for the nearest storage unit company on my phone, I make the short drive and enter the office.

I fill out the paperwork and pay for a small rental unit. No way Darius is going to let me have access to the emergency bag, so I'm creating my own. Besides, Harrison is dead, so it's not like he can take it with him. Harrison is dead because my husband killed him; having something to do with the mob money I just stole.

My wings are feeling pretty damn dirty.

CHAPTER
Thirty-Five

Lily

Answering the final question on the very last exam of my undergrad career, I walk out in the hall with a big smile on my face.

Everyone's excited, milling about. "Hey, Lily. We're going to grab a drink. You want to join us?" A friend from class asks me.

No is on the tip of my tongue, but then I think, why not? Iris is in school; I no longer have to rush to the club to make the lunch shift; and I'm avoiding Darius. "Sure, sounds like fun."

I meet up with the group at a popular bar I've never been to—my college experience hasn't exactly been the typical one—and I take a seat at the table. A tray of shots is presented, but I decline, instead ordering a beer. Spotting a familiar face being seated by a hostess, I say to everyone, "Excuse me for just a minute."

Walking across the bar, I approach Ethan. "This is a surprise," I tell him.

"Big surprise. I'm not sure I've ever seen you drink," he teases, eyeing the beer in my hand.

"I just finished my last final," I say with a huge smile. "I'm out celebrating with friends from class."

"Congrats!" He gestures for me to sit across from him, and I do so. "That's really awesome, Lily," he tells me. "I would say the next round's on me, but I'm just here for lunch; I have a shift this evening."

"Quite alright," I tell him. "One drink is my limit. I have to meet with my lawyer this afternoon about the probate stuff."

"Good. Glad you're getting that taken care of. How about we plan to meet up for coffee, and I can bring you the paperwork for Iris' benefits I was telling you about."

"Sure. Now that I'm finished for the summer, my schedule is pretty flexible. Just text me when you have some free time."

"Will do," he tells me.

"I'd better get back. I'll talk to you later."

I return to the table, and my friend announces, "Oooh, I forgot to tell everybody the news. Guess who I ran into at the physical therapy office my mom manages? *Professor Miller.* The man had a really bad cycling accident—that's why he took off the rest of the semester," she reports.

Too bad he survived the accident, I think, and then mentally cringe. God, when did I become this person?

We finish our drinks, and everyone decides to bar hop. "This is where my hop ends," I say with a smile. "But have fun."

Saying our goodbyes, I make a quick pit stop at the bathroom. Stepping inside the one-staller, I go to close the door when a large foot wearing a trainer I know all too well blocks it.

Darius flings the door open and stalks inside. I back up,

immediately on high alert, as he has the crazy *Diávolos* look about him.

He closes and locks the door before stalking over to me. There's nowhere for me to go in this tiny bathroom, and soon, my back's against the wall.

"Be careful, little angel," he says in an eerily calm tone. "Smile like that at Ethan one more time, and I'll cut out his eyes; make sure he never has the pleasure of seeing your pretty face again."

"You're crazy," I say, crossing my arms, pretending my heart isn't beating like a jackhammer.

"You know it." He cages me in with his arms, his hard dick pressed against my stomach.

I square my jaw. "Red."

He smiles, and it's a fucking terrifying sight. "You're going to give me the green light soon, wifey, and when you do?" He nudges me with his dick. "I'm going to fucking destroy this pussy, because you seem to have forgotten who it belongs to." Squatting down, he takes a deep breath with his nose at my crotch. Looking up at me, he says, "Think you can play games with the devil and not get your wings singed, *aggeloudhi mou?* Keep toying with *Diávolos*, and you'll find out."

With that, he stands and unlocks the bathroom door, flinging it open as he stalks out.

My heart racing, I catch sight of myself in the mirror. Eyes dilated, I tell myself it's because I'm afraid. Nipples hard, I likewise justify it due to fear. But there's no mental gymnastics I can do to explain why my panties are soaked with desire.

Exiting my lawyer's office, I've just signed the necessary paperwork to open the probate estate. My next task is meeting with a realtor at Harrison's place.

I let myself inside with the key, flipping on the lights. Something looks different, and it takes me a moment to realize the television and gaming system are gone. Hurrying to the guest bedroom, my eyes go wide when I find a gaping hole in the closet floor—someone's cut the safe out and taken it.

Quickly exiting the room, I hurry to the kitchen to find the back door hanging on its hinges. I sprint out of the house and hop in my SUV, getting the hell out of here just in case the intruder decides to come back.

I drive until I'm a safe distance away, pulling into the parking lot of a gas station. Texting the realtor we need to reschedule, I'm about to call Ethan next, but my hand pauses on his contact. He'll tell me to file a police report, and that's the last thing I want to do. The cops would have to survey the damage, and that would raise too many questions about the safe.

Swallowing my pride, I call Darius. "Wifey," he answers cheerfully.

"Could you send Parisi Construction over to Harrison's house to fix the back door?" I get straight to the point.

"What's wrong with the back door?"

"Someone broke into the house and stole the television and gaming system. I didn't hang around to see if anything else had been taken." I don't tell him the entire truth; the missing safe and the money I swiped my little secret.

"Good. Don't go back to the house. I'll take care of it."

"Thanks," I tell him.

"Of course. What would wifey like for dinner? Want me to stop and grab takeout?"

"We're not playing the 'happy couple' game, Darius," I warn.

"What game do you want to play?" he asks, his voice dropping in timbre. "Because I know exactly what game I want to play with you. I'd tie you to our bed, and—"

"Bye," I say, ending the call.

Darius

I've already killed Ethan in my mind twenty-seven times. My favorite version is me hanging him up by his thumbs and cutting off his dick; I'd shove the tiny, severed member in his mouth to muffle his cries of agony as I gouge out his eyes. I might even pull a Sammy—try my hand at skinning Ethan alive while I'm at it.

The only thing stopping me from turning this fantasy into a reality is Lily would never forgive me. Since I've got enough shit I need her forgiveness on, I'm not going to add Ethan's death to the list. *For now.* I make no promises about the future.

As for my pent up aggression, too bad for the fucker I've got strung up inside this warehouse. "Sorry about that," I say, walking back over to my workstation and pocketing my phone. Putting on my gloves and moving my face shield back into place, I ask, "Now, where were we?"

It's a rhetorical question, because this gentleman has already had his tongue cut out.

"Don't worry, I'll get to you momentarily," I tell his business partner who's tied up and gagged, watching in horror. *Or maybe I won't.* I might let the partner live, if only to tell the tale about *Diávolos*. A cautionary tale for anyone else who thinks they're going to pull one over on me. Gave them extra time to pay up, and they had the fucking nerve to try and give me the slip? That simply won't do.

Grabbing a scalpel, I make a large incision, removing a nice chunk of the man's liver as he makes an ungodly whimpering sound, all the while blood sprays everywhere. "You have a fatty liver, my man," I announce, slapping a piece of it onto the table next to his tongue. "I would recommend some lifestyle changes, but well, it's a little late for that."

The partner thrashes against the restraints; his terror permeating the room. I take a deep inhale, and smile. "Thought you could escape *Diávolos*? You thought wrong."

Just like Lily's wrong in thinking she can keep me at arm's length. Only a matter of time before she breaks; that, or *Diávolos* breaks her. She better hope she breaks of her own volition.

CHAPTER
Thirty-Six

Darius

"Lily Grant Angelos," the announcer calls, and Lily glides on stage, accepting her diploma. She's the only Angelos to ever have received one—with honors no less—and it makes me proud as hell she's my wife; too bad she's embarrassed by my dumb ass. She didn't want me to come, but good luck shaking me.

We've got a ways to go through the alphabet, and Iris is already getting restless. Kat's with us and brought a busy bag, as she called it. She swore to me when we spoke privately she didn't know about John Davis. She'd better be telling the truth, or the only bag my cousin will need is a *body bag*.

Kat hands Iris an activity book, and Iris gets to work peeling the stickers and placing them on the pages. Bored with that, she begins sticking them on my tie. "Looks so much nicer now," I whisper to her, and she flashes a devious little smile. *That's my kid.*

Iris' grandma and grandpa are seated on the other side of us, and they keep casting judgmental looks in my direction. I flash a smile at them, straightening my tie now adorned with unicorn stickers.

The commencement ends, and we work our way through the hordes of people to find our graduate. "Mama," Iris runs over and hops into Lily's arms.

"Congratulations," I tell Lily, kissing the top of her head.

"Thank you. Nice tie." She smiles brightly until she remembers she's mad at me. "Mother. Father," she says, giving her parents an awkward side hug.

"Let me take a picture of everyone," Kat suggests.

Lily hands her phone to Kat, and I scoot in close, placing my arm around my wife. She tenses, but doesn't shrug out of my hold. I'll take it.

"I need to get back to AC. I'm working this evening," Kat announces, handing Lily back her phone.

"What is it you do?" Mr. Grant asks Kat.

"I'm a casino dealer," Kat answers.

"How interesting," Mrs. Grant says in a rather condescending tone.

"You have no idea," Kat quips, ignoring the snobbery. She gives Lily a hug. "Congrats again."

"Thank you, and thanks for coming," Lily says.

"Of course." Squatting down and hugging Iris, Kat says, "I'll come play with you and Lucky here soon."

"Iris has a new cat," Lily explains to her parents.

"Oh," is all Mrs. Grant says.

Kat says her goodbyes, and Lily waves at some classmates. "We'll meet you at the house," Lily tells her parents.

I put Iris on my shoulders so we can maneuver easier through the crowd. Lily chats with a few classmates and professors before telling me she's ready.

We walk to the parking garage, and I drive us to neighboring Princeton. We turn into a neighborhood not as flashy as Antonio Parisi's, but a distant second. I know from looking into Lily's background, both her parents are professors at the nearby Ivy League university, as well as coasting along on old family money. It makes me hot under the collar the Grant family is well off, and yet their daughter and granddaughter had to scrape by on their own.

I find a spot on the street to park, as I don't want to get blocked in the driveway in the event we need a quick getaway. I'm not sure why we'd need a quick getaway, but old habits die hard.

Lily leads us to the backyard where the party's already started. "Who are these people?" I ask Lily quietly. Around fifty stuffy-looking men and women in country club attire are sipping on bourbon and spouting bullshit.

"My parents friends and work colleagues."

"I thought this was a party to celebrate your graduation?" I ask.

She shrugs. "Iris, you want something to eat?"

"A cupcake!"

"Lunch first, then a cupcake," Lily tells her.

"I'll grab you both a plate," I volunteer.

Walking over to the food table, I start to fill plates when I overhear the tail end of a conversation between two women in front of me. "Married a gym rat."

"Not much of a step up from the deadbeat 'baby daddy.'"

"No. I'd say more of a downgrade."

"I prefer the term 'personal trainer,'" I say loudly, and both women turn to me, eyes wide. "You might consider finding a trainer. Weightlifting is wonderful to strengthen bones—especially in elderly women dealing with osteo-porosis."

Who knows how old these women are given their exten-sive plastic surgery, but my shot must have hit the mark, because they both look offended as hell.

"Excuse me." I grab Iris a cupcake and stroll off.

Lily

I keep checking my phone; ugh, have we really only been here for an hour? "I need to go to the bathroom. Iris, do you need to potty?" I ask.

"Nope," she says, blowing bubbles with a wand Darius brought. The man really is thoughtful; and *psychotic*, I can't forget that part.

"Be back in a few," I say, stepping inside. I use the bathroom, and upon exit, I'm waived over by my father. I smile; that is until I see who he's speaking with. "Lily, you of course know Professor Miller," my father says.

"Hello." I force a smile.

"Ms. Grant," Professor Miller says politely, like that vile threat he made in his office never happened.

"Professor Miller's going to be joining my department this fall," my father says.

"Oh, you're not returning to Newark?" I ask, wanting to jump for joy.

"No," Professor Miller says, but doesn't elaborate.

Someone snags my father's attention. "Excuse me for just a moment," he says, walking off.

That leaves me alone with a sexual predator. The old Lily would be terrified, but somewhere along the way, I seemed to have discovered my backbone. "New university; new pool of women to sexually harass. You must be excited," I comment.

Professor Miller curls his lips into a snarl, only for his eyes to land over my shoulder; he turns a ghastly shade of white before hobbling away with the aid of his cane.

Turning around, I find Darius watching us from across the

room, with Iris' attention elsewhere. Our eyes lock before he squats down, saying something to my daughter.

Darius

"Excuse me, ladies. Restroom break," I announce. I've had my eye on Professor Miller all afternoon; he's been hitting the booze pretty hard, and it's only a matter of time before he needs to take a piss.

"First door down the hall on the left," Lily instructs me.

"Thanks. Be back in a little bit." Walking inside the house, I enter the guest bathroom, making sure to clog the toilet with enough paper to cause a biblical-sized flood. I give it a flush, and water begins backing up as I close the door behind me.

Positioning myself to where I can see the door, I watch another party-goer enter, only to turn right around. The guest tracks down a woman in a housekeeper uniform, who enters the bathroom and likewise exits swiftly. She takes off down the hall, returning a moment later with reinforcements—a man holding a plunger. He enters the bathroom, and the housekeeper tapes an out of order sign on the door.

I slink to the foyer and ascend the stairs, waiting for the second act of this little tragedy. I've already triple checked for security cameras; none inside. Outside, I noted five, so that just means dirty deeds will need to be performed indoors.

Exactly seven minutes pass before Professor Miller hobbles up the stairs and enters the bathroom. He exits quickly—no way he fucking washed his hands—and I creep up behind him. As soon as he reaches the first step, I give him a good heave-ho. Not because he didn't wash up, but because

I warned the fucker not to so much as look at Lily, and I'm a man of my word.

His cries echo as I hustle to the front stairs, taking them two at a time and rejoining the party outside. "Girls, can I get you anything else to eat? Drink?" I ask, appearing beside my wife and stepdaughter.

"Sweetie, are you still hungry?" Lily asks Iris.

"No. Can we go? I'm bored," Iris announces.

"Sure. Let's find my parents and tell them bye," Lily says, taking Iris' hand. Iris extends her other hand, and I smile as I take her tiny one in mine.

Lily

We step inside the living room, where everyone's congregating near the stairs. Working our way through the crowd, it's a chaotic scene: Professor Miller lies at the bottom of the stairs in a contorted position; Mother's speaking frantically on the phone, while my father is squatting down next to Professor Miller, taking his pulse.

"What is it?" Iris asks, unable to see over the adults in front of her.

"Come on, rainbow goddess. There's a traffic jam. Let's go outside until it clears." Darius leads her out; for that, I'm grateful.

"What happened?" I ask a woman standing next to me.

"Poor man took a tumble down the stairs," she tells me. "I didn't see it, but he hit every step on his way down from the sound of it."

"Oh my," is all I can come up with.

Soon, an ambulance arrives, and I work my way up to my

mother and father, who are speaking to an EMT while Professor Miller is being loaded onto a stretcher.

"Is he going to be alright?" I ask my parents as the emergency responders wheel Professor Miller out.

"He was able to move his legs, so hopefully it's not a spinal injury, but whatever recovery he's made from his cycling crash just got negated," my father tells me, shaking his head. "I'm going to drive to the hospital to meet him there." I nod, hugging my father goodbye.

"Darling, I simply don't understand this new marriage of yours. Haven't you outgrown your rebellious streak yet?" Mother chides when it's just the two of us.

"Darius is a good man, a good provider, and good to me and Iris. What's not to understand?" I find myself hotly defending him.

"A personal trainer." She scoffs. If my mother only knew I used to be an exotic dancer, she'd be the one needing EMT assistance. "What on earth could you two possibly have in common?"

"That is beyond elitist," I say, crossing my arms. "And I'll have you know Darius is an extremely intelligent man— fluent in three languages." Mother doesn't look convinced, but I continue, "If you want to go back to an estranged relationship with me, keep disparaging my husband."

"Of course I don't want that. Lily, I know your father and I made some missteps with you and Iris' father—"

"Some missteps?" I say incredulously. "You mean forbidding me from seeing Harrison because he wasn't in the same tax bracket as us, and then trying to force me to have an abortion when I told you I was pregnant?" I hiss.

"Darling, lower your voice," she says, looking over my shoulder.

Taking a deep breath, I say, "Mother, we need to go. Thanks for the party." Giving her a stilted hug, I walk out.

CHAPTER
Thirty-Seven

Lily

Having tucked Iris in for the night, I take a long bath before climbing into bed; the huge king-size bed feeling even bigger with just me in it. Somewhere along the way, I got used to snuggling next to Darius, who runs at least three degrees hotter than me. The man didn't even mind when I'd put my icy feet on his legs.

I toss and turn before throwing back the covers in frustration. Switching on the lamp, I pull on my robe and cinch it around my waist as I tiptoe down the hall. Earlier today, I accused Mother of having an elitist mentality, but looking back on my own actions, I owe Darius an apology. Of course, I didn't mean it when I called him a dumb brute, but he *thought* I did, and now's as good a time as any for my *mea culpa*.

The overhead light's off in the bonus room, but I find Darius laying on the couch under a blanket with the television muted in the background. "I owe you an apology," I start. "When I called you a dumb brute, I said that to hurt you. Please know I didn't mean it. I'm sorry."

I have his attention, and yet he's preoccupied with a strained look on his face. I find out why when he jerks the blanket down—I've caught him stroking his dick.

"What perfect timing. Do you know what the dumb brute was just imagining before you walked in here? You, on all fours; me, eating your pussy from behind."

"Don't call yourself that," I whisper in a husky tone.

"Did you know you have the sweetest pussy I've ever tasted?" He ignores my last statement as he continues to move his hand up and down his shaft. "I don't mean that poetically. I mean you fucking taste sweet—with just a hit of acidic lemon, and a back finish of saltiness. But of course my little angel is sweet."

"Darius—"

"You're being such a good girl for me, and I move my tongue from your pussy to your crack," he continues to narrate his fantasy while stroking his dick.

"Darius!" I say in shock.

"And my naughty angel likes that," he hums, noticing my painfully hard nipples. "Yes, my dirty little slut likes the devil knocking at her back door. I'm not taking your ass tonight with my dick. Soon, but not tonight. No, tonight your ass is getting acquainted with my tongue," he tells me as he tugs his dick harder.

I'll worry about this bad decision later, but for now I close the door and lock it, walking over to him. Shrugging out of my robe, I pull my tank top over my head, and slide my panties down—stepping out of them. I kneel on the floor, positioning myself on all fours.

"You ready to give yourself to me for good this time?" Darius asks, now behind me. He massages my ass cheeks with his big hands.

I shake my head. "Just for tonight."

"Why are you fighting this?" he demands. "I fucked up; I know I did. But I can't go back and change any of it."

I'm fighting this because I do live in an ivory tower, and it's scary as hell to acknowledge my own darkness and climb down. I don't admit that; instead, I go to rise off my hands and knees and walk out.

His big hand forces the upper half of my body to the carpet. "Oh, no you don't. No more toying with *Diávolos.* Face down, ass up."

He obscenely spreads my ass cheeks open and growls. "Fucking dripping for me. Keep denying us if you want, but your pussy doesn't lie," he says, running his finger through my slit. He moves that wet finger back, circling a different hole—causing my muscles to involuntarily clench. Laughing darkly, he dives in, fucking my pussy with his tongue as he roughly grips my ass cheeks.

I jerk. I writhe. I thrust my hips back. I rub my tits on the carpet. Something, anything, to get some relief from this insatiable need.

"You come when I allow you to come, little whore," he chides, shocking me when his teeth clamp down on my ass cheek.

"Oww!" I cry out, the pain only making my pussy throb that much harder.

He licks the spot where he just bit me. "Be still, or I'll hogtie you." A shudder courses through my body, and he laughs softly. "Next time; I don't have any rope up here, and no way I'm leaving this room and giving you time to over-think this."

He grazes my clit with his teeth, and I nearly jerk off the floor. "Oh, shit!"

The palm of his hand connects with my ass with a stinging *pop.* "I said be still."

My body goes rigid, and he runs his tongue from my inner thigh to my pussy lips—lapping at my dripping desire. "Only a good girl when you're desperate to squirt on my face, isn't that right, little whore?" He spreads my ass cheeks open to the point of pain, his tongue circling my tight hole.

I gasp. "Wait, I don't know—"

He smacks my ass again; this time harder, and I hiss.

"Every pretty hole of yours belongs to me, to do with as I see fit." With that declaration, he begins flicking his tongue against my rim; the fluttering sensation unlike anything I've felt before.

He spears my asshole with his tongue—the intrusion strange, and yet pleasurable. "Oh, fuck," I moan.

Holding my cheeks open with one hand, he moves his forearm between my legs, rubbing my keyed-up pussy back and forth as he continues to fuck my asshole with his tongue.

"Darius!" I cry as I dig my fingers into the carpet, my body shaking uncontrollably. "I'm coming!" Spearing his tongue inside me, he rubs his arm faster and faster, and I scream as my ass contracts around his tongue; my pussy gushing on his forearm.

He waits until my body stops shaking before helping me up. My feet a bit wobbly, I'm too much in post-orgasm bliss to be shocked at him running his tongue along his glistening forearm. Helping me to my feet, he places my robe around me and ties it. "Now, don't come to me again until you're ready to give me everything." With that, he marches over and opens the door, motioning for me to leave.

Stunned, I walk out of the room. Turning around, I open my mouth to say something, but he closes the door before I can find the words.

CHAPTER
Thirty-Eight

Darius

I should have denied Lily; waited her out until she's ready to accept us. Accept *me*. But I'm fucking weak when it comes to this woman; a feeling I despise.

Jerking off with her panties wrapped around my dick last night—and once this morning—hasn't nearly taken the edge off like I'd hoped, and that's why I'm hitting the gym extra hard this morning.

My pager sounds, and I check the encrypted message from Fabio.

> Need a trainer ASAP. Can you get to AC?

I send him a reply.

> Heading your way now.

Taking a quick shower, I change into street clothes before locking up behind me. On the drive, I start a new podcast: the story of a serial killer who was caught because he was dumb enough to swipe a trophy from the victim's house. I angrily turn off the episode, as this topic hits a little too close to home. I *never* take a trophy, and why I chose to start with that damn rainbow charm, God only know.

Arriving at Sergio's restaurant—now Fabio's restaurant—I park in the back. Fabio greets me at the door, and we fist bump before he leads me through the kitchen to a private dining room.

I whistle, taking in the scene. Men are slumped over at the table—their bullet-riddled heads having landed in their plates of pasta, with their blood and innards painting the floor and wall behind them. "They must not have liked the dinner special."

"Send food back at your own risk." Fabio chuckles as he gears up. Grabbing a hacksaw, he begins sawing a torso in half.

I open my bag, putting on my protective gear and face shield before lending a hand. "Why does Sammy always get out of the grunt work?" I complain.

"Perks of being the underboss," Fabio tells me. "How's newlywed life treating you?" he asks, grabbing a severed head by the hair and tossing it into an industrial barrel.

"Can't complain," I say, keeping my marital problems to myself as I remove an arm with effort, tossing it in the barrel. "When you going to settle down?"

"You sound like my nonna," he gripes.

"She's probably just grateful you stopped doing those fake butter commercials," I taunt. "Any more romance book covers on the horizon, or have you put away the baby oil for good?"

He snorts a laugh. "After all these years, you'd think everyone would come up with new material."

"Why, when the old shtick is so good? Anything happening at Ace's Wild?"

"Things have been quiet. Too quiet," he tells me.

"We'll flush the fucker out eventually," I say.

"That we will," he agrees.

"You been keeping an eye on my cousin, Kat?"

"And if I say yes?"

"Then you're doing your job," I assure him. "What do you think?"

"The boss gets paid the big bucks to think; I just follow orders."

I snort. "That's the biggest fucking cop out if I've ever heard one."

He pauses before saying, "Kat appears clean, but then again, she knows we're watching. Time will tell."

"True enough." I can only pray time is on my cousin's side.

We turn our attention back to finishing the dismemberment job. Making sure all body parts are accounted for, I help Fabio load the barrels onto a refrigerated truck.

"Be right back," Fabio tells me. Returning with a bucket of blood, he dumps it over the already bloody floor. "Pig's blood; muddles any DNA testing."

"Nice touch," I tell him.

I help spray down the room with a pressure washer mixed with a bleach solution; a floor drain's hidden beneath a table for such an occasion. Helping him load the barrels, we peel off our gear and stick it in a trash bag, and Fabio tosses it on the back of the truck, closing the door. "Thanks, man," he tells me.

"Any time. You need help with the trash haul?" I ask as we return inside and wash up.

"Nah, I've got it from here."

"Alright. I'm gonna head back to Newark. Text me when your restaurant opens, and I'll bring my family." At some point, Lily's gotta forgive me. "Just don't tell me you're using any of Sergio's recipes."

"That fucker couldn't cook for shit." Fabio makes a face.

"I'll save a table for your family. Thanks, again." He fist-bumps me.

"Any time you need a hand. Unless it's to help you oil up for a photo shoot. You're on your own with that."

"Your jokes are nearly as bad as Sam's," he calls after me.

Hopping in my car, I notice a small drop of blood on my shirt, and so I drive over to Kat's place. Letting myself inside with the spare key, I shower and change into clean clothes before wiping everything down with bleach.

The sound of a key jiggling in the lock has me hustling to the front.

"Darius, what the hell?" Kat exclaims, closing the door behind her. "You're seriously trying to give me a heart attack!"

"I needed to use your bathroom."

"You smell like bleach." She wrinkles her nose. "*Again.*"

I shrug. "What's going on with the poker room?"

"Don't know," she tells me. "No one's approached me about dealing."

"Be more approachable," I advise her.

Kat narrows her eyes. "Trust me, I'm trying. I can assure you I don't want your terrifying boss and his goon breathing down my neck."

"Explain to me again how you found yourself in that basement," I say, taking a seat on the couch.

"My friend, Taylor, told me about an opportunity at a private party—"

"And you didn't think to ask whose party?" I interject.

"When you put it that way, it was really dumb on my part. But no, I didn't ask. I've been a dealer at parties in private settings before; I didn't think anything about it."

"Walk me through it. How did you know where to go?" I ask.

"I rode with Taylor," she answers, taking a seat across from me in a chair.

"How did Taylor know where to go?"

"She got the details about the party from Russell, the guy who runs Aces Wild Boxing Club," Kat answers. "She's the one who recommended I start working out there. I hope the family isn't terrorizing her; she doesn't have a clue about this world."

Not my problem. "So you rode with Taylor to Ace's Wild. Then what happened?"

"Russell introduced himself. He seemed like a nice guy," she adds. Yeah, real nice asshole who shot me. "Taylor and I stashed our bags in the locker room before Russell escorted us to the basement. I set up my blackjack table, and soon the party started. I dealt for a few hours, and the party wrapped up."

"Then what?" I press.

"Then that's it. Russell paid us, and we left. I swear to you, no one mentioned anything about John Davis," she implores.

I could show her John Davis' photo from the motel—see if she recognizes him—but I decide to hold that card. Whether she meant for it to happen or not, Kat's now a player in this game; the stakes life or death.

CHAPTER
Thirty~Nine

Lily

My lawyer and I pass through security, stepping inside the courtroom. I take a seat beside her, trying not to fidget.

The bailiff announces, "All rise," and we stand.

The judge enters and takes a seat behind the bench, instructing us to be seated. A few cases are called before it's our turn. "In the matter of The Estate of Thomas Harrison, Junior," the judge announces.

I walk up to the podium with my lawyer, who introduces me and gives a brief summary of the case. "There's no will, your honor," she informs the court, "and my client is requesting to be named personal administrator on behalf of the decedent's and her minor daughter, the sole heir."

"Judge, I'm Thomas Harrison. This is my son's case, and I have his will," a voice sounds from the back of the room. Craning my neck, I spot Harrison's dad holding a piece of paper. "My son left everything to me," he announces.

"Your honor, this is the first we're hearing about a purported will," my lawyer says.

"I'm going to call the next case; give you time to speak to

this gentleman," the judge tells my lawyer, and we step down.

I follow her out in the hall, and Thomas hands over a document. She reads it before passing it to me. It's a copy of a handwritten note with today's date file-stamped with the court.

> I, Thomas Harrison, Jr., being of legal age and sound mind, herein intend this handwritten note to be my Last Will and Testament. I leave the entirety of my estate to my father, Thomas Harrison. Iris Grant is not my daughter, and I do not wish to leave anything to the child, or her lying stripper mother. I hereby appoint my father, Thomas Harrison, Sr., as the Executor.

My entire body vibrating with anger, I shove the paper back at Thomas.

"Paternity can easily be established postmortem, Mr. Harrison," my lawyer tells him, and I fucking seethe. I never took his deadbeat son to court for child support, and this is the thanks I get? "And so you know, Mr. Harrison, New Jersey law doesn't allow for a parent to disinherit a minor child, regardless of what a will says," my lawyer informs him.

"That may be true, but she's not handling my son's estate." He sneers, pointing at me. "No way I'm letting a money-grubbing stripper be in charge. Over my dead body."

I know a man who could make that happen. And as soon as I catch that thought, I realize I've taken about three steps down from my ivory tower.

I arrive at the hole-in-the-wall diner Ethan suggested. Finding him seated at a booth, I make my way over. "Hey, Lily. You're dressed sharp," he tells me as I take a seat across from him.

"Thanks," I say, straightening my blouse. "I just got out of court."

A waitress appears, and I order a cup of coffee with cream and sugar.

"Coffee. Black," Ethan says politely.

The waitress leaves, and I comment, "Only a cop orders black coffee."

"Cop or serial killer," he jokes. "How did court go?"

"Not great." I explain what went down, pulling up a copy of the will on my phone and passing it to him. "Harrison pouring salt on the wound from the grave."

Ethan examines it before shaking his head adamantly. "No way that is Harrison's handwriting."

"You don't think?" I ask.

"I don't think; I *know*. I've looked over enough reports written by my partner. Former partner," he corrects himself somberly. "His old man forged this," he says, handing me back my phone.

"Honestly, if Harrison's dad needs the money that badly, maybe I should just let him have it and be done with him," I muse.

"You know Harrison hated his old man, and I can tell you with one hundred percent certainty he wouldn't want Thomas to get a penny," Ethan tells me.

I sigh. "The last time I went to Harrison's house, it was broken into. The television and gaming system were stolen. I'm not sure what else; I didn't hang around to look."

"Harrison's old man did it; I guarantee," he spits.

"That's what I'm thinking," I admit.

"Did you report the break-in?" he asks.

"No," I say, shaking my head. "I just had someone fix the door."

"Lily," he chastises. "You should have reported it."

"So the cops could do what?" I shrug. "Isn't it something like ninety percent of property crimes go unsolved?"

"Yes, but maybe this could have been one of the ten percent that does get solved," he points out. *Exactly*, and that's why I didn't report it. Doing so would only have raised too many questions about the missing safe.

Our coffees are brought over, and I take a sip, trying not to choke—it tastes like diesel fuel. "Look, this whole thing is really triggering for me." I change the subject, pouring another packet of sugar into my coffee and giving it a stir. "Harrison didn't give a shit about me or his daughter, and if he did write the will, it just demonstrates that fact. He knew damn well Iris was his child." Harrison took my virginity, for Chrissake.

"I don't believe he wrote it," Ethan presses.

"Then if his father forged it, I'm dealing with bullshit from a Thomas Harrison either way," I point out, rubbing my temples.

"Harrison was a great friend to me, but he did you and Iris dirty. There's no argument otherwise," he says. "If I'm ever as lucky to have what he did, no way would I act that like."

"Thanks, Ethan. Are you still seeing that EMT?"

"Nah, we ended things a while back. It's tough to find a woman who wants more than just the badge," he tells me, sipping his coffee.

"Funny, Harrison never found that to be a problem," I muse.

"Yeah, well, I'm not Harrison," he says.

"I know you're not," I tell him. "You're a good guy, Ethan."

"Thanks. Now, with that thought in mind, let's talk about this husband of yours. And no blowing me off this time." He points at me.

"There's nothing to talk about," I say, my hackles raising.

"Of course there is," he says incredulously. "Lily, you're in over your head. How can you not see that?"

Ethan has no clue how 'in over my head' I really am. "Look, I appreciate the concern. But I'm married to Darius, and that's it."

"I can help you get out, all you have to do is say the word," he leans forward, telling me quietly.

This poor, naive man. All he'd accomplish would be getting himself killed. Besides, even if I could get out, I'm not so sure I *want* out. "This is the last time we're going to discuss the topic of my marriage," I tell him firmly. "Darius is my husband. He runs a gym, and anything else is just noise I don't pay attention to."

"You need to fucking be paying attention!" he says, slamming his fist down, causing the coffee cups to rattle.

"If you're this invested in my life, then why didn't Harrison's cheating get you more riled up?" I say hotly. "Unless you knew the entire time and were covering for your partner."

He rubs the back of his neck with his hand. "Lily, I swear I didn't cover for him. Sure, I heard rumors, but who was I to get involved?"

"Who are you to get involved *now*?" I throw some bills down for my coffee and march out.

"Lily, wait," he says, chasing after me. "I'm sorry if I overstepped."

"Look, we're at an impasse here," I say bluntly.

He pauses, choosing his words carefully. "Maybe I am invested now because I feel guilty for not getting involved before, but I won't make that mistake again. Let me help you."

"That's the thing, Ethan. I don't need help," I tell him, crossing my arms.

"Alright," he says, holding up his hands in surrender. "Oh, I forgot the paperwork for Iris' benefits. Next time."

"Sure," I say dismissively, marching to my SUV.

Guilt gnaws at me as I unlock the door and slip behind the wheel. I shouldn't have come down so hard on Ethan; it's not his fault Harrison was a shit father and boyfriend.

Checking my phone, there's no new messages. I don't know where Darius is today or what he's doing. Not my concern, I remind myself as I pull out of the parking lot.

What is *concerning*, though, is the twinge of disappointment I felt because a certain deranged man with a big red dog tattoo wasn't lurking outside the coffee shop waiting on me.

CHAPTER
Forty

Lily

Dropping Iris off at summer camp, I drive to the address Nicky texted me. Pulling up to the gate, I press the button and announce myself, and the gate swings open. I continue down the driveway to a house that's nice, but modest in comparison to the mega-mansion Darius and I visited for Sunday dinner.

A burly older man is waiting to greet me. "Hello, Mrs. Angelos. Let me check your bag real quick," he says, and I hand it over. He runs a wand over it before handing it back.

The front door opens and Nicky appears. "Hey, Lily," she says, holding the collar of a menacing-looking Doberman.

I instinctively take a step back.

The man whistles, and the dog runs over and heels.

"Come in." Nicky smiles at me.

I gladly follow her inside to get away from the dog. "Thanks for the invite. Now that I've graduated, I've got all this time on my hands. It feels weird," I admit.

"Congrats, by the way."

"Thank you."

"I know what you mean. It's definitely an adjustment for me now that I'm finished with school." She leads me through the house, out back to a beautiful courtyard and pool. Motioning to a lounger, she pulls off her coverup and takes a seat, and I follow suit. "What would you like to drink? Water? Smoothie? Iced Coffee?"

"Iced coffee with cream and sugar would be amazing," I say, rifling through my bag until I find my sunglasses, putting them on.

She grabs her phone and sends a text. "Is your daughter out of school for the summer?"

I nod. "Yes, but she's enrolled in an art camp for the month."

"Nice," she comments. "You and Darius get some extra honeymoon time." I must have made a face, because she asks, "Everything alright?"

"Not exactly," I admit. "I'm just having trouble adjusting to his life. *This* life." I can't air all of Darius and my dirty laundry, but that's the gist of it.

"Understandable. But it's a package deal—the man and this life," Nicky warns me gently.

"Yes, and I get that." Darius told me *Diávolos* wasn't a nickname when we first spent time together in the VIP room. My husband is, if anything, a man of his word.

An older woman approaches us, carrying a large tray. "Iced coffee with cream and sugar," she says in an Italian accent, handing me a glass with a straw.

"Thank you." I smile, accepting the glass.

"Of course. Strawberry smoothie," the woman says, handing Nicky a glass.

"Thanks," Nicky says cooly.

"And I brought cornetto and biscotti, along with juice and

sparkling water," she announces, sitting down the tray. "Please let me know if I can get you anything else."

"That will be all." Nicky nods curtly, and the woman walks off.

Nicky turns to me. "I'm not usually such a bitch, but I haven't decided if I can trust Francesca or not," she admits. "Try a chocolate cornetto. They're my favorite." She hands me a small plate.

"Amazing," I say after taking a bite.

Valentina exits the pool house holding a binder, speaking animatedly with a man I recognize from the Parisi Construction crew.

"Valentina and Nonna are moving in," Nicky explains. "Romeo's building Nonna her own house on the property, and Valentina's taking the pool house."

"How do you feel about that?" I ask, unsure if Nicky wants her in-laws so close.

"It's one less worry for Romeo, so I'm fine with it. *Except* for Nonna's incessant campaign for a great grandchild," she says with a smile, shaking her head. "I've locked up my birth control like a maximum-security prison."

"Would she really mess with it?" Even though I have an IUD, I'm suddenly grateful my mother-in-law is on the other side of the world.

She shrugs. "Probably not, but just to play it safe."

Valentina and the man walk around the pool house, with Valentina pointing to various things. She hands him a binder before making her way to us.

"Hey, Lily," she greets me, pulling her coverup over her head and plopping down on the lounge chair beside me.

"Hey, Valentina," I say.

"The crew's going to start with the renovations tomorrow," Valentina tells Nicky. "But you can tell Romeo I'm not moving in until the pool house is finished, I don't care what he says."

Nicky shakes her head. "Nope. I'm not getting in the middle of that."

"Come on! He just told me I can't walk at graduation, and he's canceled my party—which is complete bullshit," she says crossly.

"Valentina, it's just not safe right now to have that much public exposure. Or to have so many people in and out of Antonio's house," Nicky says. I'm not sure why it's not safe, but I don't ask. "And your party isn't canceled; it's just been downsized and moved to Daniella's."

"So you're taking his side?" Valentina huffs.

Nicky holds up her hands. "I'm not taking sides." Her phone goes off, and she checks the message. "Sorry to bail, but I'm needed at the clinic."

"Darius?" I ask, my stomach dropping.

"Not Darius." She pats my arm.

"Sammy?" Valentina asks, crossing her fingers.

"Sorry, also not Sammy," Nicky tells Valentina. "Hopefully the next time you come over, we can hang out longer," she tells me apologetically.

"I look forward to it," I tell her.

"Lily and I will have plenty of fun while you're gone. Go do your fancy doctor stuff." Valentina tells her, and Nicky, nods, hurrying inside.

"Ugh, just when I thought my morning couldn't get any worse," Valentina exclaims. I follow her gaze to see Sammy approaching.

"Lily. Valentina." Eyeing her skimpy bikini, he orders, "Go change."

"Fuck you." She crosses her arms. "I'm an adult, and you aren't the boss of me."

"I'm the underboss, so yes, I am the boss of you," he corrects her.

She snorts. "How can anyone forget? You might as well

wear a name tag: 'Hello, my name is Underboss.' As if your ego wasn't big enough."

"Lots of big things about me," he says suggestively.

Valentina makes a gagging sound. "Too bad a brain isn't on that 'big' list."

"Excuse me," I interject. "Is there a restroom?" I don't particularly need to go that badly, but I want to escape the line of fire.

"Inside the pool house. First door on the right," Valentina tells me, before setting her sights back on Sam and unloading in Italian.

I hurry inside the pool house, finding the bathroom. After using the toilet, I wash my hands and open the door, squealing in surprise. Darius is blocking the exit, dressed in workout clothes and drenched in sweat, looking like he's about to eat me alive.

I stumble back, and he advances, closing and locking the door behind him. "I didn't know a little whore was going to be here this morning—flaunting what's mine for every motherfucker to see," he says in a menacing tone, his eyes having gone wild.

"Nicky invited me, I'm not flaunting anything, and I'm not yours," I remind him. "Not anymore."

He spins me so fast, I have to brace my hands on the sink. Smiling at me in the mirror, he snakes his hand down, lightly tweaking my pebbled nipple through my bikini top. Moving that hand lower, he cups my pussy over my bathing suit, rubbing his palm back and forth. "Shall we see what a terrible liar you are?" he whispers, lightly grazing the shell of my ear with his teeth as he slowly inches his fingers beneath my bikini bottom.

I could say red; I *should* say red, but instead, I find myself leaning back into his body as he pushes a finger inside me. Gasping, I grip the sink so hard my knuckles blanch as he fingers me roughly while using his thumb to stroke my clit.

"Drenched," he chides, his eyes locking with mine in the mirror. "When are you going to stop lying to yourself, little angel?"

With that, he removes his hand, unlocking the door and walking out without so much as a backward glance.

Arriving at my lawyer's office, we exchange pleasantries before getting down to business.

"Here are the options," she tells me. "One: contest the validity of the will. Two: don't contest the validity of the will, but contest the clause where Mr. Harrison cuts out your minor child. Three: do nothing, and Mr. Harrison's father will receive the entirety of the estate."

"I met with Harrison's best friend and partner on the force. He looked at the will, and didn't think it was Harrison's handwriting," I tell her.

"Would he be willing to testify as to that?" she asks, leaning back in her chair.

"Probably, but I'd have to ask him."

"Do that, and let me know. We have thirty days to contest, so we need to move pretty quickly," she warns me.

"Let me think on it," I say.

Exiting the law office, I stop short when I find pink lilies on the windshield of my SUV. I smile. So it was Darius who left lilies on my car back at the club, what feels like a lifetime ago. My smile turns into a frown when I recall how he wound me up in the bathroom this morning, only to walk out leaving me a needy, confused mess.

I snatch the flowers and march back inside the office. The receptionist having stepped away, I place the bouquet on her desk and hurry out. Maybe those flowers will make her day; that, or she'll think she has a stalker.

Well, she will just have to get her own stalker, because Darius is mine. Placing a hand on my head, I sigh. I really do need help.

CHAPTER
Forty-One

Lily

On our way to Valentina's graduation party, Darius and I drop Iris off at the park with Kat. "Have fun," I tell them.

"Fun is my middle name," Kat declares.

"I thought trouble is your middle name?" Iris asks, and I laugh softly, kissing the top of my daughter's head.

"No trouble," Darius tells Kat, giving her a look I can't interpret. There's an undercurrent of tension between the cousins, but I don't know why. "Rainbow goddess." Darius gives Iris a hug.

"Bye, sweetie. Love you," I call after her, but she's already taken off to the playset.

I climb into the passenger side of the SUV, and Darius closes my door for me. "How'd the meeting with your lawyer go?" he asks when he slides behind the wheel.

"I can't talk to you about this, not when I know—" *You killed Harrison.* Sighing, I say, "I don't know anything."

"Such a good girl," Darius praises, and I berate myself for the tingling between my thighs.

"I have three options." I explain what the lawyer relayed to me.

"Can I give you my two cents?" he asks.

Pursing my lips, I tell him, "I might accept a penny."

He grins, but his face turns serious. "Iris will always be financially secure in this family. She doesn't need anything from that piece of shit excuse for a father, or his piece of shit excuse for a father."

"Maybe I expected too much from Harrison, considering his role model." Thomas abandoned Harrison and his mom chasing tail. *Where does that sound familiar?*

"That's just an excuse for lack of personal responsibility," Darius admonishes. "My old man was an abusive piece of shit, but I get to choose who I am; not his sorry ass."

I look over to my husband. Really look at him. He's big, and scary when he wants to be, and could've easily gone down the same path as his father. Sure, the path Darius has chosen isn't one of sainthood, but he'd never hurt Iris—that much I know for a fact.

"I don't want your pity, little angel," he tells me, focusing his eyes back on the road.

"Not pity, but admiration," I correct him.

Darius snorts a laugh. "Please don't call me a good man."

"You told me you're many things, but good isn't one of them," I parrot back his words.

"Are you finally ready to believe me?" he asks quietly.

Fiddling with my mood ring, I'm not sure how to answer that, so I don't.

"Why do you never talk about your family?" He breaks the silence.

"My parents and I were estranged until recently," I admit. "After I got pregnant in high school, they didn't take the news well. *A teenage pregnancy*?" I say in a shocked tone. "Nothing could be more embarrassing in their world."

"I hope they realize how wrong they were," Darius comments.

I shrug. "I'm not holding my breath."

"Well, they were wrong," he says firmly. "Iris is an amazing kid, and she has an amazing mother."

"Darius," I start, swallowing the lump that's now in my throat.

"Yes, wifey?"

Before I can decide what I want to say, we pull into the parking lot of Daniella's.

"Are you sure we don't need a gift?" I ask when he helps me out of the SUV.

"Strict no-gift policy," he assures me.

Placing his hand on the small of my back, he leads me to the lobby, and we're greeted by several intimidating-looking Italian men. One searches my purse, while another holds the leash of a German Shepard. "Name and identification?" A third man with a clipboard asks.

"Darius and Lily Angelos," Darius answers, and the man checks us off the list after we flash our IDs.

I pass through a metal detector, and the guard returns my purse to me. Waiting for Darius to clear security, I shouldn't be surprised at this point, and yet I still have to stop myself from gawking when he pulls out a gun, a knife, a pair of brass knuckles, and some other weapon I can't identify.

He steps through the metal detector, retrieving his his arsenal and putting everything back into hidden position. "Ready?" he asks, and I just nod.

We enter the restaurant decorated to the nines with flowers, balloons, and framed senior pictures of a stunning Valentina. I spot Nicky with the graduate, and they wave me over. Before I can decide if I want him to or not, Darius kisses me quickly and saunters off.

I join the ladies, who greet me with a double cheek kiss. "Congratulations. This is so lovely," I tell Valentina.

"Thanks," she says, sounding dejected. "It's not an ideal setup, but I made it work given the unreasonable restrictions." Valentina cuts her eyes to Nicky, who holds up her hands in surrender. "Come on, let's take a picture in the photo booth." Valentina grabs our hands, pulling us along.

I glance over my shoulder to find a young Italian guy following us. "The lurker is Enzo," Nicky says, as if that explains everything. "Enzo, this is Lily, Darius' wife."

"Nice to meet you," he tells me. "And congratulations."

"Thank you."

"At least Sammy is too 'busy' to be all up in my business. The one good thing about his promotion," Valentina comments.

"I'm never too busy to be all up in *principessa's* business," Sammy says, now beside us.

"How nice for me," Valentina says dryly. She ushers us inside the photo booth, closing the curtain in Sammy's face. Piling in between us, she makes silly and mock sexy faces for the camera, and Nicky and I laugh.

The machine spits out a strip of pictures, and Valentina grabs them. We walk out, and she hangs the photo strip on a large magnetic board next to the booth. "I expect couples' pics," she declares. "At least try to get Romeo to smile." she points at Nicky.

Nicky raises an eyebrow. "I've told you before—I'm not a miracle worker."

"Sammy, I guess since you're missing a plus one, take a picture with your right hand," Valentina tells him sweetly, and Nicky snorts a laugh.

He smirks, unfazed. "I'm ambidextrous."

"Gross." Valentina makes a face before scanning the crowd, her eyes landing on a diminutive man with a clipboard and walkie talkie strapped to his belt. "I need to check on the cake. Please help yourself to food and drink while I'm gone," she says, excusing herself.

"Stop harassing Valentina," Nicky warns Sammy.

"Boss told me to keep an eye on her. Last time I checked, you're not the boss." He smirks before walking off.

"I would say he's a nice guy once you get to know him, but I'm not a bald-face liar," Nicky tells me once Sammy's gone.

"Ladies and gentlemen, can I have everyone's attention?" A man with a microphone appears, and a hush falls over the crowd. "Let's give it up for our graduate, Valentina!" Music plays over the loudspeakers, and Valentina appears from a side door, waving and smiling.

Everyone applauds, and she works her way through the crowd, stopping to speak to each and every guest. "Girl knows how to work a room," Nicky comments.

"Absolutely," I agree.

The overhead lights dim, and a man rolls out a three-tier cake topped with flickering sparklers. Valentina walks over and smiles as everyone *oohs* and *aahs*.

Suddenly, there's a loud *pop*. The cake explodes, covering Valentina from head to toe in icing before Sam tackles her to the ground.

That's all I can see, as I'm now in Darius' arms on the floor, with his solid body on top of me. Nicky's beside us, with Romeo shielding her.

"Kill that motherfucker!" Valentina shrieks, wiping cake from her eyes as she shoves Sam off her.

"Language," Nonna shouts from the back of the room.

CHAPTER
Forty~Two

Darius

Having received a good ass chewing from Romeo last night, I decide a more direct approach is needed. The carrot didn't work, and now it's time for the stick.

Slipping on my brass knuckles, I punch Big Benny over and over in his disgusting stomach while he's bound to his office chair. "You fucking with me?" I menace.

"No!" he wheezes, a mixture of blood and drool spraying from his mouth.

I pummel his jiggly midsection like a feedbag. "You working with John Davis?"

"No!"

I deliver a nice jab to the liver area, and he pukes. Looking down at my white trainers now spattered with brown vomit, I growl.

"The man hasn't been back, I swear on my life!" Big Benny wheezes.

"I find out you're lying, and it will be your life. Except I won't kill you quickly. No, Big Benny, a slow and torturous death awaits you, my friend. Did you know I like to eat the organs of my victims while they watch?" I lie, using the disgusting rumor about *Diávolos* to my advantage.

He pisses his pants, and now I have vomit *and* urine on my favorite shoes; he shits on me, I don't give a fuck how potentially valuable he is, I'm gutting him right here.

"But instead of me partaking on your flesh, I'm going to force-feed you," I continue. "First your kidney; you've got two, so your body will putter sadly along. Next your left lung, followed by your spleen. Did you know, Big Benny, you can survive with quite a few organs missing. You want to hear the record number of organs removed before the poor fuck finally keeled over on me?"

He whimpers.

"Eight, but that's counting the thyroid. I'm not sure if a thyroid is considered an organ." I make a mental note to ask Nicky the next time I see her.

"Please, I swear I'll help you get your guy," he begs.

"One more chance," I tell him, balancing on one leg as I wipe my left shoe on his shirt, followed by my right. I stroll behind him, cutting him loose. "Don't make me regret this."

Walking out, I grab my bag from the trunk, changing into sandals before sticking the now ruined shoes and socks into a trash bag. Everything back in the trunk, I drive over to my gym and shower quickly before driving to school.

I take a seat on the bench, and Lily approaches, surprised to see me. "I thought you knew I was picking up Iris," she tells me with a raised eyebrow.

Before I can answer, Lily's buzzed inside; she returns a few minutes later with Iris holding her evil eye charm. Opening my arms, she comes running over to me with a big smile. I pick her up and toss her in the air before placing her on her feet. "Rainbow goddess. How about me, you, and your beautiful mama go to the park and get ice cream?"

"Yes!" She jumps up and down.

"Follow me there?" I ask Lily, who's much less enthused, but nods. I'll take it.

"Hey, Lily." Becca and her daughter walk out. I'm sure the woman's about to say something obnoxious, so I catch her line of sight and quietly snap my teeth.

"Uh, we need to go. See you later," she says, hurrying her daughter along.

Lily side-eyes me, but doesn't say anything.

We arrive at the park, and I walk over to the ice cream truck while Iris makes a beeline to the playground. "Iris, wait! Let me hold your lucky charm while you play," Lily calls, and Iris runs back to her mom and hands it over, before taking off again.

Returning a few minutes later with the ice cream, I give Lily her pistachio cone. She smiles brightly, and I'll never get tired of that sight. "Thank you."

"Of course. Iris," I call, and she makes a mad dash to me.

"Thank you," she chirps, taking her chocolate cone and getting to work, as the ice cream's already starting to melt.

Lily holds out her cone to offer me a lick, and as I go in for one, she smashes it in my face. Iris squeals, and Lily giggles as she backs away from me.

"You're going to pay for that, wifey," I tell her playfully, using the bottom of my shirt to wipe off my face.

"No!" Lily bemoans, placing a hand on her head, but she laughs.

Iris runs out of steam, and I take the rest of her cone and toss it in the trash. Now good and sugared up, she hurries to the playground. "Wait, we need to wipe your sticky hands!" Lily calls after her.

"Nah, just gives her better grip on the ladder," I assure Lily.

Iris waves at us at the top of the slide, and we wave back as she wizzes down. She sprints back to the ladder to do it again.

Lily finishes her cone and turns to me. "Those times Iris and I ran into you here at the park, was it a coincidence, or were you following me?"

"Following you," I answer honestly.

She looks at me thoughtfully. "Professor Miller's accident. You were gone for a while at the party, and then—"

"I shoved the asshole down the stairs." I go ahead and come clean. "Heard him threaten you in his office, and that does not, nor will it *ever* fly with me for someone to treat you like that."

"And Becca's mom?"

"Threatened her husband, and I'd do it again in a heartbeat, because no one is going to mess with Iris."

I expect her to run away after those admissions, but she surprises me by grabbing my stained shirt and pulling me close. Standing on her tiptoes, she presses her sweet lips to mine. "I'm ready to step down from my ivory tower," she tells me quietly.

"For good," I demand. "If you give yourself to me, there's no going back this time." What's left of my hardened heart couldn't survive it.

"For good," she promises.

"Then let's go home," I say, my voice lowering as I admire my little angel, thinking of all the filthy things I'm going to do to her.

Her cheeks shade a lovely color of pink, and I cup them before leaning in and getting one more taste of heaven, or as close to heaven as a man like me will ever get.

CHAPTER
Forty-Three

Lily

Darius and I haven't had a chance to slip away to the bedroom since we got home, and the anticipation is killing me. Finally, evening rolls around. "Come on, let's get ready for bed," I tell Iris a little too eagerly.

"I don't want to go to bed." Iris pouts.

"If you get ready for bed for your mama, I'll read you a book," Darius offers.

"Two books," Iris counters.

He chuckles. "You gonna be the family lawyer?"

"No!" I say in a panic, and Iris' eyes go wide with confusion. "I mean, of course you can be whatever you want, sweetie, when you grow up." *As long as the mob isn't involved.* "I'm just not ready for you to grow up so fast," I tell her, kissing the top of her head.

"I'm going to be a vetty-narian," she tries to say. "So I can play with cats all the time!"

"Sounds like a good plan." Darius smiles.

"You'll make an amazing veterinarian," I agree. "Now, let's get ready for bed."

We go through Iris' bedtime routine, and I hand her over to Darius for story time. "Night, sweetie. Love you."

"Love you," Iris says, hugging me.

"Be naked for me," Darius whispers in my ear before beginning a story about a dragon.

Hurrying to the bathroom, I use the toilet, take off my makeup, and brush my teeth in world-record speed. Stripping out of my clothes and climbing on top of the covers, I smile, strumming my fingers over my clit.

"Did I give the little whore permission to touch herself?" Darius chides, closing and locking the door behind him.

I drop my hand, but shake my head. "I don't want to be *Diávolos'* whore; right now, I want to be my husband's queen."

His eyes soften. "Whatever my queen wants, always." He strips out of his shirt, and next to come off are his shorts and boxers, giving me the best show in town.

Speaking of shows, that reminds me: "I still owe you a dance," I tell him as he stalks over to me.

He smiles. "Trust me, I haven't forgotten. But we have a lifetime for me to collect." He takes a seat on the bed with his legs extended and pulls me into his lap.

Now straddling him, I cup his cheeks and tell him everything he needs to hear—because it's all true. "Darius, you are so smart." He goes to interrupt, but I press my finger to his lips. "Don't make me spank your ass."

He chuckles, lapping with his tongue the wet from where I was just playing with myself. A woman on a mission, I'm not going to let myself be distracted. "You are so smart, and kind, and take such good care of me and Iris, and I'm so lucky to call you my husband." He stills his movement, and I continue, "And you're wrong: you are a good man. Be as bad as you need to out there, as long as my Darius always comes back to me," I tell him, placing my other hand over his heart. "And my *Diávolos* too, because sometimes I need to be his little whore," I whisper the last part. "I love you. *All* of you. The good. The bad. And everything in between."

Emotions swirl in his dark eyes, and I move my lips to his —baring my heart to this man in a single kiss. Tears spring from my eyes—or maybe those are from his eyes—as we kiss slowly, like we're trying to freeze this beautiful moment in time.

Eventually, I break the kiss and wrap my hand around his length. I raise my hips, and the head of his dick nudges my entrance. My body tenses, not quite sure if he's going to fit, even though I know he will. I take deep breath, impaling myself on his dick, and we both cry out.

He wraps his arms around me and holds me close as I lay my head on his chest. His hard dick is still inside me, but we stay like we are; not moving, just being connected. "Darius," I finally say, looking into his eyes.

"Yes, wifey?"

"I want you to hogtie me," I whisper.

His lips curl back into a cruel smile, and my pussy absolutely strangles his dick. "I knew this good girl act wouldn't last. Such a filthy whore."

Mmm, and there's my Diávolos.

Grabbing my hips, he lifts me off his dick and tosses me to the bed. "Don't move," he menaces, getting up and stalking to the closet.

I'm vibrating with anticipation when he returns with rope in hand. He's got that crazy *Diávolos* look, making it far too easy for me to slip into my role in this little game. "Please, no!" A heady combination of fear and desire courses through my veins as I scramble to the other side of the bed.

He laughs darkly, grabbing me by my ankle; my upper half crumbles to the bed as he drags me back to his side with ease. Now on my stomach, he holds me down as he spreads my legs. "Behave, or I'll blindfold and gag you," he threatens, his teeth scrapping the slope of my ass cheek.

"I'll behave," I promise. My body stills, even though a tiny part of me is curious to know what it would be like. Unable to see. Unable to speak. Completely at *Diávolos'* mercy.

"There's my good little slut." Grabbing my arms from behind, he ties my wrists together. Admiring his work, he hums. "Fuck if that isn't a sight." He loops the rope around my ankles until they're bound together, before pushing my legs up to where they're bent at the knees at ninety degrees—my feet in the air. With my body contorted in this position, he secures the binding around my ankles to the binding around my wrists, leaving enough slack to where I'm comfortable; as comfortable as one can be while hogtied, I suppose.

I try to tug against the restraints, causing myself to bounce on the bed; that's about as much movement as I can manage in this position. "That's right. You're *Diávolos'* plaything now." He laughs darkly, trailing his finger along my ass crack. "And I don't plan on letting you go. *Ever.*"

Sounds like heaven to me.

Darius shifts to where he's on his knees towering over me, and I have to tilt my neck up at an awkward angle to see him. Fuck, he looks so dangerous I might come from the sight of him alone. He was right: I just need to think about my bad husband to get off.

He smiles as if he can read my thoughts, smushing my cheeks together with his hand; the action causes my lips to pucker. "Look at this pouty mouth, begging for my dick." He tightens his hold as he grips his dick with his other hand, leaning in and painting my lips with his precum.

I whimper, and he squeezes my cheeks harder, bordering on painful.

"Open," Darius commands, and I open my mouth. He gathers his excitement from my lips with his index finger, shoving it inside my mouth. I take it upon myself to run my tongue over the pad of his finger, lapping the salty taste of him.

Nostrils flaring, he jerks his digit out of my mouth. "You like tempting the devil, don't you, little angel?"

"No," I lie.

"*No*?" Darius mocks. My pink vibrator is now in his hand, and he turns it on; a *whirling* sound fills the room. "You didn't tease me with this?" He slides the wand underneath my pelvis, shifting it until he finds my clit.

"I didn't know you were watching me." I moan.

"What would you have done had you known?" He muses. "Would you have gotten up and fixed your blinds, or would you have spread that filthy pussy open wider for me to see?"

Panting, I arch my ass in the air, trying to move away from the vibrator; the speed combined with his dirty words feels too intense.

He notices, and gives my ass a firm smack. "Lay down."

Lowering my pelvis back to the bed, I whimper as he presses a button on my vibrator, turning up to high speed. "Fuck!" I cry out. "It's too much!"

He *tsks*. "You should have thought about that before taunting *Diávolos* with this pussy. Bad girls get punished."

My body jerks and writhes; the sounds of the vibrator and my mewls of pleasure bordering on pain fill the room. I'm teetering on the edge when suddenly, the vibration stops. I cry out in surprise when I'm jerked to my left side, my right leg suspended in the air due to the restraints.

"Θέλω να σε σκίσω," Darius menaces. He shifts closer to me on his knees, holding onto my bent leg. Growling, he squeezes my leg so hard I'm sure it'll leave a bruise as thrusts his dick inside my pussy.

"Oh, fuck!" I cry at the huge intrusion at this unusual angle.

"Με κάνεις να χάσω τον έλεγχο." He grits his teeth, keeping himself perfectly still inside me with a pained expression. "You make me loose control."

I'm the one tied up, but I feel more powerful than maybe

I've ever felt my entire life. "Good." I hum. "Show me what *Diávolos* looks like when he loses control for his little whore."

"Be careful what you wish for," he threatens, and begins to pound into me ruthlessly.

I'm immobilized, and all I can do is take everything he's giving me. But I still want more. "Is that all *Diávolos* has got?" I goad him.

He laughs darkly, pulling out his dick coated with our combined desire, and shifts his body. Before I know what's happening, he jerks my jaw open—shoving his dick inside my mouth.

I gag, and he laughs again. "In my fucking dreams, eh wifey? And yet here we are, my little slut choking on my dick." He brutally fucks my mouth like I really am his little slut, and tears well in my eyes when he shoves himself further down my throat.

That *whirling* sound is back, and I jerk when he places the vibrator on my clit as he violently fucks my mouth.

This is hell.

This is heaven.

This is—

"Perfection," he answers my unspoken thought. "Look at the little angel, deep throating the devil."

Unable to scream. Unable to move. Unable to do anything expect fall apart as my orgasm rocks through my body like a tidal wave, my throat constricting around his dick.

"*Με τρελαίνεις!*" He growls, throwing his head back as he thrusts his hips faster and faster. "Fuck, Lily!" Hot cum shoots down my throat in violent spurts.

My eyes go wide in alarm; I try not to choke while still reeling from my own explosive orgasm. Pulling out quickly, he closes my mouth with his hand, forcing me to swallow. "Deep breaths through your nose," he reminds me, now looking and sounding more like my sweet and caring husband than *Diávolos*.

I swallow his cum while taking deep belly breaths.

He hops up out of view, returning with a knife. I'm too far spent to be afraid, but I soon realize why he's holding a weapon when my arms and legs are cut free. I roll over onto my back, and Darius gently rubs my ankles, and then my wrists. "Good, wifey?"

"Mmm. I might have died, I'm not sure," I whisper with a scratchy voice.

"I'll have to add a new tooth tattoo after that," Darius murmurs his agreement. He cradles my face like I'm the most precious thing in the world, gently pressing his lips to mine. "But it was worth tempting the Fates," he declares.

CHAPTER
Forty~Four

Darius

I follow Lily to her lawyer's office—if anything, my obsession with my little angel is even stronger now I know without a doubt she's mine. Parking across the street, I watch at a safe distance as to not be spotted.

Lily's been in the office for about twenty minutes, when a man slinks from the alley and sneaks over to her SUV. He places a bouquet of pink lilies on the windshield before sprinting away.

Well. Well. Well. Would you look who just moved to the top of my hit list?

Round one of tying up loose ends: I'm at the Jersey Motor Inn. This isn't about John Davis, but a different piece of shit excuse for a human.

A street-level dealer—can't remember his name—exits the room, and I wait. Not long after, a hooker enters. She leaves approximately eleven minutes later. My God, what pathetic bedroom prowess these Harrison men have.

I let an additional hour pass before sneaking to the door and using the key Big Benny was so nice enough to let me borrow. Entering the room, Thomas Harrison is passed out in his tighty-whities—a line of white powder and a credit card on a small mirror positioned next to him on the bed.

Grabbing my supplies out of my bag, I slip on gloves before tying off his left arm with a tourniquet. Damn, his veins are torn up all to hell with track marks. Depressing the syringe of a lethal dose of fentanyl, I poke around until I'm able to stick his vein and press the plunger.

Leaving the needle in his arm, I hurry out of the room and close the door behind me. Told the fucker when I confronted him at Tommy's house if he harassed Lily again, it'd be his last mistake. Don't believe *Diávolos*? Hide and fucking watch.

Lily

Having left my lawyer's office, I've decided to fight Thomas about the will. Despite Harrison's shortcomings, I really don't believe he would have chosen his estranged dad over his daughter. Besides, now that I've found my backbone, it's hard to ignore.

Sliding behind the wheel of my SUV, I grab my phone and text Ethan.

> Do you have a few minutes to chat about Harrison's estate?

He doesn't respond right away, and so I drop my phone in my purse and continue checking items off my to-do list while Kat's watching Iris.

Arriving at campus, I walk over to the financial services office. Canceling my payment plan, I go ahead and pay for my upcoming grad school tuition using a pre-paid credit card I loaded with some of Harrison's cash. Now *my* cash.

Who the hell said my wings had to be clean, anyway?

Next stop is the salon for some much-needed maintenance. After getting my hair done, I take a seat in the pedicure chair, texting Darius what he wants for dinner, but he doesn't reply. Trying to shake away the unease—it's his job, and he has twenty-eight teeth left, I remind myself—I toss my purse in my bag, relaxing into my foot massage.

Finishing up at the salon, I step out into the parking lot, riffling through my purse for my keys while trying not to mess up my nails. Iris' evil eye charm I took from her yesterday at the park gets jostled in the process; falling onto the pavement, it cracks in half.

"No!" Picking up the jagged pieces, I stick them in my pocket. Maybe I can glue it back together. Or better yet, maybe Darius can find her a replacement charm. The man calls me an angel, but the same could be said for him. Well, more like a dark angel, but that's even better.

Pulling out of the parking lot, I don't get very far, as the back end of my vehicle starts to make a weird *thumping* sound. I pull over and inspect the rear right tire—flat. I'm not in the safest neighborhood, so I lock my doors and call Darius, but it goes to automated voicemail.

A police cruiser pulls up behind me, and I sigh a breath of relief when I see Ethan approaching. "Need a hand?" he asks when I step out of my vehicle.

"Thanks. This is so embarrassing to admit, but I don't know how to change a tire."

"A lot of people don't know how, so don't feel too bad," he assures me.

"Perfect timing anyway, because I needed to talk to you about Harrison's estate," I tell him.

"No problem. First, let me grab my tools from my trunk. Hey, walk with me, and I'll give you the paperwork for Iris while I'm thinking about it."

"Sure," I say, following him.

He opens the trunk and calls me over. "Here's the paper-work." I join him behind his vehicle, something hard now pressed against my side. It takes my shocked brain a moment to catch up—it's a gun.

"Get in," he menaces, grabbing my wrist with his free hand.

"Ethan, what the hell are you doing?" Struggling against him, I look around for help, but the street's deserted. He slaps something heavy on one of my wrists—handcuffs—as I buck like a wild animal. He easily outmuscles me, cuffing my other hand before picking me up and tossing me in the trunk.

"Ethan, no!" I shout, kicking wildly, but my legs aren't long enough to do a damn thing; the trunk closes with a *thunk*.

The police cruiser starts moving, and I kick with all my might—trying to bust out the taillight from the inside with the hopes a driver behind us notices. I pray it's a cop. Unless they're all dirty like Harrison and Ethan?

Fuck, where's a mobster when I need one?

Darius, earlier that day…

And now to mark off the second name from my hit list. So thoughtful of Ethan to leave lilies on my wife's SUV. I'll make sure to return the favor on his headstone.

Driving over to his house, I park two streets over and make my way on foot. Having already staked out the property, I easily pick the basement lock—I have no idea why these cops are so lax with home security.

Screwing on my silencer, I go to walk upstairs but stop dead in my tracks. A rage like I've never felt before fills my veins when I see it. It's a stalker shrine—a small table with pictures of an unsuspecting Lily in various states of undress. Stepping closer, I examine the pictures—these were taken from her bedroom at her old house. *I fucking told her it wasn't safe.* Also on the table is a hair brush with light blonde strands, and a black thong with what looks to be dried cum; that fucker beats his dick with my wife's panties.

There's a television next to the table, and my hand shakes with fury as I grab the remote and hit power. It's a paused video taken from inside Lily's bedroom; Ethan was the one who broke the lock on her window, setting up a hidden camera. I should have went with my instincts and gouged the fuckers eyes out with the bubble wand.

Gritting my teeth, I hit play and watch an unsuspecting Lily strip out of her clothes and stroll to her bathroom naked. I laugh; it sounds inhuman to my own damn ears. Oh, do I have plans for Ethan.

Turning off the television, the tiniest of sounds has me spinning around, but I'm too late. A baseball bat connects with my skull with a loud *whack,* and I crumble to the floor.

CHAPTER
Forty-Five

Lily

Ethan's cruiser comes to a stop, and the trunk opens. Before my eyes can adjust to the harsh overhead light, he yanks me out. I thrash violently against his hold. "Let me go!" I shout.

He drags me through the garage to the kitchen, and my foot catches a chair leg to stop our forward progression. "Help!" I scream at the top of my lugs.

Ethan curses, grabbing me and flinging me over his shoulder. "Lily, be quiet."

I only get louder, screaming and trying to kick him in the crotch, but I can't connect at this angle. He carries me down a set of stairs to the basement.

"Oh my God," I gasp when he flips on the light. There's a table with pictures of me—some are of me naked in my bedroom—along with my hairbrush and panties I didn't even realize were missing.

"We're going to be together real soon," Ethan says, dropping me on a couch. "I just need you to tell me where the money is."

"What the hell do you think you're doing?" With some

effort, I hoist my body upright to seated position. My wrists aching, I test out the restraints, quickly learning there's no getting out of these handcuffs without the key. "When Darius finds out what you've done, he's going to kill you," I warn him. "Let me go before he finds out."

He grabs me by the cheeks, squeezing hard. "I don't ever want his name on your lips again."

"You're hurting me," I manage.

"I'm going to save you, but you have to tell me where the money is." He stands and begins pacing. "We need it to start our new life together."

"You broke the lock on my window," I say, bile rising in my throat as I glance back over to the pictures of me.

"Do you know how fucking angry it made me seeing you with him at Glitter?" He bellows, and I shirk back. It's like the nice guy facade has fallen away, and I see Ethan for what he really is—a psycho. "Shaking your tits and ass in *Diávolos'* face!" He thunders, the vein in his neck bulging.

"Ethan—"

He takes a deep breath and closes his eyes, trying to compose himself. "Look, I know when you went back to the VIP room with *Diávolos*, he forced you to marry him. That's why I'm willing to forgive you for it. Just tell me where the money is."

"What money?"

"Lily, don't play dumb," he chides. "Harrison was acting shifty as hell, and so one night, I followed him to see what he was up to. And guess who gave my partner a big ole stack of cash in a back alley? *Darius Angelos.*" He watches my reaction, and when I don't give him one, he flashes a patronizing smile. "What? No more 'my husband works at a gym' bullshit?"

"My husband does work at a gym," I tell him, squaring my jaw.

The back of his hand connects with my cheek, and my upper half tumbles to the couch. "I don't want to hurt you, baby, so don't make me," he warns, jerking me back up to seated position, my cheek throbbing. "I had to wait until the crime scene was cleared before I could search for the money. Found the safe in Harrison's closet, but couldn't get the fucking thing open. Imagine my surprise when I went to the trouble of staging a break-in and moving that heavy thing, only to get it home, cut it open, and realize you beat me to it." He shakes his head in disbelief.

"You blamed Harrison's dad for breaking into the house," I say, stunned.

He shrugs. "I'm not mad at you for taking the money. Actually, I'm impressed. I didn't think you had it in you." He chuckles. "So tell me where you hid the money. You've gotten yourself in some deep shit marrying into the mob, and we need the cash to skip town."

Thump. Thump. Thump. The sound's coming from the opposite side of the basement.

Ethan rolls his eyes. "Banging his head against the door; killing whatever brain cell the dumb fuck has left." He strolls to a closet door and opens it, and terror fills me veins when I spot Darius. He's hogtied, with his mouth duct taped, and a bulging knot on his forehead. My husband's eyes find mine, and he begins thrashing wildly.

"Did you want to join the party? Come on out, big guy," Ethan says, dragging Darius out with effort. "You'll never take Lily away from me again," he says with a crazed smile, pulling a gun from his holster.

"Ethan, wait!" I say, jumping up and getting in his face; shielding Darius. "You're right: *Diávolos* did force me to marry him. He threatened me if I ever told anyone, and I didn't want to drag you into the middle of it," I explain. "I'm sorry I hurt you. It's clear to me now how much you really love me."

"About damn time," Ethan says like a petulant child.

"I'm sorry. I just needed time to make an escape plan.

That's why I took the money," I explain. "Now, I don't have to worry about escaping *Diávolos*; you're here to save me, and we can finally be together."

"Yeah?" He says, licking his lips.

"Yeah." I give him a shy smile. "I'm so sorry you had to watch me dance for him. Please, let me make it up to you now. Uncuff me and let me dance for you. He can watch and know what it feels like. After, you can handle him however you think best, and we'll go get the money."

Ethan cocks his head, considering, and I try to keep my heart from beating out of my chest. "Baby, I like that idea," he finally says, and I flash him a smile as he holsters his gun. Reaching in his pocket, he grabs the key to my cuffs. He leans in and kisses me, his disgusting tongue invading my mouth.

Don't puke. Don't puke. Don't puke. I repeat it like a mantra, trying to kiss him back convincingly, all the while Darius' muffled cries are ringing in my ears.

"Fuck, baby. You don't know how long I've waited for that." Ethan leans his forehead against mine, and I force myself not to recoil.

"Uncuff me, and let me show you it was worth the wait," I tell him with a flirty smile. My Pearl smile.

"Like the sound of that," he says in a husky tone, unlocking my left cuff, then my right. "Where do you want me?"

"Sit over here on the couch." I smile brightly when he takes a seat. "Do you have any music?"

He pulls out his phone. Scrolling, he hits play on a club song. "How's that?"

"Perfect," I tell him.

Darius' muffled cries have become louder, and I desperately want to comfort him, but I don't dare make eye contact.

Swaying my hips side to side, I promised my husband a dance, but this isn't what either of us had in mind.

Darius

Have I blacked out? Is a hallucination?

Lily smiles at Ethan as she moves her hips sensually, running her hands through her blonde waves. She turns around shakes her ass for a few beats before bending her upper half over, her dress now hiked up to where there's a peek of her ass in a thong.

Mamá warned me Lily was going to be the death of me. She wasn't wrong—because watching my wife dance for another man is killing me.

Or maybe I'm already dead?

She raises her arms and turns around, lifting the hem of her dress and tossing it on the floor.

"Fuck, yes," Ethan says, rubbing his dick through his shorts at the sight of Lily in her sexy black bra and thong. "Come here and dance on my lap," he says, motioning her over with the crook of his finger.

"My pleasure," Lily purrs.

That settles it. I'm dead, and this is hell.

Lily

I shake my hips over to Ethan. Turning around and bouncing my ass for him, I lift one leg, then the other, straddling him. He places both hands on my ass cheeks and massages them, making disgusting grunting sounds. "Damn, baby. You are so sexy. Bounce that ass on my lap."

"Like this" I say, grinding my ass on his erection, and he groans.

Ethan's distracted, and now's my chance. Running my hands over my tits, I reach into my bra cups and pull out the broken shards of Iris' lucky charm I stashed there just moments ago when I was dancing with my back to him. Wrapping my right hand around a jagged piece, I bring it down with all my might to Ethan's right inner thigh.

"Fuck!" he screams.

It's my turn to grunt as I push the glass chard deeper and twist—blood squirting violently from his thigh.

"You cunt!" He knocks my hand away, trying to pull out the glass imbedded deep in his thigh.

I bring the other half of the charm down—stabbing the vein of his left inner thigh.

He screams, shoving me off his lap into the floor, but not before I grab the gun holstered on his hip. Raising to my knees, I point it at him.

"Lily, no!" Ethan lunges for me.

I don't hesitate, pulling the trigger. The kickback nearly knocks me over, but I keep firing until there's nothing but empty clicks.

CHAPTER
Forty-Six

Darius

Lily's frozen in shock. I try to shout to get her attention, thrashing my body on the ground until finally she notices me. Her hand shaking, she drops the gun and stands, running over. Squatting down, she rips off the duck tape from my mouth—looking like a deer in the headlights.

"Little angel, you did so good," I praise her. "Can you find something to cut these zip ties? Go upstairs and bring me a knife or shears from the kitchen."

She looks back over to Ethan's slumped body; part of his skull's missing, and blood and brain spatter covers the back of the couch.

Oh no.

Turning a violent shade of green, she doubles over and vomits.

"Lily, it's alright." I try to soothe her sobs, but I can't fucking comfort her like she needs right now, not with me tied up. "Wifey, look at me."

"I can't," she says, tears streaming down her face as she clutches her stomach.

"Yes, you can. Be a good girl and look at me," I tell her in an authoritative voice, and her eyes meet mine; so much pain and fear in them, it fucking kills me all over again. "Walk upstairs. Find a knife or pair of scissors. Bring them back down to me. Go now. We've got to get home to Iris," I remind her.

She nods resolutely, running up the steps.

Glancing over to Ethan's slumped remains, the motherfucker better be grateful I didn't get my hands on him.

It feels like an eternity, but I hear footsteps, and Lily appears with a pair of kitchen shears. Her hands are shaking so badly, I'm afraid she'll accidentally cut me, and that would only upset her more. "Good girl. Take a deep breath for me. Hold it for a count of three, and let it out," I coach her.

She does so while I count, and I tell her, "That's it. Now, cut the ties."

Craning my neck, and I watch her trembling hand use the shears to cut the zip ties cut, and my hands and legs are free.

Pulling myself off the floor, I hold out my hand to take the sheers from her, because she's still got a death grip on them.

Looking down to her hands coated in blood from where she stabbed Ethan in both his femoral arteries—fucker would've died from that alone, even if she hadn't shot him point-blank in the head—she drops the shears. "There's blood on my hands," Lily whispers.

"Hey, it's alright," I tell her, taking her hands and wiping them on my own. I'm not sure if she's talking physically or metaphorically, but I tell her, "See, blood's on my hands, not yours. Never yours, little angel." I wrap my arms around her trembling body as she sobs. "Just let it all out. Give it to me; I'll carry all the darkness and pain for the both of us. Always," I assure her, holding her tight until she's cried herself out.

Scooping Lily up in my arms, she burrows her head in my

chest as I carry her upstairs and away from the scene. Finding my phones on the table, I call Sammy.

"Need help ASAP moving equipment for my home gym." Meaning this is a personal situation, not family business. I give him the address.

"If I didn't know any better, I'd say you're asking me for a favor," Sammy says with laughter in his voice.

I grit my teeth. "Yes, I'm asking for a favor."

He chuckles. "Be there in about twenty."

"I'm going to drop Lily off at the clinic first. I'll meet you back at the house. Tell Nicky this is an emergency."

"Will do," he says, hanging up.

Lily

I don't remember the drive, but somehow we've arrived at a warehouse, and Darius carries me inside what looks like a hospital room. I'm greeted by Nicky, with Enzo standing in the corner. He takes one look at me and turns white as a sheet.

Do I look that bad? I glance down to my blood-spattered body. Yes, yes I do.

"Lily, I don't want to leave you, but I have to go clean things up," Darius tells me, kissing the top of my head.

Clean things up—meaning clean up the crime scene. *Because I killed Ethan.* I give my head a shake, trying to make it stop.

"I'll take good care of her," Nicky promises. "And if we wrap up here before you, Lily can just come home with me; we'll hang out until you're finished, and you can come to the house to pick her up." Nicky assures him.

"Thanks, Nicky," Darius tells her. "Everything's going to be alright. I love you," he tells me quietly, giving me one more kiss on the top of my head before reluctantly walking out.

Nicky looks over to Enzo. "Outside."

"But boss said—"

"Boss isn't here. Outside," she says firmly.

He mutters something under his breath as he walks out.

"Heard that," Nicky calls. She turns her attention to me. "I don't know the details of what happened. Do you need a pelvic exam?" she gently asks.

"No," I tell her quietly.

"Alright. Let's start by washing up." She leads me over to the sink, and I wash the dried blood from my hands and arms. Looking in the mirror, I have blood splattered all over my face. I duck my head under the spray—hoping to wash away the events of this evening like they never happened. Rising up from underneath the faucet, I look back at myself in the mirror. I don't recognize the woman staring back at me.

"Here's a towel," Nicky says, and I dart my eyes away from my reflection, taking it and drying off. "You want me to step out while you change into a hospital gown?"

"No," I say quickly, not wanting to be left alone.

"We've seen each other practically naked anyway, right?" Nicky jokes, trying to lighten the mood as I strip out of my dress—I don't even remember putting my dress back on.

"Come sit for me," she says once I'm wearing the stiff hospital gown, and I climb up on the exam table. "I'm going to take your blood pressure." She wraps a sleeve around my arm before giving it a few pumps. It tightens around me, and the air releases. "Your blood pressure's a bit high, but understandable given the events of the evening, I'm guessing."

"Can I tell you something in confidence since you're a doctor?" I ask.

"I'm not a—" Nicky starts, but then says, "Sure."

"I killed someone tonight," I whisper.

"Did this person deserve to die?" Nicky asks, not in the least bit shocked by my admission.

"If I didn't kill him, he would have killed Darius," I say, choking up.

"Then the fucker deserved to die," Nicky declares matter-of-factly. "Lily, listen to me. Drop that guilt you're carrying, and don't you dare pick it back up. *Ever*," she tells me. "In this family, you've got to be fierce to survive. Welcome to the family." She holds up her hand, and I smile, giving her a high five.

"Don't tell anyone," I warn her.

"Who, me? I don't know *nothing*." Nicky winks.

Epilogue

Darius

We arrive at court and go through security. It makes me antsy as hell not being able to carry any weapons, but I suck it up.

Lily slides in beside the lawyer, then Kat, Iris, and me on the end of the aisle. Court begins, and it's about as dull as watching paint dry. Iris agrees with me; she begins decorating my tie with stickers, her little lips quirked in a devious smile. *That's my kid.*

And now, to make it official.

Our case is called, and Lily and I take Iris' hands as we step up to the podium. "Your honor, the Angelos' family is here to finalize this adoption," our lawyer announces. I paid off the caseworker to skip the home study and background check—expediting this process. Plus, I've listened to enough true crime podcasts to know *not* to give the government my fingerprints or access to my home. Thanks, Nonna. "The minor child, Iris, is in court with us today," our lawyer continues.

"Welcome. And hello, young lady," the judge says to Iris.

"Hi," she says politely.

"I see Mr. Angelos is the stepfather. And the biological father, Thomas Harrison, Junior?" The judge asks, looking up from the file.

"Sadly, your Honor, the biological father passed away," our lawyer's quick to answer. Did I kill Tommy to take his place? *No.* Would I have? *Hell, yes.* And I don't feel bad about that one fucking bit.

"He had a dangerous job," Iris volunteers, and I give her hand a reassuring squeeze.

"Ah, I see in the file he was a police officer. My condolences," the judge says. "And what is it you do, Mr. Angelos?" he asks me.

"Personal trainer."

"Good for you. Wouldn't hurt me to hit the gym, with as much time as I spend sitting all day," the judge comments.

"Sitting is a silent killer," I agree, and I can feel Lily side-eye me.

"Iris, do you understand why we're here today?" the judge asks her.

"Darius is going to be my dad," she answers.

"And how do you feel about that?" the judge asks.

"It's awesome!" she says animatedly, and the judge chuckles.

"And Mr. Angelos, you understand if I grant these proceedings, you will become the legal father, with all the rights and responsibilities as that of a biological father?"

"Yes, your honor," I answer.

The judge reads over something from our file, and I hold my breath. "Counselor, do you have the Order of Adoption for me to sign?"

"Right here," our lawyer holds up a paper and walks to the front, where a bailiff takes the document and passes it to the judge.

The judge signs it with a smile. "Congratulations, Angelos' family. And congratulations to you, Iris Angelos."

I pick Iris up and wrap my arms around her, squeezing tight. Leaning over, I give Lily a quick kiss, who's dabbing at her eyes with a tissue.

Kat snaps a few pictures of us before we step down from the podium, and we walk outside.

"It's official: you're an Angelos now," I tell Iris with a huge grin.

"You're my dad, right?" Iris asks.

"Right," I tell her unequivocally, picking her up.

She smiles brightly, placing her tiny arms around me, and I soak in her sunshine. "Dad," she tries out the word, and I nearly melt into a puddle. "I need another cat."

Kat howls with laughter. "I love this kid."

"Iris, one cat's more than enough," Lily starts.

"But Lucky needs a friend!" Iris makes her case; she's gonna be a lawyer, mark my words.

"She has you as her best friend, and how lucky for her," Lily smoothly replies.

"Listen to your mama, rainbow goddess." But if one day another cat happens to show up at our house, who am I to interfere with the Fates?

"Come to bed," Lily says, appearing in the doorway of the bonus room, dressed in my white T-shirt.

"Είσαι ένα όραμα," I tell her, sitting down my phone as I devour her with my eyes. Not a stitch of makeup. Hair pulled back in a messy bun. Barefoot. She is a fucking vision. It's beyond me how this woman fails to see how perfect she is, but I strive to tell her every chance I get.

"Thank you, Darius," she says sweetly, her rosy nipples now visible beneath the fabric of my shirt.

"Such a good girl," I say in a low tone I know makes her pussy drip. Stalking over to her, I squat down and lift my shirt, placing my nose against the crotch of her panties. Inhaling deeply; oh yeah, already dripping for me.

"What's this?" Lily asks with concern as she touches the edge of a bandage peeking out of my v-neck tee.

"See for yourself." Smiling, I shrug out of my shirt and peel off the bandage from my left pec—revealing the tribute to my girls.

Tears well in her eyes as she leans down and kisses my new ink: it's my hand yanking out of the bloody dirt a pink lily and a purple iris by the roots. "Darius, I love it."

The shrill *beep* from my pager puts a damper on the moment. "Give me just a few minutes. Go to bed and be naked for me. Don't fucking touch that needy pussy until I get in there."

Eyes heavy with desire *and* defiance, she smirks before walking out. I know I'll walk into our bedroom and find her playing with her clit, and I can't wait to spank that tight little ass of hers for it.

"Darius," I return the call to the number on my pager.

"Jersey Delight," is all Big Benny says.

"Excellent," I tell him, hanging up.

Walking to the bedroom, sure enough, Lily's splayed out naked on our bed—touching herself with her thighs spread wide.

What terrible fucking timing. "Wifey, I have to go take care of some business."

"Right now?" She huffs, dropping her hand from her clit in frustration.

"I'll make it up to you later," I promise her. Walking over to the bed, I have a seat on the edge and snatch her hand, bringing it to my mouth. "A little appetizer to take the edge off." I lick the juices from her fingers, one-by-one.

"Darius," Lily says in that throaty voice she doesn't even

realize she uses when she's turned on. "It's late. Why do you have to—"

I silence her by thrusting my tongue in her mouth—giving her a taste of herself; a taste of perfection. Pulling back, I press my lips to her forehead before standing and walking into my closet—gearing up quickly while ignoring my throbbing dick.

Lily's sitting on the bed when I join her, having put my shirt back on and hugging her knees. "Please be careful," she begs.

"Always for you and Iris," I tell her, giving her one more reassuring kiss. "I love you."

"Love you too," she tells me with a sigh, and I'll never get tired of hearing those sweet words from her pouty lips.

Locking up behind me, I switch plates on my car before making the drive to the motel. "I want the adjoining room to the Jersey Delight for the entire evening," I tell a different clerk from the one I dealt with last time. This guy's watching a cop procedural show; I'll have to ask Nonna if she knows about this one.

"That room's unavailable until ten," the man tells me with a heavy smoker's cough.

Waving a Benjamin, I tell him, "Make it available now."

He perks up at that, opening the deal tray, and I drop the cash inside. Eagerly retrieving the money, he says, "Gimmie just a few minutes." The man takes off through the back—probably to move a hooker and her john currently occupying the room I need. Fine by me, as I'm after a different John.

The man returns a few minutes later. "You're in luck. The Velvet Room is all yours. I'll need a copy of your driver's license."

Waving another hundred, I say, "You don't." I pay for the room, and the man passes a key through the deal tray. "You never saw me," I warn him.

"Never saw you," he agrees, returning to his television show.

Entering my room, I try not to think about the bodily fluids covering every square inch of this dump as I pick up the dresser—really wish I hadn't seen what was under there —and move it to the adjoining wall. Climbing on top of it, I remove the mirror. There's three small holes—two for viewing pleasure, and one for shooting pleasure.

I smile, setting my sights on John Davis. Let's see if this man rises from the ashes like his Phoenix tattoo. John's on his knees on the bed, going to town fucking someone who's on all fours. I'm many things, but a cockblocker isn't one of them, so I'll at least give my target the courtesy of nutting before I kill him. As for the individual getting fucked, all I can tell them is choose your partner wiser in the next life.

John gives a final thrust before shooting his load. And now time for me to *unload*. I move my finger to the trigger, but lower my gun when I see the face of John's fuck buddy.

Bloody hell.

The End

Sneak Peek of Forgotten Deal:
Parisi Family Book 3

Kat

My phone buzzes in my purse, and I sigh. There's only so many of my *mamá's* calls I can dodge, and so I drive to her bakery. Parking, I step inside; the delicious smells of childhood overtaking my senses.

Mamá appears from the back, hands on her hips. She proceeds to chew me a new one in Greek. "Katerina, you give me these gray hairs!" She points to her head, switching over to English.

"Sorry, *Mamá*. I've just been busy."

"Sit," she orders, and I take a seat at the table as she busies herself behind the counter making me *ellinikos kafes*. "What's this I hear about Darius' new wife? *Not Greek*," she says the last part as an indictment.

"No, Lily isn't Greek. But she's so sweet, and really good for Darius. And he adores her, and his stepdaughter, Iris. They're such a cute family," I tell her.

"At this point, I approve any man for you—Greek or not." She sighs dramatically.

"Thanks, *mamá*." I roll my eyes.

"Except Dominic," she adds. "Don't think I haven't heard he's back. You stay away from him." She points her bony finger at me.

I make no promises about my ex as she carries over a tray with a tiny cup. "*Efcharistó*," I tell her, taking a sip of coffee with the perfect amount of *kaimaki*.

"Oh, no," *Mamá* says warily.

"What?" I turn around, my eyes going wide.

"Mr. Mazza. Let me make you something to eat." *Mamá* smiles tightly.

"That would be lovely, thank you," the man from The Diamond bar says, straightening his tie.

"Katerina, come help me." *Mamá* practically jerks my arm off as she drags me to the back.

"Who is that man? How do you know him?"

"Fabio Mazza. Says he runs AC now, and the Parisi family's demanding a weekly protection fee," she whispers anxiously.

"Fix the man something to eat while I speak to him," I tell her, patting her hand. "He's new to AC, and obviously doesn't know how things works around here."

Returning to the front, I fling the door open to find Fabio taking a sip of my coffee. He coughs, making a terrible face. "Why the fuck does this have coffee grinds in it?"

"Why the fuck are you shaking down my *mamá*? This is bullshit! Sergio didn't even do that!"

"I handle AC business now, not Sergio," he informs me.

"How much is 'protection?' I'll cover it, but you leave my *mamá* out of this." I'll pay Fabio, and then snitch to my cousin. That'll be the last time this dickhead steps foot inside our bakery.

"Five hundred a week." Fabio flashes his dimples.

I balk. "That is fucking outrageous!"

He lifts a shoulder lazily. "Extortion typically is."

"One hundred a month. No more, no less. You want to bust my kneecaps over it, go ahead," I bluff.

He *tsks*. "But then how would you crawl back to that loser ex-boyfriend of yours who just got out of prison?"

"And you know that how?" I challenge.

"You'd better fucking believe you can't take a step in this town without me knowing about it," he menaces.

It's my turn to smirk. "Wouldn't it be a crawl?"

"That depends entirely on you," he says, flicking an invisible piece of lint from the lapel of his three-piece suit.

Grabbing my purse from the table, I nearly rip off the

zipper as I open it and shove my hand inside, grabbing the hundred dollar bill I keep stashed in the interior pocket for emergencies. "Here you go," I say, tossing the wadded bill across the table. "This month's 'security' payment. Since you're the man harassing this business establishment now under your protection, kindly see yourself out. That's what I pay you the big bucks for, after all."

He chuckles, and I want to dump the cup of coffee over his pretty head—grinds and all, because that's how you fucking drink Greek coffee. "Still owe me four hundred this *week*."

I flick my hand like I'm shooing away a pesky fly. "Then run along and fetch your bat, because you're not getting a penny more from me."

He considers, and I'm worried he might call my bluff. Finally, he says, "I'll make a deal with you: I'll waive protection payments, if you teach me everything there is to know about gambling."

"Why?" I raise my eyebrow.

His face gives nothing away. "I have my reasons."

Crossing my arms, I warn him, "A private gaming coach will run you three hundred bucks an hour. You'll wind up owing me money."

"So be it. Do we have a deal?"

I try not to smile; this chump's about to be taken to the cleaners.

Pre-Order Now!

Acknowledgments

As always, a big shoutout to my beta readers, ARC Team, and Street Team. Thank you to my amazing editor, Carissa, for all the love and support. And last but not least, thank you, dear reader, for choosing this book. *Alla prossima*!

About the Author

Andrea Hagan has an accounting degree and a law degree, but she neither launders money nor represents members of the Mafia. She lives in the Southern United States with her husband and kids. Join Andrea in a non-blood in, blood out way on social media, and don't forget to sign up for her newsletter at andreahaganauthor.com for more Parisi family fun!